"Did you seduce me?"

"Holly, let me explain," he whispered, eyeing the guard in the room.

"Explain what, Logan? How you tricked me into trusting you? Defending you? Lying for you? Why did you do it? Did you decide it would be more fun to seduce me into silence than to kill me?"

"No," Logan said gruffly.

Holly had allowed herself to love Logan again and the pain of his betrayal was a thousand times worse than it had been a decade ago. "I'll never believe you again, Logan," she said, turning on her heel, then fleeing from the room.

But Holly was in danger. And Logan had just been arrested for murder.

"The inspector's waiting," the guard said. "It's time to go."

Logan extended his wrists, allowing himself to be cuffed. There was no way he could protect Holly now—not if he went to jail.

ABOUT THE AUTHOR

Although this is Connie Bennett's first Harlequin Intrigue, she in no stranger to the mystery genre. In 1991, she won the *Romantic Times* achievement award for Best Romantic Mystery with her Superromance *Playing by the Rules,* and her most recent Superromance mystery, *Single...With Children,* debuted on the Waldenbooks Romance Bestseller list. To date, Connie has penned sixteen contemporary and historical romances, with many more to come—she hopes.

Books by Connie Bennett

HARLEQUIN AMERICAN ROMANCE
547—FIFTY WAYS TO BE YOUR LOVER

HARLEQUIN SUPERROMANCE
373—CHANGES IN THE WIND
416—PLAYING BY THE RULES
436—BELIEVE IN ME
513—TOURIST ATTRACTION
562—WINDSTORM
586—SINGLE...WITH CHILDREN

Suspicions
Connie Bennett

Harlequin Books

TORONTO • NEW YORK • LONDON
AMSTERDAM • PARIS • SYDNEY • HAMBURG
STOCKHOLM • ATHENS • TOKYO • MILAN
MADRID • WARSAW • BUDAPEST • AUCKLAND

To Suzanne Ellison for service above and beyond the call of friendship

ISBN 0-373-22311-0

SUSPICIONS

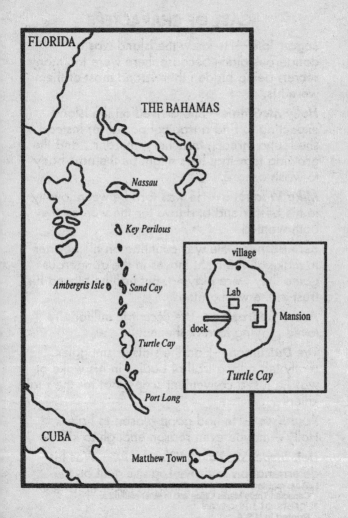

FLORIDA

THE BAHAMAS

Nassau

Key Perilous

Ambergris Isle   Sand Cay

Turtle Cay

Port Long

CUBA

Matthew Town

village

Lab

dock

Mansion

Turtle Cay

CAST OF CHARACTERS

Logan Tate—He knew the island was a dangerous place because there were too many secrets being hidden there...and most of them were his.

Holly McGinnis—She arrived on the island expecting to find a tropical paradise; instead, she found threats, treachery, murder...and the growing fear that hers might be the next body to wash ashore.

Mike Villanova—He was torn between loyalty to his best friend and love for the woman they both wanted.

Seth Barnes—He was counting on his partner to make all the right moves in the dangerous game they were playing. But had he placed his trust in the wrong man?

Avery Bedrosian—The eccentric millionaire loved playing lord of the manor.

The Dutchman—Had the sinister smuggler really left a long trail of bodies in his wake or was he just a convenient scapegoat for the real killer?

Paul Kyte—He had good reason to hate Holly—maybe even reason enough to kill.

Det. Inspector Xavier Giradeaux—Was his determination to prove Logan's guilt on the level, or was he just trying to cover up a few secrets of his own?

Prologue

Seth Barnes wasn't a patient man. He didn't like skulking around in dark places for secret meetings, and he didn't like being kept waiting. Standing alone on a beach afforded too many opportunities to be caught, captured or even killed, and Barnes had a definite aversion to death.

Behind him, the incoming tide swept around the little boat he'd dragged ashore, threatening to carry it back out to sea. He heard the distinctive scraping of the hull on the sand and dashed out of his shadowy hiding place to grab the bow line. He tugged, pulling the boat farther onto shore, and dashed back toward the shelter of the junglelike foliage that edged the beach on this part of the island.

"Having problems with the tide, Barnes?"

The deep, quiet voice seemed to come from nowhere, and Barnes cursed as his heart leapt into his throat. He regained control of his nerves quickly, though, and peered into the darkness as a tall, broad-shouldered shadow stepped out of the underbrush. "The tide is the least of my worries," he growled. "Where the hell have you been? We were supposed to meet half an hour ago."

The broad shoulders went up and down in a negligent shrug. "I had trouble getting away from my so-called *partner.*"

Barnes heard the venom that was applied to the word partner, but ignored it. "Why? Does he suspect—"

"Not a thing. He's just celebrating, that's all."

"Celebrating?" Barnes almost held his breath. "Then you finally found it?"

The tall man nodded and smiled. "Yes. We uncovered a large section of the cargo hold today. There's no doubt that we've located the *Ambergris Isle.*"

Barnes digested the news. He'd waited a long time for this, but the sense of excitement he'd expected to feel didn't come. Instead, a vague feeling of unease settled over him. "Now what?"

"Now the fireworks start. Exactly as planned."

Barnes frowned. "I don't think I like the sound of that. You're enjoying this too much," he said sternly.

"What's not to enjoy? I just located one of the richest treasure ships that ever sank in the Bahamas."

"That's not what I mean. Things are going to get ugly now," Barnes reminded him. "We're talking about murder."

"I know that."

"Then you also know it would be a big mistake for you to get too cocky. One false move, and—"

"I know. I know," the tall man said, his voice hard. "Stop worrying. I've seen the inside of a jail cell before, and I have no intention of repeating the experience." He peered at Barnes in the darkness. "You're not getting squeamish, are you? You're the one who got me into this and it's a little late to think about backing out."

"I'm not backing out, and I'm not squeamish," Barnes replied defensively as he ran one hand over the slick, shiny surface of his bald head. The nervous habit reminded him that it had been a long time since he'd had hair to run his fingers through, and he felt a momentary flash of jealousy as he looked at the thick, leonine mane that adorned his accomplice's head. His irrational envy made him even more irritable. "I just don't want you to take anything for granted. We're all going to be walking a very thin line until your *so-called partner* is . . . taken out of the picture."

The tall man's frown evolved into a dazzling smile. "That's a very sanitary way of putting it," he said, and even in the darkness Barnes could see a sparkle in his eyes that was frightening to behold.

"Nothing about this is sanitary! It's not easy to make murder look like an accident, but—"

"But it can be done. Believe me, I've considered a dozen ways." The tall man clapped Barnes on the shoulder. "There's half a billion dollars at stake, and by the time this is over, only one person will be left to enjoy it."

Barnes shuddered, wondering how he could sound so casual. "Just make sure that person is you, all right?"

"Of course." The tall man glanced over his shoulder, down the long expanse of empty beach. "Now, let's get down to business. Have you got the key?"

"Yes." Barnes dug into the pocket of his windbreaker, extracted an envelope and handed it over.

"What's the locker number?"

"Twenty-seven, at the Windjammer. It's the perfect drop-off point. Whatever you leave in the locker, I'll pick up within twenty-four hours. We'll meet here on the beach only if it's absolutely necessary."

The tall man nodded. "All right. Is there anything else to report? Anything you need to know?"

"Has Dr. McGinnis arrived yet?"

The tall man went very still. "No. She's not expected until the end of the week."

"Is she going to cause trouble?"

The short pause that followed took on an ominous quality. Barnes didn't find that surprising, considering the way this man felt about Holly McGinnis. "Probably," the man answered. "That is why she's being brought here, after all."

"You know what I mean," Barnes said testily. Dr. McGinnis had a reputation for being hotheaded and impulsive, but she was also a woman of great integrity. Her involvement was going to make things a lot more complicated. "Can you keep her under control?"

"I'm not worried about one crippled archaeologist. I can handle the high-and-mighty Dr. McGinnis."

"And if you can't?"

"Then I'll get rid of her."

"How?" Barnes asked suspiciously as a chill snaked down his spine.

The tall man's laugh was quick and cynical. "Don't worry, Barnes. I've already got a plan in place and it won't affect you in the least. Now, you'd better shove off. I've got to get back to the house before I'm missed."

Barnes was still frowning, wondering what this man had in store for Dr. McGinnis. "All right, but just don't do anything stupid, okay? We've come too far."

"Stop worrying so much, Barnes. Everything is under control. *Even* Holly McGinnis."

Chapter One

"Holly, please don't go. You don't know what you're getting yourself into."

Holly McGinnis wedged her cosmetic bag into the last available space in her suitcase, then turned toward her older sister who was sitting on the foot of the bed practically wringing her hands. "Lois...correct me if I'm wrong, but haven't we had this conversation before?"

"Yes, and we're having it again. Unless you come to your senses, we'll continue to have it until the taxi arrives to take you to the airport. You can't handle a job like this."

"Don't be ridiculous," Holly said, striving to keep her tone light. "I'm a marine archaeologist. Locating and excavating ancient shipwrecks is what I do for a living."

"It's what you *used* to do," Lois replied. "It's been three years since your last job, and you haven't exactly been in top form during that time." She paused significantly before adding, "You know better than anyone how dangerous wreck diving can be."

Holly bristled at her sister's blatant manipulation. Lois meant well, but Holly didn't need a reminder of the accident that confined her to a wheelchair for a large portion of the last three years. The doctors had told her she'd never walk again, but Holly had defied them all and she was ready to go back to work. She still had a slight limp and a moderate amount of pain, but she was sick of being an invalid. Moreover, she was sick of having everyone—family, friends and colleagues—think of her as a cripple.

She had been offered what could turn out to be the most important job of her career, and she was going to take it, no matter what. "Lois, I know you think you're looking out for my best interests, but believe me, I'm more than ready to oversee the excavation of the *Ambergris Isle.*"

"No matter what it costs you in terms of your recovery?"

"I've already recovered!" she exclaimed, then spread her arms wide to emphasize her point. "Look, Ma, no crutches...no braces...no wheelchair. I'm standing on my own two feet now. Finally! Dr. Paniterri did give me a clean bill of health, didn't he?"

"But he didn't know what you had in mind," Lois argued. "Endless hours of diving, living in primitive conditions—"

Holly prayed for patience. "You were here when Avery Bedrosian came to offer me this job, Lois. You heard him say the conditions weren't primitive. Our base camp is a thirty-five-room mansion, for crying out loud. I'll even have a pool and gymnasium available to me so I can continue my exercises."

"But you'll be on a deserted island, cut off from everything!"

"Turtle Cay is not deserted. It's a private island. There's a difference."

"But it doesn't even have a doctor."

Holly's patience snapped. "I don't need a doctor!" she exclaimed in frustration.

"Maybe not, but I don't like the idea of your being down there in such a desolate place."

"Oh, for heaven's sake," Holly muttered, flipping the lid of her suitcase closed. "I've worked marine excavations in far more remote areas than this one."

"That's right. And at the last one, a two-ton cannon fell, pinned you underwater and crushed your spine! The nearest decent medical facility was two hundred miles away!"

"Lois...that's enough," Holly said quietly but firmly, trying not to shout at the sister who had taken her in after the accident and done everything in her power to aid Holly's recovery. Holly owed her the right to speak her mind, at least.

And Lois did, though she tried a new tactic. "I know why you're so adamant about doing this," she said slyly. "It's because Logan Tate is involved, isn't it?"

Holly looked at her, aghast. "How can you even suggest that? This has *nothing* to do with Logan!"

"Are you sure?"

"Of course I am," she snapped. "I haven't made any secret of how I feel about Logan Tate and the horrible things he's done. He's an unscrupulous treasure salvor who has made a fortune plundering the environment and destroying historically priceless shipwrecks."

"Then why did you agree to work with him?"

Trying to ignore the peculiar way her pulse had begun to race, Holly turned her attention to zipping up the overloaded suitcase. "Because I didn't have a choice," she said striving for an equanimity she really didn't feel. "Logan and Mr. Bedrosian are partners in this venture."

"Then you're really involved in a treasure hunt, not an archaeological dig," Lois said smugly, knowing there was nothing that would make her sister any angrier. And she was right.

"This is not a treasure hunt!" Holly exclaimed hotly. "I'll be conducting the excavation my way under the auspices of the Bedrosian Museum. If I hadn't been guaranteed complete control, I never would have taken the job. I'm anxious to resume my career, but I would *never* jeopardize my reputation by being associated with a treasure hunt."

Lois just looked at her. "So, it has nothing to do with seeing your former fiancé for the first time in twelve years?"

Holly glared at her. "Absolutely nothing. Can we drop this, please?" She grabbed her suitcase and pulled it off the bed. It settled onto its four wheels with a clatter and Holly glanced around the room. "Now, what am I forgetting?"

"Your common sense."

Holly grinned at her sister. "How can I forget something I never had?"

"That would be funny if it weren't so true," Lois said with a sigh, then pointed to the small desk in the corner. "But you do have mail this morning. I put it over there."

"Oh. Thanks." Holly crossed to the desk, trying to keep her gait even so as not to give Lois any more ammunition to use against her. She glanced through her mail quickly, taking note of the return addresses—an archaeological journal subscription renewal, an unresolved medical bill, insurance red tape . . . the usual minutiae she had become accustomed to.

But the last envelope had no return address.

Frowning, Holly glanced at the postmark and realized it had been mailed in the Bahamas. There was nothing unusual about that, of course. Holly had received several updates on the work being done there ever since Avery Bedrosian had hired her. This was probably another report from the wealthy antiquities dealer.

Holly was understandably anxious to learn the latest developments. Bedrosian and his partner, Logan Tate, had made one of the most important archaeological discoveries of the century—the *Ambergris Isle*, the first eighteenth-century English privateer ever recovered. The ship, long believed to be nothing more than a colorful legend, had gone down in the Bahamas during a hurricane shortly after it had taken on several tons of cargo from a galleon that had been part of the Spanish treasure flota.

Until a few months ago, the ship had been just a fanciful tale told by Bahamian tour guides to gullible tourists. But then, several volumes of the journal written by the ship's captain after he returned to England had been discovered in a dusty library in London, and the race to find the ship had begun.

Avery Bedrosian had purchased the journals at a London auction house, bidding against treasure salvor Logan Tate, and though Bedrosian had won the journals, the price had been exorbitant. To finance the recovery of the shipwreck, Bedrosian had joined forces with Tate. Logan's highly successful, Bahamas-based salvage operation already had all the equipment and divers that would be needed to find the wreck, and their partnership had cut Bedrosian's start-up costs in half.

It had taken several months, but their search had finally been successful. At first, only small pockets of artifacts had been discovered, but they had been promising enough to prompt Avery Bedrosian to begin assembling the team of archaeologists he wanted to conduct the actual excavation and restoration. Then, just days ago, a major portion of the ship had been located.

Holly was disappointed that she hadn't been on hand for that discovery, and she was anxious to know if anything new had developed in the last few days. She sliced into the envelope with a letter opener, but before she could extract the contents the sharp blare of a car horn gave her a more pressing priority. She had a plane to catch this morning, and it was getting late.

"Oops. Taxi's here," she said, moving quickly back to the bed. "Grab something, will you, Sis?"

"Only under protest," Lois replied, taking up the leash of the suitcase as Holly stuffed the envelope and other mail into her huge purse and grabbed her carry-on bag.

She took one last glance around the room. "That's it, I guess." She looked at her sister. "You can have your guest room back now, Sis."

"I'd rather have you in it. Safe and sound."

Holly gave her an encouraging smile. "I'll be fine."

"You'd better be," Lois replied sternly, dragging the suitcase across the room. Together, they hurried outside, with Holly stopping just long enough to retrieve one last item from the front hall closet.

Lois frowned as Holly joined her on the front porch. "If you're so fine, why are you taking that?" she asked as though it proved the point she'd been trying to make earlier.

Holly motioned to the taxi driver using the elegant brass-headed cane she'd taken from the hall closet. "It's just a precaution," she said evenly without looking at Lois. "You know how I stiffen up if I sit for too long, and it's a six-hour plane ride to the Bahamas."

"And that's the only reason?"

"What other one would there be?"

"Sentimental value?" Lois suggested.

"Don't start that again," Holly warned her softly as the taxi driver bounded onto the porch to relieve them of her luggage. She told him her destination, then looked at her sister again. "I'm taking the cane because it might come in handy before the day is over. I'm taking this job because if I don't, it might be years before anyone trusts me with my own excavation. I have to prove that I'm not a cripple."

Lois let the issue of the cane drop and looked at Holly imploringly. "That's not a good enough reason to place yourself in danger."

Holly couldn't help but laugh. "Oh, for heaven's sake. Don't be so melodramatic. I'm going to be working on a private island in the Bahamas with professional archaeologists, not cavorting with slave traders on the Barbary Coast. I'll be fine."

Tears welled in Lois's eyes. "I hope you're right."

Holly opened her arms, and the two women clung to each other for a long moment. "I'll miss you, Sis," Holly whispered, trying and failing to fight her own tears. "Thank you for everything."

Lois cleared her throat, gathered her composure and stepped back. "Just be careful, Holly. I've got a bad feeling about this. You may be standing on two legs again, but you're walking into something dangerous down there. I can feel it."

Holly started to laugh at her sister's ridiculous premonition, but the sincerity in Lois's eyes stopped her. Lois wasn't given to flights of fancy. She had never before spouted prophecies of doom. She was levelheaded, rational and down-to-earth. Holly, on the other hand, was an impulsive hothead who had been known to leap before she looked.

Maybe Lois was right. Maybe there was something fishy about this whole situation, and Holly was just too thrilled to be working again to see it.

And maybe Lois was being overprotective.

Convincing herself that was the case, Holly shook off the pall that Lois's warning had momentarily cast. She smiled brightly, kissed her sister goodbye and hugged her again when they reached the cab.

"I'll keep in touch," Holly promised as she climbed into the back seat and slammed the door. Instantly, the cab roared away from the curb, and as Holly turned to wave goodbye, she barely heard Lois shout one final, "Be careful!"

Shaking her head at the warning, Holly settled into the seat. Lois really was going overboard, but Holly refused to allow that to spoil her enthusiasm for this exciting new project. Instead of dwelling on her sister's premonition of gloom and doom, Holly turned her attention to more important things. A renewed thrill of expectation swept

through her as she fished into her purse for the update
Bedrosian had sent her.

A flash of red and green caught Holly's attention as she
took the folded sheet of paper from the envelope, and she
grinned in disbelief. Christmas stationery in March? she
wondered, looking at the colorful row of holly and berries
that lined the lower edge of the paper below the fold. Apparently Avery Bedrosian was even more eccentric than
Holly had thought when they met. She certainly hadn't
taken him for the type who would make cutesy jokes about
her name.

Then she unfolded the decorative sheet.

The single sentence written there erased her smile instantly. Her pulse began pounding when she read the big
block letters that offered a simple, straightforward, terrifying warning. *Holly: Don't come to Turtle Cay or you may
not leave here alive.*

Suddenly, Lois's premonition of danger didn't seem silly
at all.

SEVEN HOURS LATER, Holly shifted uncomfortably in the
passenger seat of the helicopter. Below her, the pristine waters of the Bahamas stretched in endless ribbons of azure
and turquoise; a beautiful but lonely expanse punctuated by
emerald islands with sparkling, white sand beaches. Under
other circumstances, Holly might have found the scenery
inspiring, but she was still preoccupied by the menacing note
that had arrived that morning.

She'd had hours to speculate on who might have sent it
and why. She was acquainted with a number of the people
who would be working on this project. One was her dearest
friend, and several others were archaeologists she knew
mainly by their sterling reputations.

But to the best of her knowledge, only one of them had
any reason to hate her enough to make a threat like this.

That ugly little note was probably just the kind of thing Logan Tate would find amusing.

Fourteen years ago, Logan and Holly had both been graduate students in marine archaeology at Harvard. Young idealists who had shared a passion for history and adventure—and each other—they fell madly in love and had planned to spend their lives together as the premier marine archaeologists of their day.

But then Logan had shattered that image of perfection. After their second year of grad school, he'd taken a summer job in the Bahamas to help pay for his tuition, and when he returned to Holly in the fall, he'd been a different person. Without warning, he announced his decision to abandon his degree and start his own treasure salvage company.

Holly had been appalled. His decision was a betrayal of everything she believed in—and everything she had *thought* Logan believed in. Their relationship had ended bitterly, and while Holly had established herself as a respected member of the archaeological community, Logan had become one of the most successful treasure salvors in the Bahamas.

Unfortunately, he had achieved that success through means that were often unethical and occasionally illegal. He had become the antithesis of everything Holly represented; what he did and the way he did it were reprehensible to her and every other member of Holly's profession.

She hadn't seen Logan since then, but five years ago, Holly had been given the opportunity to dive on a site he had just finished excavating. What she had seen had made her physically ill. An entire reef and countless historically priceless artifacts had been destroyed by indiscriminate dynamite blasts. Outraged, Holly had publicized the atrocity in several archaeological journals, condemning treasure salvors in general and citing Logan Tate as the worst of a bad lot.

That public condemnation had clearly illustrated Holly's dislike and distrust of Logan, and she couldn't help but wonder now if his hatred of her had prodded him into sending the threatening missive as some sort of warped revenge.

Or perhaps he just wanted her out of his way because he knew she would be watching his every move like a hawk to be certain that he didn't try anything illegal over the coming months. He was hoping that his silly, melodramatic threat would scare her off.

At least that's what Holly wanted to believe, because if she was wrong—if Logan wasn't the one who sent the note—she could be walking into real danger.

It was that sliver of doubt that persuaded Holly not to confront Logan about the note. He would only deny that he had sent it, and Holly didn't want anyone on the island to know about the threat. In fact, she derived a certain amount of pleasure thinking of the sender stewing over whether or not she'd received his message.

A pain stabbed through Holly's spine, and she shifted uncomfortably in the helicopter seat. She desperately needed to work out the kinks in her back and legs. She'd been sitting much too long today.

"Are you uncomfortable, Doc?"

Holly glanced at the pilot to her left. Young, blond and deeply tanned, Judd Cunningham looked more like a beach bum than a helicopter pilot. "I'll survive," she said, adjusting the transmitter of her headset. "How much longer to the island?"

"We're about five minutes from the wreck site near Sand Cay, and another ten from there to the base at Turtle Cay. Can you hang on that long?" he asked.

"Oh, sure. I've endured a lot worse, believe me."

Cunningham gave her a speculative glance that made Holly wish she wasn't alone with him. "You know, Doc, you're not exactly what I expected."

She tensed a bit and tightened her grip on the ornate brass handle of the cane resting against her legs. "Oh? Why not?" she asked, ready for a fight if Cunningham even hinted that she wasn't capable of doing the job she'd been hired for.

"Well, for one thing, you're a damned sight prettier than any of the other archaeologists I've transported to Turtle Cay."

Holly relaxed, but only a little. Cunningham was just handsome enough to convince himself he was God's gift to women, and this was just another of the flirtatious passes he'd been making at her since he'd picked her up in Nassau. Though she wasn't comfortable with his flirting, it was better than the criticism she'd anticipated. "Fortunately you don't have to win a beauty contest in order to get your doctorate degree, Judd," she told him.

"It's a good thing," he said with a roguish grin. "Otherwise, some of those guys would be up a creek. Until today, the best looking thing I've transported to Turtle Cay was a backup generator for the restoration laboratory."

Holly tried to smile politely at his joke. "Mr. Bedrosian told me he spared no expense setting up this operation. The generator ought to look good."

"Avery Bedrosian spares no expense on anything, Doc," Judd told her. "This is a first-class gig all the way. The latest in high-tech diving gear and communications equipment, full archaeology staff, a cartographer, a movie crew to film a documentary, even a helicopter and pilot on full-time standby. But then, considering the stakes, I guess Avery and Logan can afford it. They say the *Ambergris Isle* was the richest ship that ever went down in the Bahamas. Worth maybe half a billion dollars on today's market."

"It's the historical value that interests me," Holly told him, trying not to sound as if she were sermonizing. "And fortunately, that's Mr. Bedrosian's interest, as well. Otherwise, the world would be losing an incredible opportunity to learn more about the lives of the eighteenth-century privateers who sailed that ship."

"Yeah, right," Judd said skeptically. "Would you like to take a look at the site? It's just ahead."

Holly let the lecture drop. "Yes, I would."

Judd fished a pair of high-powered binoculars from beneath his seat and handed them to Holly. He pointed, and she trained the glasses on the area directly ahead of the helicopter. It took a moment, but she finally spotted a cluster of boats sitting just off the shore of a tiny, uninhabited island. As the dots grew larger, she was able to distinguish three vessels that were lashed together—a huge, flat pontoon with a large deckhouse and a shaded canopy, a sleek runabout speedboat and a large salvage vessel.

Probably Logan Tate's *Fortune Hunter*, Holly thought with disgust.

"Well, what do you think, Doc?" Judd asked.

"It's quite a setup," she commented.

"You can see it close-up in about a minute," he told her. "It will give you a chance to stretch your legs."

Holly frowned at the pilot. "We're stopping at the site?"

"Yep. There's a makeshift chopper pad by the divers' barracks on Sand Cay."

"But Mr. Bedrosian is waiting for me on Turtle Cay."

"These are his orders, Doc. He told me to put down on Sand Cay so you could get a look."

Holly hadn't expected this and she wasn't quite sure how to react. She was anxious to get her first look at the wreck site, but she was certainly in no shape to dive this afternoon. The most she could hope for was a tour of the recovery setup—conducted by Logan Tate, no doubt.

Something that felt like excitement twisted in her stomach, but Holly convinced herself it was only the natural anticipation of finally getting back to work. It had absolutely nothing to do with seeing Logan.

Tamping down her excitement and replacing it with professional calm, Holly trained the binoculars on the boats again. As they took on more detail, she finally saw several men lounging around on the pontoon. One in particular drew her attention and she lowered the binoculars, frowning. "Why is that man carrying a rifle?" she demanded.

Judd glanced at the boats. "Just a security measure. The government sends a cruiser by to check on the site from time to time, but that's not enough to keep the bad guys away." He grinned at her. "If you think that's something, wait till you get a load of Turtle Cay. It's like living in Fort Knox. Security fences, guards, electronic surveillance ... everything. It's a miracle we don't have to memorize a password to get into the place."

Holly sank back in the seat, stunned. An armed fortress? This was something she hadn't foreseen. Of course, considering the value of the artifacts, it did make sense to take a few precautions. But guns on the salvage boats? In Holly's opinion, guns and boats didn't mix.

The helicopter lurched downward, catching Holly off guard and making her stomach roll. In the flash of an eye, Cunningham had the chopper skimming the crystal blue water at a dizzying speed. He grinned at Holly as though he were proud of his daredevil stunt, and she was tempted to give the hotshot a piece of her mind.

Instead, she held her tongue and looked at the boats. Apparently, the men had seen the aerobatic stunt because they snapped to attention, and more weapons appeared, all aimed at the chopper. For an instant, Holly had a horrible vision of them opening fire on the helicopter, shooting it down in flames. But then they spotted the chopper's familiar blue-and-orange markings and lowered their guns.

Holly breathed a sigh of relief and made a mental note to discuss these security measures—and Judd Cunningham—with Avery Bedrosian.

The chopper stirred up a whirlwind of white powder as Judd guided it over the broad expanse of sand on the beach, heading for a grassy area beside a large Quonset hut. With pinpoint precision, he avoided a grove of palm trees and set the chopper gently on the grass.

Craning her neck toward the boats that sat fifty yards offshore, Holly removed her headset and reached for the handle of the door, but Judd took hold of her arm to stop her. He pointed toward the roof of the chopper, indicating the blades that were still whirling sluggishly overhead. "Wait for them to stop," he advised, then quickly slipped out of his harness, opened his own door and jumped to the ground.

Keeping his head low, he circled the craft and opened Holly's door himself. She unhitched her seat belt, took hold of her cane, twisted on the seat and looked down. It wasn't far to the ground, but she had been sitting a long time and was none too certain about the ability of her legs to hold her up. Fortunately, Judd had the same doubts. He offered his hand and Holly took it, irritated that she needed his help.

She allowed him to support some of her weight as she came out of the chopper, but she was pleased to discover that her legs were in better shape than she had feared. Somehow, though, Judd's steadying hands ended up on her waist—and stayed there.

"Thank you," she said, giving him a thin, polite smile that indicated she could make it on her own.

"My pleasure, Dr. McGinnis," he said huskily.

Trapped between Judd and the helicopter, there wasn't much she could do but glance sternly down at his hand on her waist. "You can let go now, Judd," she said tersely.

"Are you sure? I wouldn't want you to fall."

"*Oh, don't worry about that, Judd.*" The deep, masculine voice came from out of nowhere, startling Holly and bringing back a flood of unwanted memories. "Holly's like a cat. She always lands on her feet, don't you Holly-love?"

Judd stepped back and Holly whirled around to find the only man who'd ever broken her heart leaning negligently against the trunk of a palm tree.

Chapter Two

It took Holly a second to catch her breath. It had been twelve years since she'd seen Logan, and her memory had shrunk him some because he seemed taller than she remembered. His shoulders were broader, his waist leaner. His hair was as fair and silky as spun gold, a haphazard mane that ended just above his collar and framed a face that was . . . gorgeous. Simply gorgeous. All sun-bronzed flesh and hard, masculine angles, with deep-set crystalline blue eyes that could melt stone—or a young woman's heart.

But Holly wasn't that young anymore, and what she felt for the handsome man in front of her had nothing to do with love. She had good reason to loathe him. If he was the one who had sent her the threatening letter, she might have good reason to fear him, too.

Strangely enough, Holly found that knowledge more invigorating than terrifying. Ready for battle, she moved toward the shady patch of ground beneath the palm, making sure that her stride was as smooth and graceful as possible under the circumstances. She had no idea that her slow, deliberate steps gave her movements a sensual quality that quickened the pulse of both the men watching her.

She moved as close to Logan as she dared and stopped. Even from several feet away, she could feel the full impact of her former lover's magnetic presence. She had felt it the day she'd met him, and its effect hadn't worn off since the day she told him she never wanted to see him again.

"Hello, Logan."

"Holly."

"Are you disappointed to see me up and about?" she asked.

"On the contrary." A cynical smile teased his full lips as he studied her from head to toe. His gaze stopped for a moment on the cane she was barely leaning on, and Holly clenched it a bit tighter. He smiled but didn't comment on the elegant walking stick. "I never doubted that you'd walk again, Holly-love. The only thing that disappoints me is finding you here."

Holly bristled at his use of the pet name that had once meant so much to her. "Why? Are you afraid I might finally get enough proof of your criminal activities to put you out of business—or behind bars?"

His answering laugh was a deep, rich, musical sound that evoked too many memories for Holly's comfort. "Not at all," he assured her. "I'm just disillusioned that the high-and-mighty Dr. Holland McGinnis would involve herself with something as crass as a treasure hunt. I didn't think you'd ever compromise your precious principles, no matter what the price tag."

Taking a deep, calming breath, Holly moved a step closer, then another, until she was close enough to smell his distinctive masculine fragrance. The sensory impression reminded her of the countless hours she had spent in his arms, but she was too angry to be swayed by those deeply erotic memories.

"Let's get something straight, Logan," she said, keeping her voice low and purposeful. "Money has nothing to do with my involvement in this project. I'm working under the auspices of the Bedrosian Museum, where Mr. Bedrosian's share of the artifacts will be on display for the benefit of the public, not lining the pockets of greedy fortune hunters like you."

Logan snorted disdainfully. "Still as self-righteous as ever, aren't you?"

"You can call me whatever you want, Logan, so long as you remember one thing. I'm the boss here. The excavation of the *Ambergris Isle* is going to be conducted *my* way, and I intend to keep my eye on you every minute."

"Really?" he asked lightly. "And what does that mean, exactly?"

"It means I don't trust you any further than I could throw your worthless carcass, and if you have any plans to...shall we say, *misappropriate* any of the artifacts, you can forget it right now. You're being watched, Logan."

"Shucks!" Logan snapped his fingers and affected a look of disappointment. "All those devious schemes, down the drain. Holly-love, you've got me shaking in my boots already."

"Can the sarcasm," she snapped, infuriated that he refused to take her seriously. "I don't like the idea of working with you any more than you enjoy the thought of taking orders from me. That's just the way it is."

"Who says I'm going to take orders from you?" His blue eyes glittered dangerously, but Holly refused to be intimidated.

"Bedrosian put me in charge of the excavation. That means I give the orders until he tells me otherwise," she said, calming herself.

"And if I don't agree? I am a full partner, you know."

"That's between you and Bedrosian. But if you can't or won't accept my authority, you'd better make that clear to Bedrosian now so that he can find himself another archaeologist."

Logan's grin was maddening. "You mean I have the power to send you packing?"

"I don't know, Logan. Do you?" she asked pointedly. "Is your partnership as full as you claim, or is Bedrosian really calling the shots?"

Logan's smile disappeared and the searing flare of anger in his eyes told Holly that her instincts were right. Despite the rosy picture Avery had painted for Holly, there was definitely friction between Logan and his partner—a *lot* of friction, if the intensity of his anger was any indication.

But Logan didn't let that anger get out of control. It took only a second for him to summon a cool, cynical air of indifference. "Oh, what difference does it make, Holly-love? You might as well stay," he said silkily. "You're already here, and as far as I'm concerned, one archaeologist is as bad as another." He gave her an insolent grin. "At least your presence will improve the scenery and provide a little... diversion."

"Not in your wildest dreams," Holly promised him coldly. "I've been your *little diversion* before, and I don't care for a repeat performance."

"Are you sure about that? I seem to remember a time when you enjoyed our repeat performances very much."

Holly wasn't sure how she did it, but she managed to meet his arrogance with a little of her own. "Logan, it will be a cold day in hell before you ever touch me again."

The grin that spread over his rugged, handsome face made Holly's heart slip into double time. "Holly-love, that has the ring of a challenge—and you know there's nothing I like more."

She shrugged diffidently. "Do your worst. Having had the disease once, I can safely promise you that I'm now immune."

"Wanna bet?"

She shook her head. "I don't take money from fools. I'll tell you one thing you can take to the bank, though."

"What's that?"

She took a step closer and lowered her voice seductively. "If you call me *Holly-love* one more time, I'll cut out your heart and serve it on a platter for supper."

She turned abruptly and stalked toward the helicopter where a wide-eyed Judd Cunningham was waiting for her.

"Come on, Judd. Let's go," she ordered sternly.

"B-but the tour of the site."

"It can wait until tomorrow. I want to get to Turtle Cay and inspect the restoration lab before dark." Holly brushed past him, trying to ignore the infuriating sound of Logan's laughter that followed her all the way to the chopper.

"I GUESS YOU AND LOGAN already know each other, huh?" Judd said once they were airborne again.

Holly didn't want to talk, but she couldn't very well ignore the pilot. "Intimately."

"Uh, right. It ended badly?"

She shot him an irritated glance. "What was your first clue?"

Judd shrugged. "Sorry. In case you're wondering, I couldn't hear all of your conversation, but I got a few bits and pieces. Logan raised quite a ruckus when he found out Mr. Bedrosian had hired you. I wondered then what you had done to get on his bad side."

"I publicly accused him of being a greedy wreck rapist who was systematically plundering the treasures of the Americas without regard for history or the ecosystems he was destroying," she said dispassionately, quoting from the journal article she had written.

Judd gave a little whistle. "A wreck rapist? Yeah, that would do it. I guess that was after you two—"

"Look, Judd, could we drop this discussion?" Holly asked tersely. "The less I have to think about Logan Tate, the better I'll like it. Just get me to Turtle Cay. Please."

"Sure, Doc."

They fell silent and Holly finally had the opportunity to get her errant emotions back under control. She was a professional, and it was important that she act with professional calm and detachment. Allowing Logan to make her angry or letting him distract her with reminders of their previous relationship would only make the next few months more difficult.

The problem was, she didn't need Logan's sly sexual innuendos to remind her of what they had shared. It was permanently imprinted on her soul. She'd been fighting her own memories for years, and now she was going to be fighting the man who haunted those memories, as well. Working with him every day was going to be a nightmare.

Holly's adrenaline flow and heartbeat had just barely returned to normal when Judd finally pointed out Turtle Cay to her. She made use of the binoculars to study the lush, green island and found that it was comparatively small—only a few square miles of land, with pristine white beaches lining its coast. A quaint little village with a marina sat on the northern tip, but the interior of the island looked wild and untamed. Tall stands of pines were tangled with dense undergrowth, making the area seem impenetrable and forbidding.

And then they were hovering over the mansion, a sprawling, U-shaped estate two stories high with a gallery encircling the house on the first floor, and a balcony on the second. The north and south wings of the house reached toward the white beach and turquoise water of the cove just below the enormous, immaculate lawn. It seemed beautiful and inviting—until she noticed the high fences around the perimeter and the uniformed guards who were carrying machine guns.

The discordant images were unsettling. Holly had expected to find a tropical paradise on Turtle Cay. Instead she was entering a pretty prison.

The helicopter circled over the house, then landed on the lawn between a large, nondescript building and the boat dock that jutted into the cove. Holly looked toward the house just as Avery Bedrosian and Miguel Villanova emerged, and Holly forgot all about guards, guns and fences.

Not waiting for Judd's assistance, she climbed out of the helicopter and hurried up the lawn, heedless of the way her speed made her limp more pronounced than usual.

On the steps of the house, Miguel Villanova's smile was no dimmer than the one that had lit up Holly's face. "Please excuse me, Avery," he muttered. Without waiting for Bedrosian's answer, he took off down the sloping lawn.

"Oh, Mike, it's so good to see you," Holly murmured as her best friend swept her into his arms.

"You, too, Holly." Mike kissed her cheek, then stood back to examine her thoroughly from head to foot. She had regained some of the weight she'd lost since the last time he had seen her in the hospital, but she was still thinner than she'd been before the accident. She was pale, too, and her blond hair—unstreaked by the sun—was darker than usual. Other than that, she was exactly the same—stunningly lovely, with eyes the color of emeralds and a smile that lit up the world.

When Mike completed his inspection and was satisfied that the reports of her recovery were accurate, the look he gave her was a mixture of intense pride and happiness. "I *knew* you'd fool those ridiculous doctors, Holly. Nothing has ever kept you down for long."

Holly took both of his hands and squeezed them. "Thank you, Mike." With the irritating exception of Logan Tate, Miguel Villanova was the most extraordinarily handsome man Holly had ever known. The youngest son of a wealthy Mexican businessman, he had been educated in the U.S. and had done research in marine archaeology all over the world. He was quite tall, with aristocratic, Latin-lover looks and a deep, cultured voice that had lost all traces of his ancestral accent. He was also intelligent, charming, kind and exceedingly gentle . . . in short, the kind of man any woman would be a fool not to fall in love with.

Holly considered the fact that she had never done so to be the stupidest mistake of her life. No matter how hard she tried, though, she had never been able to view Mike Villanova as anything more than her dearest friend.

"You'll never know how much your letters helped," she told him earnestly, weaving one arm through his. "Every time I got frustrated and started to give up, another letter would arrive to remind me of everything I had to look forward to."

"And now, we're together again, just like the old days— you, me and Logan," Mike said, watching closely for her reaction. "The three musketeers, reunited."

Holly's smile faded. "Not like the old days, Mike," she said quietly. "This is the real world, not college. Those days are gone, thanks to Logan."

"Dr. McGinnis! Welcome to Turtle Cay!" Avery Bedrosian said when he finally reached them.

Holly smiled at her new boss. "Thank you, Mr. Bedrosian. It's good to be here."

Tall and heavyset, with dark eyes and thick, wavy hair that was more silver than gray, Avery Bedrosian was a very unusual man. Holly had liked him on sight when they met, and his obvious love of antiquities had solidified the bond between them. She had found his old-world manners and charm a trifle eccentric in a harmless sort of way, and she wasn't surprised to see him now dressed in an impeccable white linen suit and Panama hat that made him look like a nineteenth-century gentleman planter out for an afternoon stroll around the plantation. It was an image well supported by the magnificent house in the background.

Avery glanced speculatively from Holly to Villanova. "Obviously, this is a happy reunion."

"Yes, it is," Holly said. Though she knew that Mike was one of the first professionals Bedrosian had hired, she felt compelled to tell Avery, "You're very lucky that Mike was available to take this job. He's the best marine cartographer in the world."

Mike laughed. "As you can see, Avery, she hasn't let fourteen years of friendship prejudice her in the least."

"And he's too modest," Holly said, looking up at her friend. "When did you arrive?"

"Last week."

"Then you've already started mapping the site?"

Mike nodded. "Actually, Logan started the mapping, but I've continued his work. Thanks to him, my job is going to be ridiculously simple."

Holly knew otherwise, but she made no comment about that, or about the work Logan had done thus far.

"Did you stop off at Sand Cay, Doctor?" Bedrosian asked.

"Briefly," she replied.

"What did you think of our setup?"

Holly hesitated. She didn't want to displease her new boss, but she didn't want to lie to him, either. "I'm afraid I didn't see much of it, except from the air. Since it was too late for me to dive today, I thought my time would be better spent looking over the facilities here. I can inspect the dive site tomorrow morning."

"Did you see Logan?" Mike asked, searching her face for a sign of what she was feeling.

Holly simply nodded.

"How did it go?" he asked quietly.

"About as well as could be expected."

Mike looked concerned. "Holly—"

She placed her hand on his arm. "Later, Mike. Please." She smiled at Bedrosian. "For now, I'd love a tour of the grounds. I could use a good stretch."

"It would be my pleasure." Bedrosian turned and called to Judd, who was still at the helicopter. "Cunningham! Take Dr. McGinnis's luggage to the house, please."

Judd saluted briskly. "Yes, sir."

If Bedrosian found the gesture insolent, he gave no indication of it. He turned and began strolling up the lawn with Holly and Mike beside him.

The tour began at the house, which was as spectacular inside as it was out. There were eighteen bedrooms, a parlor, library, den, gymnasium, kitchen ... thirty-five rooms in all—not counting the ten baths, or the pool house and the servants' quarters in the rear. Every room Holly saw was impeccably furnished. All the rooms had high ceilings, huge windows, and at least one tall set of French doors that led to the gallery and balconies that encircled the house.

The grounds were no less impressive, and the restoration lab was remarkably sophisticated, which Holly found surprising because it had been furnished by Logan with equipment he'd brought up from his headquarters on Great Inagua Island.

But Holly had difficulty appreciating the grounds or the lab. The electrified fences and ever present guards were too disturbing. She felt as though she had fallen into the midst of a third world army gearing up for a revolution, and she couldn't escape the irritating thought that the security precautions were far more serious than the situation called for.

Unless, of course, the situation was far more serious than Holly had been told. She thought of the threatening note and realized with mounting alarm that something strange was happening on Turtle Cay.

"And the vault is back here," Bedrosian said, moving toward the rear of the enormous laboratory to a walk-in safe that was worthy of any bank.

Holly followed him in and immediately regretted it. It was like walking into a tomb. "Are the gold coins you found last week still in here?'' she asked, trying to ignore the panicky feeling of claustrophobia that hit her.

"Not any longer," he assured her. "As you know, the Bahamian government is entitled to twenty-five percent of whatever we find. As a consequence, all precious metal or gemstone artifacts must be transported by helicopter to the Bahamas Trust Bank in Nassau as soon as they have been recorded and restored. Since gold requires no more than a freshwater bath, Logan and I flew everything up to the bank yesterday."

"I see." Holly stepped out of the vault and took a deep breath. She saw Mike looking at her with concern and she gave him a reassuring smile that probably looked as false as it felt, but she wasn't about to admit to anyone that she'd been having problems tolerating confined spaces ever since her accident.

Bedrosian continued the tour, taking her through the barracks at the back of the building where sleeping cubicles and a large community room had been created for the non-supervisory members of Holly's archaeology staff and the guards.

"It's a marvelous facility, Avery," Holly said with an enthusiasm she really didn't feel as they returned to the main section of the lab. "I'm very impressed."

"I told you that my museum was committed to conducting this project professionally. I never do anything halfway."

"Obviously. This is the first time I've ever had an X-ray machine on-site. And the other equipment is—" Holly broke off in midsentence when she spotted a movement on the far side of the room. A man walked out of one of the office cubicles, and Holly couldn't quite believe her eyes. "Paul?" she murmured, then looked at Bedrosian. "Is that Paul Kyte?"

Bedrosian glanced across the room. "Indeed it is." He raised his voice. "Dr. Kyte! Please join us."

Holly's surprise turned to displeasure as the archaeologist made his way toward them. "You didn't tell me he was a member of my staff," Holly said to Bedrosian, keeping her voice low.

Avery frowned. "He's a recent addition. Dr. Kyte signed on after Dr. Tomas Ludvik received an offer to work on an excavation for the University of Mexico. I never dreamed that there would be a problem because I knew that you had worked with Dr. Kyte before."

Holly couldn't believe what she was hearing. "You mean Paul is one of my restoration supervisors?"

"Yes. Unless you disapprove of the selection," Avery said, clearly upset and confused by Holly's reaction to this change in personnel.

Holly did disapprove. Wholeheartedly. In her entire career, she'd made only one enemy among her fellow archaeologists—and it was the man walking toward her now. Eight years ago they had worked together on an excavation in the Mediterranean that had been sponsored by the Smithsonian Institute. For reasons Holly still didn't understand, Kyte had taken an instant dislike to her, and their working relationship had been the most unpleasant Holly had ever endured.

They had disagreed on everything from restoration methodology to interpretation of data, and Holly had been overjoyed that the Smithsonian hadn't picked up Paul's contract when the excavation had resumed the following season. Unfortunately, Paul had blamed Holly for his dismissal, and he had been trying to destroy her reputation in the archaeological community ever since. He had told outrageous lies about her and had even published papers designed solely to contradict her own publications.

If he was working on the *Ambergris Isle* excavation now... Holly didn't want to think about the problems this was going to cause her, but she knew she had to acknowledge one important fact: Logan Tate wasn't the only person on the island who might have sent her that threatening note. Paul Kyte was an equally likely suspect.

All her defenses went on the alert as Kyte approached her. "Hello, Paul," she said, doing her best to conceal her displeasure.

He gave her a strained smile. "Holly. It's good to see you again. I'm glad that the reports of your injuries from that accident in Mexico were exaggerated."

"Are you?" she couldn't keep herself from asking.

Kyte looked down at the floor and shifted his weight from one foot to the other. "I suppose I deserved that." He darted a glance at her, but had trouble holding her gaze. "I know we've had trouble in the past, Holly, but I hope we can put it behind us."

"I hope so, too, Paul," she replied. "You're an excellent restoration specialist and I'd like to think that we can work together as a team."

He seemed pleased by her compliment. "That's what I want, too."

She didn't trust his contrite act for a minute, but she gave him the benefit of the doubt, chatting politely with him a few minutes longer before moving off toward the exit.

"Holly, I am truly sorry," Avery said once they were out of the building. "I had no idea there was friction between you and Dr. Kyte."

Holly frowned at him. That didn't make sense for several reasons. When Bedrosian had approached her about the job, he had known all about her history with Logan because he had done extensive research on her background. He had claimed that her animosity toward his partner didn't bother him, and Holly had even gotten the impression that he approved.

But she supposed it was possible that his research hadn't turned up this problem with Paul, so she merely asked, "Mike didn't tell you that Dr. Kyte and I have had what you might call a professional rivalry?"

"No, I didn't, Holly," Mike answered for him. "It's been so long since we've discussed Paul that I thought maybe he'd given up his ridiculous vendetta. I didn't want to stir up trouble before I talked to you."

"Do you want me to let him go?" Avery asked her.

Holly laughed shortly. "Absolutely not. Many of my most recent problems with Paul started because he mistakenly believed that I'd gotten him fired. There's no telling what he might do if I was responsible for him losing this job. Just let it go. I'll deal with him in my own way."

"As you wish," Avery said, then brightened. "Why don't we return to the house now? I'm sure you'd like an opportunity to rest and freshen up before dinner. I've hired an excellent chef, by the way, and he's promised something truly spectacular in honor of your arrival."

Holly was relying heavily on her cane as she proceeded down the path from the lab. "That sounds wonderful," she said, thinking how good a shower was going to feel on her back. But then she spotted Logan coming toward them from the direction of the boat dock. His long, leisurely strides reminded Holly of the sensual movements of a feline predator, and the anxiety she was already feeling multiplied. "Well, look what the cat dragged in," she muttered.

Avery raised one hand in greeting. "Ah, Logan! Did you have a productive day?"

"Moderately," he replied as he approached, his gaze sweeping over the trio. It settled for a moment on Holly, then shifted to Bedrosian. "You can send Judd down to Sand Cay to pick up the core samples and some other items we recovered that were too small to be left lying around. They were being packed for transport when I left."

Holly looked at him archly. "You couldn't have waited a few minutes and brought them yourself?"

His blue eyes widened in mock disbelief. "And miss spending these precious moments with you? Don't be absurd."

Mike cleared his throat. "Actually, Holly, Logan was merely acting in accord with the security measures he and Mr. Bedrosian have established."

She cast a questioning gaze at Avery. "*More* security measures?"

"Given the value of the artifacts and the threat of theft, we feel that the helicopter is a safer method of transport than the runabout."

Holly frowned. "All right, that's enough. Would someone please enlighten me? This is the twentieth century, for God's sake. You people are behaving as though you expect an attack from Blackbeard the Pirate at any minute. Now, what's going on?" She looked directly at Mike because she knew he'd tell her the truth.

But Mike glanced uncertainly at Logan, as though he wasn't sure what he should say, and Holly realized that her old friend was trying to protect her.

Holly was furious. "Damn it, Mike. I'm not a silly, fainting female. Tell me—"

Logan cut her off. "An old acquaintance of mine is lurking about, Holly. His name is Dutch Voorhees, but everyone calls him the Dutchman. You'll like him," Logan added sarcastically. "He's a smuggler, a murderer and a wreck rapist of the first order who'd slit his own mother's throat for a piece of eight. We're taking security precautions to keep the treasure *in* the compound and the Dutchman *out*."

"Great." Holly met Logan's gaze evenly. "That gives us *two* crooks to worry about, doesn't it?"

"Why don't we return to the house," Mike suggested quickly before Logan could respond to Holly's insinuation. "Holly has had a long day."

"Good idea, Mike," Logan said. "Maybe a little rest will improve her disposition."

Holly bristled. "There's nothing wrong with my disposition, Logan. Just the company I'm being forced to keep."

"Forced?" Logan's eyebrows shot up and he glanced around. "I don't see anyone holding a gun on you." He looked straight at her. "Yet."

Holly's heart skipped a beat. "Is that a threat, Logan?" she asked with a coolness she didn't feel. She hadn't expected this kind of overt intimidation.

"Of course not. I just meant, that considering your charming personality, it shouldn't take long for you to irritate the wrong person."

Holly didn't believe him for a minute. He'd been making a threat, not a joke, but she refused to give him the satisfaction of knowing that she was rattled. "I'm ready to go back to the house now, Avery," she said. "I'd like to take a shower and rest before dinner."

"Certainly," Bedrosian replied. "I'll show you to your room." With Avery leading the way, the trio began strolling up the hill to the house.

Logan remained behind, unable to tear his gaze away from Holly.

Damn her, he thought with a surge of disgust directed wholly at himself. How could she possibly be even more beautiful than he remembered? The woman he'd once loved—the girlish colt, full of energy and fresh-faced innocence—was gone, but in her place was a vivacious, vibrantly lovely woman. The years had added a maturity and confidence that Logan found incredibly compelling, and her hatred of him added a fire to her emerald-colored eyes that reminded him of a different kind of fire he used to see there.

Holly McGinnis was the most passionate woman Logan had ever known, and he had loved her with a youthful intensity that had nearly killed him when she broke off their engagement. Fighting the memories of what they had once shared was going to be a thousand times more difficult than Logan had imagined, but he could do it. Considering what was happening on Turtle Cay, he didn't have a choice. He couldn't afford a romantic entanglement right now. There were too many secrets on the island.

And most of them were his.

Chapter Three

Holly's luggage was already in her room when she stepped in and surveyed her new quarters. It was luxuriously appointed, decorated entirely in white, with a private bath and French windows that opened onto a balcony that overlooked the courtyard where the swimming pool was located. That would make it much easier for her to continue her physical therapy, and Holly made a mental note to thank Bedrosian for his consideration.

And she also made a note to thank him for the lovely welcome gifts she saw when she turned away from the window. A bowl of fruit and a huge vase of tropical flowers were sitting on the vanity, and though she couldn't have complimented the haphazard arrangement of the bouquet, she appreciated the gesture. It was the first truly comforting, reassuring thing she'd seen since her arrival—a gesture of consideration that made her feel like a welcome guest instead of a visitor to a war zone.

Smiling, she crossed to the vanity and plucked a bird of paradise from the vase.

That's when she saw it . . . the piece of white paper stuck in the center of the bouquet. A paper that had been folded once, with a border of holly exposed on the edge.

The bird of paradise fell from Holly's nerveless fingers and she reached for the note with an unsteady hand. Dreading what she would find, she unfolded it.

You should have taken my warning, Holly. Leave now before it's too late.

The threat went through her like a hand that had reached out to touch her from the grave, and she crumpled the warning into her fist.

"The hell I will," she muttered, then dropped into the nearest chair because she didn't know how much longer her trembling legs would hold her up.

BY THE TIME she finished dressing for dinner, Holly had convinced herself that she was more angry about the note than frightened. Still, she had taken her shower and changed into a summery sundress with all the doors securely bolted. Even with that precaution, though, her hands were still trembling slightly as she clipped on a pair of dangling earrings.

Irritated with her bout of nerves, she made a final inspection of herself in the bathroom mirror and returned to the bedroom.

Holly heard the distinctive *click* the moment she entered the room. She froze and looked at the door. Sure enough, the bolt had been unlocked.

And the door handle was turning.

Acting on instinct, she looked around for a weapon and grabbed a brass candlestick from the bureau. Flicking the candle out of the holder, she stepped toward the door just as it swung open.

"That's far enough!" she commanded, using her free hand to yank the door open wider with the candlestick drawn back to strike.

The lovely, dark-skinned maid in the doorway screeched and stepped back in alarm.

"Damn," Holly muttered, feeling like ten kinds of a fool. She lowered the candlestick. "I'm sorry. It's all right. I'm not going to hurt you," she tried to reassure the frightened girl. "You just startled me."

The girl struggled to find her voice, but didn't make any effort to enter the room. "I'm so sorry, Ma'am. I—I thought you had already gone down to dinner." She lifted her arm to display the linens draped across it. "I wanted to bring you fresh towels before bedtime."

"Thank you. But in the future, please knock," Holly said shakily, returning the candlestick to the bureau.

"Yes, Ma'am." The girl edged into the room and kept a nervous eye on Holly as she slipped into the bathroom.

Holly silently cursed the man who had caused this, but she was just as angry at herself for allowing his stupid notes to turn her into a Nervous Nellie. Holly didn't like feeling vulnerable, and she hated being afraid even more. She wasn't too happy about looking like an idiot, either.

Collecting herself, she began searching for the candle she had dislodged from the holder. It had rolled under the edge of the bed, and Holly had to hold on to the nightstand for support as she knelt to retrieve it. Her back was as stiff as a board, and she wished she'd had time for a swim to work out the knots.

"May I help you, Ma'am?" the maid asked cautiously when she came out of the bathroom with an armload of wet towels.

"No. But thank you," Holly said, gritting her teeth against the pain as she came to her feet, candle in hand. "What's your name?"

"Marianna. This is my wing of the house," she said with a touch of pride. "If you need anything, I will be happy to provide it."

"Thank you, Marianna. I'll let you know."

"Yes, Ma'am." The girl nodded politely and started for the door.

"Wait," Holly said as an afterthought when her gaze fell on the flowers. "There is one thing you can tell me. Do you know where those flowers came from?" She motioned toward the vanity.

The girl looked at the vase. "I believe they came from the garden in the courtyard," she replied. "The bird of paradise are blooming there now."

"Did you bring them to my room?"

Marianna shook her head. "No, Ma'am."

"Do you have any idea who did?"

"No, Ma'am. I brought the bowl of fruit early this morning and there were no flowers. I have not been here since, and I saw no one near your room."

So much for playing Sherlock Holmes, Holly thought with disgust. Logan was still her number one suspect, but she couldn't discount Paul as a possibility, either. Until she knew for certain which of them had sent the notes, she couldn't very well go around making accusations. Assuming, of course, that the mystery letter-writer was one of them. Given the strange state of affairs on the island, Holly couldn't completely discount the possibility that there was an unknown entity intent on doing her harm.

The maid departed and Holly limped to the vanity to retrieve her cane. She started for the door, then stopped, a defiant smile playing over her mouth as she thought of a way to send a message of her own to the man who had sent her the bouquet.

Moving back to the vanity, she plucked a bird of paradise from the vase, snapped off the stem, and stuck the blossom behind her ear.

"Let's see what you think of that, guys," she murmured as she left the room.

"WHAT I DON'T UNDERSTAND is why we call it a wreck site when there's no boat down there," Judd Cunningham commented as he moved away from the bar that sat in the corner of the parlor. Everyone was enjoying a drink before dinner, but Judd seemed to be enjoying his a little too much.

"After more than two hundred years, it would be very rare to find many of the ship's timbers intact, Judd," Avery told him. "Unless wood is buried very quickly in sand or silt, worms devour it. But what Logan thinks we've found is the spot where the ship first broke up during the hurricane. Isn't that right, Logan?" he asked pointedly, forcing his partner to acknowledge the existence of the other people in the room with him. When Holly had entered the parlor, Logan had given her one hard, searching look, then moved to the French windows overlooking the front lawn. Holly didn't know whether he was irritated with her presence in general, or by the saucy bird of paradise she wore in her hair, but Logan had stayed at the window with his back to the room, completely ignoring the other team members, ever since.

Apparently, Avery was fed up with Logan's bad manners, and Holly couldn't blame him. She mentally applauded Avery's tactic when Logan turned grudgingly to answer his question. "That's right. It looks like the *Ambergris Isle* hit the coral reef, but the storm lifted her over the reef onto the sandy plain where we're finding her cargo now."

"And since that's where the wreckage lies, we call it the wreck site, even though we don't expect to find much of the ship itself," Avery concluded. Logan gave a terse nod in agreement and turned his back on the room once again.

The conversation went on without him, and Holly couldn't say that it was much of a loss. Even discounting Logan's ill-tempered presence, the group seemed decidedly tense despite Avery's efforts to put everyone at ease.

"That is a gorgeous cane you're using, Holly," Neal Scanlon, the documentary filmmaker on the project, said, gesturing to the walking stick that was resting against the side of her chair. "I noticed it the moment you came in."

Holly's glance darted toward Logan again and she tensed when he turned around, this time appearing far more interested in the conversation. She looked away from him quickly and addressed the athletic-looking director. "Thank you, Neal," she replied, hoping he wouldn't pursue the subject.

But Edgar Franklin, the government's representative in the recovery operation, jumped onto the bandwagon. "Yes, it's quite stunning. It's eighteenth-century Spanish, isn't it?"

"Yes," she said, keenly aware that Logan was now watching her.

"You know, Holly, it hadn't occurred to me until now, but I don't remember seeing you carrying a cane when we met at your home," Avery commented.

Holly desperately wanted this conversation to end. "I rarely use it at all anymore, Avery. As long as I can maintain a high activity level, I don't need it, but with all the hours I spent on a plane today, it seemed like a wise precaution."

Franklin rose and moved to her. "May I take a closer look at it?"

He held out his hand and Holly was surprised to find that the prospect of handing the cane to him was not a pleasant one. There was something about the thin, bespectacled bureaucrat that made her skin crawl, but she chided herself for being irrational. "Of course."

"Remarkable," he said, running his fingers lightly over the brass handle that had been sculpted into a stylized pheasant. The polished mahogany shaft melded into the bird's slender body, with the head and the long, beautifully detailed tail feathers forming a lopsided, T-shaped handle. "This isn't a reproduction, is it?"

Holly had to give him credit for knowing a genuine artifact from a cheap copy. "No," she admitted.

Franklin cocked one eyebrow as he looked down at her. "A souvenir from one of your excavations?"

Holly frowned. "Of course not. That would be highly unethical—not to mention illegal."

"I'm sorry. I didn't mean to imply that you had purloined the cane. I thought perhaps you had purchased it."

"No. It was a present from—" her gaze darted to Logan again, who was still lounging at the door, watching her with unnerving intensity "—an acquaintance."

Franklin twirled the shaft between his thumb and forefinger as though testing its balance. "A very generous gift," he said, then returned the cane to Holly.

"I'm afraid generosity was not the giver's motive," she said, unable to keep a touch of bitterness out of her voice. "The cane arrived while I was still in the hospital, shortly after I had been told I would spend the rest of my life in a wheelchair. At the time, it was a very cruel practical joke."

"A joke?" Logan pushed away from the door frame.

Holly's head came up defiantly as she met his gaze. "That's right."

"Are you certain? Perhaps your *acquaintance* meant the gift as a gesture of his confidence in your ability to outwit your doctors."

"That's not likely."

"Then why did you keep it?" he asked, his voice hard.

"Because I wanted the satisfaction of returning it in person, while standing on two healthy legs."

Logan's gaze slid insolently over her, making Holly's pulse quicken. "They look pretty good to me."

Holly bit back a curse, keenly aware that the tension between them had everyone riveted to their exchange. Fortunately, one of the servants chose that moment to announce dinner. Bedrosian began shepherding his guests out of the room, but Logan was still glaring at Holly when Mike offered her his arm.

She stood. "In a minute, Mike," she said softly in a hard voice as she waited for the room to clear.

Logan and Holly were facing each other squarely, like fighters in an arena, and Mike looked anxiously from one friend to the other. "Please. This doesn't serve any purpose. Logan—"

Logan shot a killing glance at his old friend. "Stay out of this, Mike. In case you hadn't noticed, Holly is more than capable of fighting her own battles."

"He's right, Mike. I can." She held out the cane defiantly. "Here, Logan. It served its purpose. Now, why don't you take it and sell it?"

Logan just looked at the cane. "It's not mine. I gave it to you."

"And now I'm giving it back."

Logan's eyes held a strange mixture of anger and something that Holly would have said was pain if she hadn't known better. "I don't want it, Holly," he said harshly. "Believe what you like, but I sent you that cane because I knew nothing was going to keep you from walking again. I wanted you to know I had faith in you."

Deep in Holly's heart, a little voice cried out for her to believe him, but she didn't dare. "Don't give me that, Logan. You didn't care if I walked again, you just wanted to pay me back for the article I wrote about you."

Logan laughed harshly. "Holly, if I wanted to pay you back for that piece of trash, I'd have sent you a present from the wreck of the *Nuestra Señora Suerte* and called it poetic justice."

Holly felt sick. "Did you?" she demanded, clutching the cane a little tighter as she held it up in front of his face. "Is this from the wreck you dynamited?"

"Don't you mean the wreck you *accused* me of dynamiting?"

"Damn it, answer me! Is this from the *Nuestra*—"

"No!"

Holly wasn't sure she believed him. She opened her hand and the cane clattered to the floor between them. "Take it,

Logan. And I'd better not ever find out that you're lying to me. I *won't* be made an accessory to your crimes."

"My only crimes are the ones you invented!"

"I didn't *invent* the fact that you were arrested for dynamiting that reef!" she flung back at him.

The cold fury that came over Logan's face was terrifying. "That's right, Holly. I was arrested, but the only charge that anyone was able to make stick was *yours*. Logan Tate, wreck rapist. Tried, convicted and sentenced by the righteous Dr. Holly McGinnis!"

"Holly? Is everything all right?"

Relief flooded through Holly at the interruption, and she turned to find Avery looking at her solicitously from the door. "Yes. Everything is fine," she told him, trying to calm herself.

"May I escort you into the dining room?" he asked, coming closer to offer her his arm.

"Thank you." She threw one last look of disgust at Logan, then allowed Bedrosian to escort her from the room.

Still seething, Logan watched her go. Mike picked up the cane and held it out to him, but Logan just glared at it. "Didn't you hear me say I don't want it, Mike? It was a gift to Holly."

"From the *Nuestra Señora Suerte?*"

Logan's eyes narrowed. "Don't you believe me, either?"

"If you say it wasn't salvage from that wreck, then I believe you," Mike assured him. "Where did you get it? Another salvage?"

"No." He hesitated a moment before admitting, "I bought the handle at an auction at Christie's and had it restored."

Mike remembered that Logan had been in London for the Christie's auction at the time of Holly's accident. In fact, Logan had called the hospital from there when he'd learned she had been injured, and Mike had taken the call. He also remembered how concerned Logan had been. It made sense that with Holly on his mind, he would have chosen this particular gift for her.

Mike looked at his friend beseechingly. "Logan, this feud with Holly can't continue. She's only been here a few hours and already you two are at each other's throats."

Logan scowled at him. "And you think that's my fault?"

"No. But if you're going to work together, you're going to have to make peace somehow."

"Tell that to Holly."

"I'm telling it to you," Mike replied sternly. "I love you both, and I don't like being caught in the middle. Now, bury the hatchet and let go of the past."

Logan shook his head. "I didn't start this feud, Mike. Holly did, twelve years ago when she threw our engagement ring in my face. And she's the one who's been keeping it alive ever since. So give her your little peace speech and let me know how it goes, all right?" he said as he snatched the cane out of Mike's hand and started toward the door.

"Logan—"

"Save it, Mike," he said without turning. "Tell Holly the boat leaves for Sand Cay at six a.m. sharp. If anyone wants me, I'll be eating dinner with the guards."

STILL SEETHING from her argument with Logan, Holly returned to her room right after supper. She was exhausted, but sleep was the last thing on her mind. Her suspicion that Logan had actually given her an artifact from the *Neustra Señora Suerte* ate away at her, and she was almost as angry with herself as she was with him. She should never have kept the cane to begin with, but she had, and she still wasn't sure why.

She had been furious when she received it, but it had represented a challenge she was too much of a fighter to ignore. During the long months that she had been confined to a wheelchair, she had kept the cane in sight always, using it to prod her forward when the pain was so great that she could almost believe the doctors were right.

It had been both a talisman and an incentive to recover, and she had always intended to return it to Logan just as she had told him tonight—while standing on two good legs. If she was honest with herself, though, she also had to admit that a small part of her had always wanted to believe Logan's reason for sending it was exactly as he had claimed tonight.

But would a man who had sent her a cane as a tender gesture of encouragement and support also have sent her two notes threatening her life?

It was improbable, to say the least, and Holly still felt that Logan was the most likely candidate for the man behind the threats. Paul hadn't shown any reaction whatsoever to the bird of paradise in her hair tonight, whereas Logan had hardly been able to look at her. That wasn't proof, but it was enough to tip the scales back toward Logan.

Too restless to sleep, Holly turned her attention to the updated transcript of the journal written by the captain of the *Ambergris Isle*. Riva Thompson, Avery's secretary, had provided Holly with the new material, and she settled into a chair to study it.

Though it was fascinating reading, Holly was vividly aware of every sound around her. She had been forced to open the French doors because the room was unbearably stuffy, and she could hear footsteps and the faint sound of voices outside or in the hall as servants went about their business and members of the team returned to their own rooms for the night.

The house settled into an eerie quiet as the hour grew late, and Holly tried to familiarize herself with the creaks and thumps the old mansion made. A light breeze stirred the curtains and rustled through the coarse leaves of the palms outside. But all else was quiet.

Shortly after midnight, when Holly realized that she had read the same page three times, she decided it was time to turn in. It had been a long, grueling day and she didn't expect tomorrow to be much better. She placed the manuscript on the vanity that would double as her work desk, pulled a nightgown from the bureau and moved into the bathroom.

By the time she washed off her makeup and changed into the gown, Holly was yawning and more than ready for bed. She moved back into the bedroom and froze. Pages of the journal transcript littered the floor around the vanity like fallen leaves. The cool night breeze still ruffled the curtains, but the French windows and the vanity were on opposite ends of the same wall—not even a stiff wind could have sent them flying like that.

Someone had been in her room.

Twin surges of fear and anger hit Holly at the same time. She was *not* going to allow herself to be terrorized! Furious, she ran through the French windows onto the balcony, determined to confront her midnight prowler.

But no one was there. All the lights were out in the rooms on either side of her. There was nothing on the balcony but an ocean-scented breeze and deep shadows. Whoever had been in her room was gone now.

Frustrated, Holly stepped to the balcony rail. "What is happening here?" she murmured. Only the breeze answered her.

The darkness made her feel even more vulnerable, but before she could turn to go back indoors a movement in the courtyard below caught her eye. A man-size shadow was moving swiftly through the garden on the other side of the pool, then it melted into the night and vanished. But the moonlight had been strong enough to provide Holly with the distinct impression of a large silhouette and striking blond hair.

Or had it been silver? she wondered, thinking of all the men in the compound who might fit that description. Logan, Judd Cunningham, Avery and even Paul Kyte, whose light brown hair was turning prematurely gray. Any of them could have made the shadow. Any of them could have entered her room and scattered the manuscript, then run down the stairs into the garden.

Or it could have been none of them. Between the divers, archaeology staff and security personnel, there were more than fifty people—nearly all of them men—involved with the project.

Holly realized that her midnight caller could have been anyone.

It was the most frightening thought she'd had since she arrived on the island. At that moment, Holly wanted more than anything to call her sister, just to hear a voice of sanity in a world that had suddenly tilted upside down. But she didn't dare call Lois, because her sister would only tell her she should come home immediately.

And Holly was afraid that she would agree.

SHE LOOKED LIKE AN ANGEL standing there on the balcony. Her hair tumbled around her shoulders, the breeze rustled her flowing white nightgown, and the light from the room behind her bathed her in a soft golden halo.

Even from this distance, hidden by the darkness of the garden, he could see her hands gripping the rail as she searched the shadows for a sign of the intruder who had been in her room. Even from this distance, he could tell she was frightened.

Good. That was very good. He wanted her to be frightened. He wanted her to jump at shadows and look for the hidden motives of everyone she met. He wanted her to trust no one. To feel cut off... alone... vulnerable.

It was all part of the plan he'd told Barnes about on the beach, and it was working.

Beautiful, strong-willed Holly McGinnis was afraid.

Now, if he could just convince her to turn to him, confide in him, trust him, it would be the icing on the cake.

Assuming, of course, that she lived that long.

Chapter Four

At five minutes till six the next morning, Holly was on her way down to the dock despite having had precious little rest. Mike had given her Logan's message, and she had no doubt that he'd leave without her if she was so much as a minute late. She wasn't about to give him that satisfaction.

Sure enough, Logan was already there, casually dressed in shorts and a white cotton pullover, checking the mooring lines on one of the runabouts.

Holly stopped in front of Logan and he looked at her, his expression bland and completely unreadable. "Are you ready?" he asked.

Since he hadn't bothered with a greeting, Holly didn't either. "Do you have scuba equipment for me at the site?"

He nodded. "Avery gave me your shopping list, and it was pretty standard stuff. It wasn't hard to fill."

"Then I'm ready." She glanced around. "Mike isn't here yet?"

Logan pointed toward the house. "He's coming down now." He paused a moment and a look of hesitancy came over his face. It was the first honest emotion other than anger that Holly had witnessed, and she couldn't help but wonder what he was thinking. She didn't hold out any hope that he was about to confess to having sent her those threats, but whatever was on his mind was serious.

"If you've got something to say to me, Logan, spit it out," she suggested.

His eyes narrowed in irritation, but he went ahead. "Mike thinks we should settle our differences once and for all," he told her. "For the sake of this project, I think he may be right."

It took Holly a moment to realize that he was proffering an olive branch, and she almost laughed in his face. Just what kind of a simpleton did he take her for, anyway? She glared at him coldly. "Mike is a peacemaker, but he doesn't understand that the issues between us are too complex to be settled with a handshake. The best we can hope for is some kind of polite working relationship."

Logan didn't take the rebuff kindly. "Based on mutual respect?" he asked mockingly.

"Hardly. You just do your job, I'll do mine and we'll stay out of each other's way as much as possible."

Logan shrugged. "Sounds like a plan to me. Are you ready to climb aboard?" He stepped into the runabout, keeping one foot on the dock to steady the swaying of the little boat.

Holly hesitated when he held out his hand to her, but she knew better than to refuse his offer of assistance. She tossed her shoulder bag onto one of the seats, then placed her hand in Logan's.

Holly felt the jolt of the contact all the way up her arm, a hot current of electricity that twisted and curled inside her. She tried to ignore the sensation, pretending it didn't exist, but as soon as she had stepped on board and was sure of her balance, she jerked her hand away. As she edged past him she made the mistake of looking up, and found a knowing and infuriatingly sexy grin hovering around his lips.

"Too hot to handle?" he asked lightly.

Holly glared at him. "No. I just don't want to catch anything."

"Don't worry, Holly-love. Scruples—or the lack thereof—aren't contagious."

"More's the pity," she snapped as she took her seat. "You could benefit from a good dose of ethics."

"Good morning, Logan. Holly," Mike said as he came down the dock looking anxiously from one to the other. "I hope I haven't held you up."

"No. You're just in time to referee," Logan snapped.

Mike dropped his bag into the stern and frowned at both of them, but Holly put an end to his lecture before he had a chance to start. "It's all right, Mike," she said as she dug into her bag for a pair of sunglasses. "Logan and I have agreed to be civil to each other."

"In public, anyway," Logan added as he leaned forward to untie the bow line. "If you'll get the stern line, we can shove off."

Mike complied and had barely enough time to take his seat before Logan revved the engine and sped away from the dock. Forty-five minutes later, they reached the wreck site where Logan's salvage boat and the pontoon were lashed together. Logan threw a line to one of the armed guards who had been monitoring their approach, and the man put down his high-powered rifle long enough to secure the runabout to the pontoon.

Holly eyed the guard and the gun nervously. "I don't think I'll ever get used to this," she murmured. "I don't like guns."

"Just ignore them," Logan advised her as he vaulted out of the speedboat onto the deck. "Before we finish excavating this wreck, you'll be grateful for their presence, I promise you."

"I doubt that." Holly picked up her bag and used the back of the seat to steady herself against the pitching of the runabout.

"Your equipment is on the *Fortune Hunter*," Logan told her. "Mike already knows his way around. He'll show you where everything is."

"Thank you," Holly replied. "I can be ready to dive in about thirty minutes."

"Suit yourself. No pun intended." He turned and disappeared into the deckhouse.

Mike climbed onto the pontoon and helped Holly do the same. "If this is what you and Logan call a truce—"

"I'm doing the best I can, Mike. Just leave it alone, okay?"

Though everything was well organized, Holly had to pick her way through a minefield of salvage equipment and diving gear to reach the ladder that provided access to the *Fortune Hunter*.

"Can I give you a hand with your bag, Dr. McGinnis?"

Holly shaded her eyes as she looked up to the salvage boat. A middle-aged man with a wild mane of long gray hair was leaning over the ladder, his hand extended to her. His hair spilled over his shoulders, framing one of the kindest faces Holly had ever seen. She couldn't help but return the smile he gave her.

"Thanks." She tossed her bag up to him and scaled the ladder with Mike right behind her.

"Welcome aboard, Dr. McGinnis. It's a pleasure to finally meet you."

Holly was pleased that his greeting seemed genuine. Since he was clad in a wet suit he was obviously a member of the dive team; she hadn't expected a warm welcome from any of Logan's people. "I'm afraid you have me at a disadvantage," she said as she shook his hand.

"Sorry. Rupert Duffey, at your service. I'm the dive master around here, so if you need anything, you see me."

Holly's smile faded. "You're Duffey?"

"That's right."

Holly wasn't sure how to feel. Twelve years ago, she had hated this man without ever having met him. It was Rupert Duffey who had given Logan a summer job as a diving instructor and filled his head with visions of Spanish gold. For a long time, she'd held Duffey responsible for Logan's decision to leave grad school. Blaming a stranger had been easier than admitting that Logan wasn't the man she'd thought he was.

But Holly had long ago realized how wrong she'd been about Logan, and now she found that she really didn't feel anything at all about Duffey except a healthy dose of distrust. "I didn't know you and Logan were working together," she said when she found her voice again.

"He's the best in the business, and I like working with the best."

Holly could have disputed his assessment, but she didn't see any point in starting an argument. "I need to suit up, Duffey. Can you point me toward the equipment lockers?"

"Yours is in the main cabin along with Logan's, Mike's and mine," he told her. "All the other divers have lockers down on the pontoon. You'll find your name stenciled on your locker and your air tanks."

"Thanks."

She departed, but Mike remained behind a moment watching her with a puzzled expression on his face.

Duffey watched her, too, but when he spared a glance at Mike he had to chuckle. "You look more surprised than I am, Mike. Considering some of the things Logan told me she said about me twelve years ago, that wasn't quite what I expected from our first meeting."

"Nor I," Mike replied almost reflectively. "Maybe she'll learn to be as indifferent toward Logan one of these days."

"That would make things easier for you, wouldn't it?"

Mike looked at him with some surprise. "Am I that transparent?"

Duffey grinned. "I seem to recall a drinking bout between you and Logan that I sat in on a few years back in Matthew Town. It was very enlightening. Until then I didn't know it was possible for two men to be in love with the same woman and remain good friends."

Mike frowned. "Obviously you remember more of that evening than I do. You believe Logan is still in love with Holly?"

Duffey shrugged. "Let's just say that he's been carrying around a lot of dead weight these last twelve years. One way or another, he's going to have to jettison some of it."

"I suppose you're right," Mike said reluctantly, then gave Duffey a thin smile. "I should change now. There's a lot of work to be done."

"Sure. Yell if you need anything. I'll be on the bridge."

When Mike finally entered the main cabin, Holly was already zipping up her red-and-black wet suit. "These high-tech dive helmets are going to spoil me rotten, Mike," she told him, taking the helmet and her buoyancy vest from her locker. "If I get used to it, I may never be able to go back to normal scuba equipment."

He moved to his locker. "You'll enjoy the freedom it gives you," he promised her. "The sound quality is remarkable, and there are four communications channels that allow teams to work together without confusion."

"I've been away too long." Holly moved to the tank rack at the end of the locker bay and retrieved the scuba tank with her name on it. "I'll be on deck checking out my equipment whenever you're ready to dive."

"I'll join you in a minute."

Holly emerged from the cabin onto the deserted deck. There was a dive team already at work beneath the boat, and she was grateful for the few minutes of privacy. She had nervous knots in her stomach and she needed to collect herself.

To that end, she focused on her dive gear, carefully studying the new helmet. It was designed to encase the head completely, making a regulator and face mask obsolete. The built-in microphone allowed divers to communicate freely, and the angled acrylic faceplate would give her a wide field of vision. It was a revolutionary system.

The other equipment was more familiar, but she checked it thoroughly, letting the steady, familiar rhythm of the boat at anchor soothe her.

She was kneeling on the deck attaching a scuba tank to her buoyancy vest when Logan finally came aboard the *Fortune Hunter*. "Well, did you find everything you need?" he inquired politely.

"Yes, thank you."

Logan sat on the transom in front of her, giving Holly a too-close-for-comfort view of his well-muscled calves and thighs. Twelve years hadn't diminished his impressive physique in the slightest. If anything, he looked stronger and more powerful than ever. "Are you nervous, Holly?" he asked softly.

She stiffened, fearing that he had somehow read her thoughts, but when she looked up at him she found no hint of smugness in his expression; just a sincere concern that she knew better than to trust. "Of course not. Why would I be?"

"This is your first dive since the accident in Mexico, isn't it?"

"Not really," she said, returning her attention to the vest. "I've been swimming nearly every day for the last eighteen months, and I've even managed to get in a little tank time."

"That's not the same thing."

She looked up at him, perturbed. "Don't worry, Logan. I'm not going to fall apart down there. I wouldn't give you that pleasure."

He sighed heavily. "I thought we were operating under a flag of truce."

She craned her head, looking pointedly around the deck. "In public, remember? I don't see anyone else around, so I don't see any reason to pretend we're buddies."

"We were never buddies, Holly," he reminded her, his voice soft and husky. "We never could be. But that doesn't mean we have to be enemies."

Holly tried to ignore the shiver that his intimate tone sent down her spine. "What is this, Logan? A new tactic? Intimidation didn't work, so you're going for the soft sell?"

All traces of tenderness left Logan's face as he stood abruptly. "No, I was just worried about you. Excuse me for being human."

He stalked off and Holly realized that she had made a serious mistake. She wasn't about to be taken in by Logan's phony solicitude, but forcing confrontations with him would only be counterproductive. She didn't have to trust him, but she *did* have to work with him whether she liked it or not. "Logan..."

He stopped and frowned at her. "What?"

"Thank you for your concern, but I'll be fine."

He gave her a nod, acknowledging the giant step she'd just taken. "I'm glad." A faint smile played around his lips. "As long as we're making nice, would you like some help getting into your gear? It takes two to attach the helmet."

Holly didn't like the idea of Logan assisting her. Part of her rebelled because she didn't trust him to attach the rig safely; another part of her just didn't want him that close. "Thanks, but Mike will be out in a minute. I'm sure he can give me a hand."

Logan stiffened at the rebuff. "Whatever you want," he said, then disappeared into the cabin.

Holly picked up her dive tanks and wiggled into the vest. By the time she got the harness latched, she was wishing she had accepted Logan's offer of help.

"Heads up, Logan! We've got company!"

Holly whirled toward the urgent cry and found Duffey leaning over the bridge rail. Logan came charging out of the cabin wearing nothing but his swim trunks, and Mike was right on his heels.

"Who is it?" Logan asked, reaching up to take the pair of binoculars Duffey lowered over the rail.

"Who do you think?"

"Damn," Logan muttered. Duffey pointed to the north, and Logan moved aft to train the binoculars on the horizon.

"What's going on?" Holly asked.

"The Dutchman is paying us a social call," Duffey replied, tension written all over his weathered face.

"What does that mean?" she asked him.

"Trouble," Duffey replied. "Nothing but trouble."

"How much longer before team one comes up?" Logan called out, keeping the binoculars focused on the approaching boat.

"About ten minutes," the dive master replied.

"Get on the horn to Skip. Tell him to get his people up now. And have them use the pontoon. I don't want them bringing anything aboard while Dutch is here."

"Done." Duffey disappeared into the bridge cabin.

"I'll help the dive team," Mike offered. He hurried to the ladder, and Holly looked down at the pontoon as he descended.

She wasn't surprised to find that all the guards were displaying their weapons very prominently.

She went to Logan. "Are we really going to have trouble?" she asked skeptically.

Logan lowered the binoculars. "Anywhere the Dutchman goes, there's trouble," he replied. "Usually he just watches us from a distance, but I guess he feels like dropping by to say hello. There won't be any shooting today, though, if that's what you're worried about. The first dive team hasn't brought anything up this morning."

The stress he put on the word *today* worried Holly. It indicated that eventually there *would* be shooting. "Aren't you being a little melodramatic about this, Logan? Given the security here, this Dutchman person would have to be a lunatic to attack us. And what purpose would it serve? It would make him a fugitive from the law, and any artifacts he got hold of would be stolen plunder that he couldn't possibly sell on the open market."

"Holly, Dutch Voorhees doesn't give a damn about the law. He has a half dozen government officials in his back pocket and his black market contacts are endless. You know how lucrative the antiquities trade is—even for stolen goods."

She couldn't argue that point. "So you think he'll eventually make a run on us?"

Logan nodded. "In one way or another. And subtlety isn't usually the Dutchman's style." He raised the binoculars again to study the incoming boat.

"Has he attacked you before on salvage jobs?"

"He's looted several of my sites. That's why we're leaving the *Fortune Hunter* and the pontoon at anchor here whenever the weather permits it." Logan lowered the binoculars and looked at her. His blue eyes clouded, becoming almost smoky in color, and Holly felt the jolt of an intimate memory. She'd seen that look before when Logan was wrestling with an important decision. In fact, it had been very evident the day he'd told her he planned to leave the university and become a private salvage operator.

Holly shoved the painful memory of that day aside and waited until Logan finished wrestling with whatever was on his mind. It was a moment before he finally told her, "Just so you'll know, Holly, it was the Dutchman who dynamited that reef to get at the *Nuestra Señora Suerte,* not me."

He sounded so convincing that Holly almost bought it. His eyes were filled with sincerity, as though he not only wanted her to believe it, he *needed* her to believe it. For just a second, he was the old Logan—the one Holly had loved with every fiber of her being. The one she had never really stopped loving. But that Logan didn't exist. He never had; he was only a blind romantic fantasy created by a young woman in love. Holly knew she couldn't trust the real Logan.

She managed a thin, skeptical smile. "Well, I guess it's only to be expected that you'd find a convenient scapegoat."

"Jeez—" Logan ran a hand through his hair in disgust. "Why did I bother? You're going to believe the worst of me, no matter what, aren't you?" he demanded.

"Why shouldn't I?"

"Because you know me, Holly," he said with an intensity that startled her. "There was a time when you knew me better than anyone."

A sickening wave of pain and grief washed over her at the thought of how much she'd lost. "Don't make me laugh, Logan. I didn't know you at all. I just *thought* I did. The man I was in love with never could have done the things you've done."

"All I did was decide I didn't want to spend the rest of my life chasing research grants and writing boring papers for stuffy academic journals. Why the hell is that such a crime?"

"Because doing it this way—*your* way—is wrong!"

"According to whom? All those publish-or-perish professors we had? Those stuffy academics who think you have to be affiliated with a university or museum to do research? To have ethics?"

"Yes!" she flung back.

"Well, you're wrong, Holly. Open your—"

"*Oh, chil-dren...*" Duffey's singsong voice cut Logan off in midsentence. "Could you kids postpone this debate until later? Our company is just about to knock on the back door."

Logan cursed and returned his full attention to the Dutchman's salvage boat, the *Treasure Trove*. He didn't need the binoculars this time to see Dutch Voorhees on the deck. The boat had slowed and was pulling up to the port side of the *Fortune Hunter*, close enough for Logan to see his nemesis's broad, phony smile.

Holly saw it, too, and shuddered. The man standing at the starboard rail was as big as a bear and a lot less appealing. He had a long, scraggly beard, and his dark hair was slicked back from his face. He reminded Holly of an eighteenth-century pirate captain, but there was nothing romantic about the image.

"Is that the Dutchman?" she asked.

"In the flesh."

Holly suppressed another shudder. She didn't need Logan's warning to know that this was a dangerous man. And the crewmen she could see on the boat didn't look any too harmless, either. One in particular caught her eye, and Holly felt a chill sweep over her. He was a large man, completely bald-headed, with a scowl aimed directly at her.

For the first time since she'd joined this project, Holly was grateful for the guards and their guns.

"Dutch is very good at provoking people, Holly," Logan told her quietly. "If you know what's good for you, you'll keep your mouth shut and let me do the talking."

Holly resented the advice, but she didn't dispute it. A foul smell from the *Treasure Trove* was wafting though the air, and it was almost as distasteful as the Dutchman himself. At the moment, Holly would have preferred being anywhere but on the deck of the *Fortune Hunter*, but she wasn't about to slink away like a frightened rabbit. "By all means. He's your friend. You deal with him."

Logan shot her a disgusted glance, then moved to the port rail. He looked relaxed and confident, but Holly knew the tension she'd seen in him earlier was still there. She glanced over her shoulder, and saw Duffey standing guard on the bridge with a shotgun resting in his arms. She looked at the bald man again, and was tempted to ask Duffey if he had another gun.

"Ahoy there, Tate! How's the fishing this morning?" Voorhees called out jovially once his boat was parallel to the *Fortune Hunter*.

"We're throwing the little ones back," Logan replied. "What do you want, Dutch?"

"Just dropped by for a neighborly visit. Thought I might borrow a cup of sugar."

Logan snapped his fingers. "Shucks. We just ran out."

"That's too bad." The Dutchman fastened his gaze on Holly. "My, my, Tate. You've certainly improved the looks of your crew since the last time I was here."

Holly saw Logan's shoulders stiffen. "She does her job."

The Dutchman's booming, lascivious laugh cut across the otherwise silent water. "I'll bet she does. And from the looks of her, she could do it pretty well, too. I don't suppose this is the crippled archaeologist I've heard so much about?"

Outraged, Holly balled her hands into fists, but any retort she might have made died when Logan's eyes met hers with a look that commanded her to be silent. "I don't know, Dutch," he said casually, his gaze sweeping over her. "She doesn't look crippled to me."

Holly was stunned by Logan's defense of her. It certainly wasn't what she'd expected.

The Dutchman laughed boisterously. "Well, I guess you ought to know, Tate. I wouldn't mind having a tasty morsel like that on my crew." He looked directly at Holly. "How 'bout it, little lady? You wanna come work for me?"

"No, thanks," she called back, willing herself to appear unruffled. "I don't think I could stand the stench."

Dutch's booming laugh echoed over the water, but Logan overrode the irritating noise. "Have you seen what you came to see, Dutch, or was there something else you wanted?"

Voorhees shook his head. "Nope. That's all. I just wanted to get a look at the lady egghead who was savvy enough to call you a wreck rapist."

Logan's hands clenched into white-knuckled fists, and Holly felt an unwanted stab of pity for him. If he'd been telling her the truth, he was being taunted for a crime that Voorhees himself had committed. That would be galling, in the extreme. But Holly reminded herself that she had only Logan's word that it was the Dutchman who had dynamited the wreck—and Logan wasn't exactly high on her list of trustworthy sources.

When Logan didn't respond to the taunt, Dutch laughed again and raised his hand in a farewell salute. "Take care of yourself—and my treasure—Logan. I'll be back for it. Eventually." The diesel engines aboard the *Treasure Trove* roared to life. "Be seeing you, Doc!" he yelled over the din. The boat edged forward and made a slow circle of the *Fortune Hunter* before speeding off the way it had come.

Holly watched them go, conscious of the fact that the bald crewman had never taken his eyes off her.

Shaking his head, Logan watched his nemesis depart. Then he looked at Holly. "'Couldn't stand the stench'?" he asked her with an approving grin.

Holly shrugged. "It was the truth. Did you get a whiff of his boat? It smelled like a fishing scow."

"Dutch never put too much stock in the saying, 'Cleanliness is next to godliness.'"

"I don't doubt that." Holly glanced at the departing *Treasure Trove*. "Do our security precautions include alarm sensors in each of the excavated craters?"

Logan nodded. "Absolutely. If divers approach the craters at night, the security guards will know about it." He gestured toward the Quonset hut on Sand Cay. "And the alarm rings in the divers' barracks, too."

"Good. Now, I think we've wasted enough time on the Dutchman," she said, bending to retrieve her helmet. The tank on her back was getting unbearably heavy and she was going to have to dive or get out of it. "Attach this thing for me, would you?"

Logan grinned at her. "What? You mean you're not worried anymore that I'll cross your hoses just for spite?"

Holly had forgotten all about that concern, but she wasn't about to admit to forgetting it—or to having had it, for that matter. "Just shut up and connect me," she snapped, turning her back on him as she donned the helmet.

"Yes, Your Majesty," Logan said insolently, but he moved to her and quickly attached the hoses while Holly tucked the flaps into her suit.

Holly felt the rush of air into the helmet immediately and took a deep breath. It wasn't nearly as comforting as it should have been, and Holly realized that she was on the verge of a panic attack. She'd had one the first time she'd dived after the accident, and that had been nothing more than a ten-minute submersion in a swimming pool. Now she was about to go into the ocean again for the first time in three years, and she was terrified.

But under absolutely no condition was she going to let Logan—or anyone else—know that. "Thanks," she said, moving aft to the transom. "I'll see you down there."

Logan frowned as she sat and slipped into her fins. "All right. But be sure and wait for Mike. All the divers are up and I don't want you on the bottom alone."

His voice sounded muffled thanks to the insulation of her helmet, but she got his message loud and clear. "I don't need your permission to dive, Logan. It's only thirty-five feet." She swung her legs over the transom and eased herself down to the dive platform.

"Damn it, Holly!" Logan swore at her, but it was too late. She stepped off the platform and the ocean swallowed her. "Stubborn idiot! Hasn't she ever heard of the buddy system?'' he muttered as he rushed for his dive tanks in the cabin so that he could join her.

"Logan! Look to port!" Duffey shouted. "Get Holly back up!"

Logan stopped short of the cabin and looked out over the water. His heart leapt into his throat when he saw the unmistakable notched tail fins of reef sharks circling the area where the *Treasure Trove* had stopped so briefly. A red stain of blood was spreading across the surface, and the agitated sharks were making the water churn.

Chapter Five

The panic hit Holly the instant the ocean closed over her head. The momentum of her feetfirst dive and the weights on her vest propelled her downward…ten feet, fifteen, then twenty, but Holly's preservation instincts had her flailing blindly to return to the surface long before her natural buoyancy equalized the effects of gravity. Her breath came in short, panting gasps, and the oxygen-rich mixture of her air supply made her light-headed.

This was why she had defied Logan. She wanted no one to witness her humiliating reaction to the underwater environment that had once been as natural to her as it was to the permanent residents of the ocean. She had to learn to control her panic in private.

And she did. Willing herself to breath naturally, she stopped fighting her descent. She closed her eyes, shoving away the terrifying memories of her accident—memories of being pinned beneath two tons of iron with her scuba tank crushing into her spine, her dive mask cracked, her air supply cut off and water rushing into her lungs. She willed herself not to remember the pain, the terror and the knowledge that she'd been more dead than alive when Mike and her other colleagues had freed her from what could have been her watery grave.

But she wasn't trapped now. This wasn't the same dive in the Gulf of Mexico that had nearly killed her. She was free to maneuver. She wasn't in pain. She wasn't going to die.

The panic receded, and Holly opened her eyes. Once she'd stopped struggling, her weights had carried her all the way to the sandy ocean floor, and the first thing she saw were the thin grid wires that had been secured over the excavation crater.

The second thing she saw were the frenzied sharks churning the water above the crater—a dozen or more of them fighting over what appeared to be bloody scraps of fish. They were reef sharks, the largest no bigger than six feet in length. They weren't man-eaters by nature, but that didn't offer Holly any peace of mind. A shark—any shark—in a feeding frenzy would attack anything that crossed its path.

Considering all the thrashing about she had done on her descent, Holly knew that she was lucky to be alive. It was a miracle that she hadn't attracted their attention—and it was going to take another miracle to get her back aboard the *Fortune Hunter* in one piece. A diver's most dangerous moment in shark-infested waters was the precious seconds it took to get out of the water and back onto a boat.

With her heart pounding, Holly stayed very still on the bottom, fighting to remain calm while she weighed her options. There weren't many.

"But don't panic," she murmured. The words echoed in her helmet, and she realized like a complete idiot that she had a communication system built into her headgear. There was no way anyone on the ship could help her without placing himself in mortal danger, but at the very least she could warn Mike and the others not to dive.

"Duffey? Duffey, can you hear me?" she said softly. "Duffey?"

Silence.

Great. She had means of communication, but she'd forgotten to ask how to turn it on. Moving slowly, never taking her eyes off the sharks, she fingered one side of the helmet, searching for anything that might be a switch.

Nothing.

She tried the other side and found a small dial, but when she turned it she realized that there were several settings. She tried all of them, murmuring Duffy's name at each new notch. Still no response.

The sharks were spreading out now, making darting turns as they snapped at bits of fish and other sharks that happened to get in their way. One made a wide circle, diving directly toward Holly, then careered away to rejoin the others.

Holly knew she had to do something quickly. She had no idea how the fish bait that had attracted the sharks had gotten into the water, but there was very little of it left. Once the sharks ran out of easy food they would start looking for other prey. It wouldn't take them long to find her.

When she saw the shadow pass over her, Holly's heart slammed into her chest. She looked up, expecting to find a shark circling over her head . . . expecting an attack at any second.

What she found instead was another diver, pumping his legs as hard as he could to reach her—and attracting the attention of the sharks in the process.

Holly couldn't believe her eyes. It was Logan. He hadn't even taken the time to put on a wet suit and he was wearing an old-fashioned tank and regulator, not a communication helmet like Holly's. But he was here, and he was carrying two high-powered shark billies.

"Logan, what do you think you're doing?" she demanded as he settled next to her on the sand. In answer, he shoved one of the long black sticks at her and jerked his thumb upward.

"Are you nuts?" she asked.

Though Logan had no communication link, he either heard her or read her lips because he motioned upward again, then reached out and yanked the release on Holly's dive weights. She heard a hiss of air as her buoyancy vest inflated and brought her up off the ocean floor, floating toward the surface.

He's trying to kill me, Holly thought as a wave of panic that approached hysteria ripped through her. The sharks were circling overhead now, attracted by the shock waves of Logan's dive. They were darting this way and that, making circles that brought them ever closer, and Logan had just condemned her to an ascent right in the middle of them.

Anger replaced her panic, and Holly's well-honed survival instincts took over. Moving her arms and legs as little as possible, she adopted a defensive posture with the billy as she continued her ascent. A shark made a tight circle not three feet from her and then slipped out of view. Another took its place, a little closer this time, and Holly fought the urge to strike blindly with the billy. If the club was like ones she had used before, it had only two or three small explosive charges. The concussion rarely proved fatal to the shark, but one good pop on the snout was sometimes enough to discourage it. As long as the sharks were circling, not attacking, she would hang on to the slim piece of protection Logan had given her.

Holly didn't know that Logan was ascending, too, until she heard the muffled pop of his billy. She turned just enough to see that he had placed his back to hers, covering the blind area behind her. There was no time to consider the implications of his protective gesture because a shark darted past her, then, in a move almost too swift to see, it lunged for her legs with its mouth gaping.

Grasping the billy in both hands, Holly jabbed downward with all her might. The percussion shook her, and the dazed shark floated toward the bottom then wiggled away. Another took its place, diving at her from above.

Holly had barely enough time to stab at the shark's soft underbelly. It careered away and she heard another pop from Logan's billy.

The sharks widened their circle. Holly looked up and saw only a few feet of clear blue water between her and the surface. The dive platform of the *Fortune Hunter* was just to her right, and she could see Mike there, waiting.

She knew she'd never have another chance. Pumping her legs with all her might, she burst through to the surface, grabbing for the dive platform to lever herself out of the water. Mike clutched at her, pulling her up and shoving her toward the transom.

His maneuver had her out of the water and out of the reach of the sharks' jaws in the wink of an eye, but in yanking her to safety he inadvertently disconnected the intake hose on her tank. Holly's supply of oxygen was immediately cut off, but the exhaust valve was still working perfectly. The imbalance created a vacuum inside her helmet and left her gasping for air as she struggled to climb over the transom.

She felt another pair of hands join Mike's, helping her onto the deck, and Holly collapsed to her knees, tearing frantically at the zipper of her suit. The world started to go gray as she clawed at the helmet, and then suddenly it was lifted free from her head and she could breathe.

Holly gasped for air, sucking in deep gulps, and somehow managed to ask, "Logan? Is he up?"

"Right here." It was Logan's voice. He was kneeling beside her removing his dive tanks, almost as breathless as she was. "Are you all right?" he asked.

Holly didn't know whether to be grateful to him or furious. In one sense, he had saved her life, but in so doing he had placed her in deadly peril. Had his rescue been nothing more than pretense? When he released her weights, had he been hoping that the sharks would get to her before she reached the surface?

Those doubts and the residue of adrenaline that still pumped through Holly's body tipped the balance of the scale toward fury.

"Yes, I'm all right," she snapped. "No thanks to you."

Logan stared at her in disbelief. "What do you mean? I saved your life down there."

"By dropping my weights without any warning?"

"Holly, if we'd stayed on the bottom those sharks would have started ripping us to pieces and we'd still have been thirty-five feet from the surface."

"You sent me straight into that feeding frenzy," she accused him. "If that's what you call a lifesaving technique, don't do me any favors next time!"

Anger clouded Logan's handsome features. "Don't worry, Your Majesty. I won't," he said, coming to his feet. He glared down at her coldly. "I never make the same mistake twice."

Furious, he whirled toward Duffey, who had helped him into the boat. "Keep the divers up, Duffey. No one's going down again until those sharks clear out," he ordered, then stalked off, disappearing down the ladder to the pontoon. Duffey shot her a disgusted glance, and returned to the bridge, shaking his head as he went.

Holly sank back onto her heels and realized that Mike was on his knees beside her, staring at her in disbelief. She suddenly felt ashamed of herself. "Don't look at me like that," she ordered as she unlatched her vest.

"Holly, he saved your life," Mike told her.

"Did he?" She eased out of the vest and Mike took it from her.

"Of course," he replied. "As soon as he realized that the Dutchman had baited the sharks, Logan grabbed the billies and the emergency scuba gear from the transom locker and went in after you. By the time I got up to the *Fortune Hunter* and realized what had happened, he was already in the water."

"That doesn't prove he was trying to save me," she told him, coming to her feet on legs that were unsteady at best. "He released my weights without any warning, Mike. The sharks were circling over my head and Logan sent me straight into them. Even with the billy I could have been attacked before I reached the boat."

"And so could have Logan," he reminded her.

Mike was right. Logan had risked his life, and now he was a hero. Was that what he'd been after all along? To earn her trust by saving her life? Had he expected her to fall into his arms and thank him?

If so, he had to be very disappointed about now. "Look, Mike, I applaud your loyalty, but there are things you don't know," Holly said as she limped toward the cabin. "Logan is dangerous."

"What?" he said incredulously. "What on earth are you talking about?"

Holly cursed her tongue. She didn't want Mike hovering over her like an overprotective mother hen, but that's exactly what would happen if she told him about the notes and her midnight visitor.

"Nothing," she said, moving into the cabin.

Mike wasn't going to let her accusation go, though. He followed her and shut the door. "Holly, I want to know what you meant by that. Why would you think Logan wants to hurt you?"

She hesitated a moment before confessing, "I received two threatening letters yesterday."

"What?"

She nodded. "You heard me right. One came in the mail before I left home and the other was waiting in my room when I got here. Then last night, a man sneaked into my room about midnight and scattered things around. Someone involved in this project is trying to frighten me into leaving."

Mike's alarm was obvious. "Holly, this is horrible. Why didn't you tell me about the notes yesterday?"

"Because I didn't want you involved. And I still don't."

"But if you need protection—"

"I don't," she insisted. "I can take care of myself. I just wanted you to know that I have good reason to be suspicious of Logan."

Mike frowned. "You think he sent the notes?"

"I can't prove it," she admitted reluctantly. "But he's the most likely culprit."

"Why?"

"Any number of reasons. The most obvious is that he wants to pay me back for the articles I wrote about him. But there's also the very real possibility that he needs me out of the way in order to pull off some scheme he's working on to smuggle artifacts away from the site."

Mike shook his head. "Holly, that's insane. Paul Kyte has been trying to destroy your career for years. Surely he's—"

"He's on my list," she admitted. "I'm not stupid. I've considered the possibility that it was Paul. But in light of what just happened, I'd say Logan is the front-runner." A half-formed thought finally clicked into place, and Holly took two steps toward her friend. "Mike, how much do you know about the Dutchman?"

Mike frowned, puzzled by the abrupt change of subject. "Not much. I heard that he's done two terms in prison, one for antiquities smuggling and the other for assault with a deadly weapon. He was also arrested for murder once, but the charge didn't stick."

"Whom did he kill?"

"I'm not sure. I heard that it had something to do with a wreck he was looting," Mike told her. "He used to be a legitimate salvor, but the government won't lease sites to him anymore because of his smuggling conviction. So he makes his living stealing from his former colleagues. And he still does some smuggling, of course, but the police haven't been able to catch him at it.''

"A smuggler." Holly nodded. "It fits."

Mike frowned again. "What fits?"

"I'm just wondering if it's possible that Logan's feud with the Dutchman is just for show," she said, running the possibilities quickly through her mind. "What if they're working together in a plot to steal artifacts from the wreck and smuggle them out of the islands? Maybe Logan arranged what just happened with the Dutchman to get rid of me.''

Mike looked at Holly as though she had stepped off the deep end and sunk to the bottom. "Do you know how paranoid that sounds, Holly?"

"Of course I do. But as the saying goes—just because you're paranoid, it doesn't mean someone's not out to get you. Think about it, Mike. The Dutchman's arrival was timed almost perfectly with my preparations to dive. And the first thing Logan did when he heard Dutch was on his way was to order the divers out of the water! Maybe Duffey gave Dutch some kind of signal that brought him in to start that feeding frenzy.''

"Holly, that theory is so farfetched that it's hovering out there somewhere around Venus," Mike told her. "And there's a huge hole in it. How could Logan possibly have known that you would dive alone before you noticed the sharks?''

Mike had a point. "I don't know," she said, searching for something that would allow her theory to hold together. "Maybe...maybe he was sure that if he ordered me not to dive, I'd plunge in blindly just to defy him," she suggested.

Mike conceded that point to her. "You're right. Anyone who knows you as well as Logan does would know that it's pointless to give you a direct command and expect you not to rebel.''

Holly didn't like the readiness with which Mike agreed with her. Obviously he thought that she was stubborn and

bullheaded, but she couldn't argue the point without telling
him the real reason that she had dived so quickly—that she
had been afraid she'd panic and hadn't wanted any witnesses.

Mike moved to the table in the galley across from the
lockers and sat down. "I'm sorry, Holly, but I can't believe
any of this."

She wasn't surprised, and she felt truly sorry for him. She
had lost all of her illusions about Logan years ago, but Mike
had held on to his. Seeing Logan in this new light wasn't
going to be easy for him.

She moved to sit across the table from him. "Mike, I
know that you still consider Logan to be a good friend—"

"Yes, I do," he said forcefully, cutting her off. "When I
came to America to begin my graduate studies, Logan be-
friended me and made me feel less of an outsider. He guided
me through the difficult process of assimilating into American culture. He was the one who introduced me to you, and
together you and Logan made me feel as though I belonged
somewhere for the first time in my life. You were closer to
me than my own family."

He reached out and covered Holly's hands with his own
as he continued, "I loved you both for that then, and I will
always be grateful."

"But Mike, Logan has changed. Surely you can see that."

"We all have, but that doesn't mean he's become a murderer," Mike argued.

Holly admired his loyalty. More than that, she envied it.
But she didn't share it. She couldn't. "Mike, someone has
made threats against me, and it could have been Logan,"
she said with finality as she came to her feet. "You can believe he's innocent if you want to, but I don't have that luxury. I don't plan to lower my guard with Logan for a
minute, and I'd advise anyone else who's working with him
to take the same precaution!"

Chapter Six

Holly found it harder to hold on to her resolve than she'd imagined. Over the next three weeks, she divided her time between the wreck site and the restoration lab, and on more than one occasion she found herself working side by side with Logan. Their relationship slipped into a pattern that couldn't be called friendly, but it rarely erupted into adversarial confrontations. There had even been a few times when they forgot about their differences and seemed to be on the verge of working together as an efficient team, just as they had in the old days.

Ultimately, Holly found that the further she got from the incident with the sharks, the more farfetched her accusations against Logan seemed. A plot that intricate, with that many variables, would have taken incredible planning. And besides, Logan's animosity for the Dutchman had seemed entirely genuine. In the final analysis, she decided she had simply overreacted.

Of course, it helped that there had been no more threatening notes and no more midnight visitors. Yet, even though the weather was gorgeous and the island was beautiful, that undercurrent of tension Holly had felt herself and sensed in others when she'd arrived hadn't abated.

Paul Kyte was partly responsible for it. Though he hadn't yet staged an outright mutiny, Holly sometimes caught him watching her with an intensity she could only describe as malicious. And the officious little Edgar Franklin added to the tension with constant demands for the shipment of artifacts that Holly wasn't ready to release.

Neal Scanlon, the film director, was a shameless offender, too. One never knew when the documentary director was going to stick a camera and microphone in someone's face. Holly was particularly sensitive to Scanlon's presence because it added to her feeling that she was constantly being watched.

All those little irritations added up, but Holly finally realized that Logan and Avery were at the heart of the friction on the island. The partners didn't trust each other for a minute. For every guard Avery had hired, another was on Logan's payroll, and the same was true of the divers. Logan's people watched Avery's like a hawk, and vice versa, creating a never-ending cycle of paranoia.

"Sounds like it's show time," Paul Kyte said, and Holly almost jumped out of her skin. She hadn't realized that he had left his work station in the lab. It wasn't the first time he'd sneaked up on her, and she was getting tired of it.

"Show time?" she said, regaining control of her nerves.

Paul pointed toward the sky. "The chopper. I wonder what Logan's bringing us today."

Holly cocked her head and listened. Sure enough, she heard the droning of Judd's helicopter returning from Sand Cay with the day's finds. It was a routine she'd come to expect—and enjoy—on days like this when she worked at the lab instead of the site.

"By this time we know to be ready for anything," Holly told Paul. She gestured to the gold coins she had been polishing. "Would you put these in the vault for me, please, and then come on out with the transport dolly? I'll go see what the cargo looks like."

She stripped off her rubber gloves and hurried out to the helicopter pad as the craft made its slow descent. One of the security guards was riding shotgun in the passenger seat, and Holly caught a glimpse of Logan peering out the window of the cargo bay. Her heartbeat accelerated in a rhythm that seemed to match the beating of the chopper blades.

It had nothing to do with seeing Logan, of course, she told herself sternly. They spent no more time together than was absolutely necessary, and that suited Holly just fine. If she was excited now, it was only her natural anticipation of seeing the wonderful new discoveries he had made today.

The chopper settled onto the pad and Logan threw open the cargo doors. His broad smile seemed to mirror the excitement Holly felt, and she hurried to him.

"Well, you look like the cat that ate the canary," she told him. "What did you find today?"

Logan crouched in the doorway and settled back on his heels. "Not much. We just located the captain's cabin," he said casually.

Holly felt a jolt of adrenaline. "What?"

"The captain's cabin," he repeated, deliberately misunderstanding her exclamation. "You know. The room on a ship where the captain sleeps and keeps a lot of the most valuable pieces of treasure."

Holly sighed in exasperation. "I know what a captain's cabin is. What makes you so certain you've found it?"

Logan made a show of glancing thoughtfully at the numerous crates and watertight containers lining the cargo bay. "Oh, let's see. There was the nocturnal, the astrolabe... a few odds and ends that Ashcroft described as being stored in his cabin. And... hmm... what else?"

He was teasing her, drawing out the suspense. If he had found something more rare than the navigational instruments it had to be special, indeed. "Logan..."

He grinned at her, making his sapphire eyes twinkle merrily. "And these." He reached into a barrel, pulled out a water-soaked rag, and slowly peeled the fabric away to reveal a tiny gold box, which he held out to Holly.

"Oh, Logan..." Awestruck, she took the fragile, intricately engraved box, cradling it in her palm as she inspected it. "You found one of the snuff boxes."

He chuckled. "One? My dear Dr. McGinnis, you underestimate me. According to Ashcroft's manifest, he had a chest of two hundred and fifty gold, jewel-encrusted snuff boxes in his cabin. No two exactly alike." He patted the side of the barrel. "We found over a hundred of them today."

Holly's gasp of delight quickly evolved into a laugh. "A hundred? Let me see!" She levered herself up and twisted around to sit on the cargo bay floor with her legs dangling over the side. Logan handed her one rag after another, each one containing a tiny accessory box more elegant than the last.

"Enough! Enough!" she said with a laugh when she had more than she could possibly handle.

Logan settled back against a crate and watched Holly as she reverently inspected each box. Her face was glowing, her eyes were sparkling, and she was more radiantly beautiful than he had ever seen her before. A knot of pure, unadulterated lust settled in his loins, but he was too moved by Holly's excitement and his own to make any effort to reject the sensation. A memory surged to the surface of his consciousness, and he let himself enjoy it.

"Oh, I wish I could open them, but I don't dare until they've been through a bath," she murmured, more to herself than Logan. "The sand and salt in the hinges could damage—" She glanced up and stopped abruptly when she saw the strange look on Logan's face. "What's wrong?"

"Nothing. I was just enjoying the view."

"View?"

He nodded. "The expression on your face. I've seen it before. Remember the Carruthers excavation in Belize? We brought up that ivory comb with the little roses carved on it.... You studied it with the same awe, the same look of reverence and wonder shining in your eyes."

Holly found it too painful to meet Logan's searching gaze, because she remembered the incident all too well. It had happened the first summer she and Logan had worked together . . . the summer they had fallen in love. She shifted uncomfortably. "Why don't we focus on *this* excavation, Logan? That summer in Belize was a long time ago."

"But you do remember, don't you?" he asked softly.

"I remember being young and in love, if that's what you want to know," she said with a touch of defiance. "It's amazing the way tropical heat can addle a woman's mind."

"Oh, but that's not all it can do." Logan reached out and gently touched Holly's cheek, but she twisted her head away, then looked at him coldly.

"Don't, Logan. This isn't Belize. I'm not that young anymore, it's not that hot and I'm sure as hell not in love." She jumped out of the cargo bay and began rewrapping the snuff boxes just as Judd arrived with three security guards trailing him. Paul wasn't far behind with the transport dolly.

Logan silently cursed himself for having let sentiment get the better of him. Holly hadn't lost any of the childlike wonder that had drawn her to the study of antiquities, but that was the only thing about her that hadn't changed over the years. Where he was concerned, she had a heart as cold as stone and a suspicious, cynical shell that not even dynamite could crack. But oh, how he wanted to try.

To fight that urge, he had stayed away from her as much as possible. He'd reminded himself a thousand times that she didn't trust him, didn't believe in him, and wasn't about to change her opinion of him. She thought he was morally corrupt, and when she looked at him, her eyes usually expressed her utter contempt very well. But none of that stopped Logan from remembering what it had felt like years ago when her eyes had sparkled with love every time she looked at him. He missed that Holly very much; and more than that, he missed the way her love and trust had made him feel.

If the circumstances had been different, Logan knew he'd be doing everything in his power to regain that trust—and maybe even her love. But that was a luxury he couldn't afford right now. He was beginning to hate the labyrinth of lies and intrigue he'd been drawn into, but he was in too deep to back out now.

Holly was never going to forgive him for things he *hadn't* done. It was a sure bet she would never forgive him for the things he still had to do.

"What have you brought us, Logan?" Paul arrived with the dolly and stepped up to the chopper. When he got a look at the number of boxes in the cargo bay, he let out an appreciative whistle. "All this came from Crater Three? I thought that site had just about dried up."

Logan shoved a crate to the edge of the bay. "It has. While Mike was finishing it up this morning, I moved the *Fortune Hunter* and started excavating Crater Four. It's the biggest find so far."

"I'd say so," Paul murmured as he put the crate onto the dolly.

"And this isn't the end of it," Logan continued. "We're taking everything out of this one as quickly as we can bring it up."

"Everything?" Holly said sharply, glaring up at him. "You haven't started gridding the site?"

Her suspicious, contemptuous look was back in full force, and it made Logan furious. "There's no time for the niceties on this one, Holly."

"But—"

"Before you get on your high horse, *Doctor* McGinnis, Mike agreed with my decision," he said tersely. "We've set out reference markers and Scanlon is using them to do videos of the area. Mike can chart all the finds from that."

"I don't care, Logan. We're doing this excavation my way," she replied hotly, a dozen alarm bells ringing in her head. The methodology she had insisted on was designed to make certain that none of the divers could confiscate artifacts without being detected. Deviating from that process meant abandoning some of her safeguards. Those warning bells told Holly that Logan was up to something. "That's not the procedure we agreed on."

"To hell with procedure," Logan argued. "Haven't you heard the weather report?"

"No," she admitted reluctantly. "I've been in the lab all afternoon."

"There's a big storm brewing. It's expected to strike sometime tomorrow afternoon, and anything that's not nailed down will be scattered from here to Cuba by the time the storm clears."

If that was true, Logan had a valid reason for changing procedure, but Holly wasn't convinced. "Then you shouldn't have opened up a new crater!"

"I didn't know about the storm at the time."

Holly wasn't sure she believed him, but the damage was already done. If a storm was coming in, the crater had to be excavated immediately. "How much is left to bring up?"

"A lot," Logan replied. "And most of the pieces are gold. I'm going to need every diver we've got on the site by dawn tomorrow morning, and even then we'll be cutting it close."

"All right. I'll plan to dive again tomorrow," she told him, then lowered her voice to keep the others from hearing. "But I'm warning you, Logan. I'll be watching. I wouldn't try anything if I were you."

The warning made him furious, and it was everything Holly could do to keep from cringing when Logan brought his face close to hers. "Watch all you like, Holly, but don't make threats. You have no idea just how expendable you are around here."

"NEAL, I WANT YOU to forget about the documentary today. Your one and only assignment is to get video footage of everything down there in its exact location." Holly turned in a circle on the deck of the pontoon, looking at each and every diver. The sun was barely established on the horizon, and the light cast a pinkish glow over everything on the boat. On any other day, Holly might have appreciated the aesthetic beauty of it, but she was focused on more important things this morning.

"Dr. Villanova will be supervising the filming," she went on to tell them. "His communications frequency will be set on four, and I don't want any of you to touch anything until you get approval from him. Is that clear?" There were nods of assent all around her, and that was all Holly needed. "All right, then. Let's go to work." The men scrambled to obey and Holly turned to Logan. "Have you got airlifts ready?"

He nodded tersely. "You know, Holly, there have been a couple of days out here that we actually managed to get work done without you barking orders like a drill sergeant."

Holly wasn't going to let him rile her. "But I'm here today and I'm in charge, so let's get to it."

She let Logan help her secure her helmet, then performed the same service for him. They did one last equipment check, but before they moved down to the dive platform, Logan stopped and looked off toward the horizon.

"What is it?" she asked.

"The Dutchman is out there."

"Again?"

"He is almost every day, Holly. He sits out there with a high-powered telescope watching everything we do."

Waiting for a signal? Holly wondered. She hadn't totally abandoned her suspicion that Logan and Dutch were working together somehow, but since she had absolutely no proof of it there were more pressing problems to occupy her. "Logan, worrying about that smuggler is the last thing we need today. He is *not* going to launch a full frontal assault, no matter what you think to the contrary."

"You're right," he replied thoughtfully. "There are too many men and too many guns here. But he's planning something. I know it."

"Well, worry about it later. Let's dive." Without waiting for Logan, she moved down to the dive platform and went in feetfirst.

Panic gripped her instantly, but it was becoming easier to control with every dive she made, and Holly was reasonably confident that no one noticed her accelerated breathing. She went to work, and gradually the panic eased.

The crater Logan had created was thirty feet long and nearly as wide. The concentration of artifacts in the area was amazing; Holly had never seen anything like it. As one layer was removed, pipe dredges suctioned up the sand revealing another layer beneath it. It was like a bottomless wishing well.

The teams worked in two-hour shifts throughout the morning. Mike directed Neal Scanlon's filming, staying one step ahead of the divers, who put smaller items into the nylon mesh goody bags attached to their belts. Larger items were placed in large, flat sieves that were airlifted or winched up to the boats as soon as they were filled to capacity.

Holly stationed herself at one of the sieves on the upper edge of the crater, loading the basket as the men brought artifacts to her.

"Is this the last of them?" she asked as Logan handed her another bar of gold bullion.

"It looks like it for the time being," he told her. "How many bars have we found in all? I've lost count."

"Thirty-seven."

Logan whistled softly. "That's amazing. But of course, we're still several hundred shy of what Ashcroft listed on his manifest."

"Well, they're down here somewhere," Holly told him. "We'll uncover them eventually. You haven't been wrong about where to dig yet."

Logan couldn't believe what he was hearing and he tapped the communication link on his helmet. "I beg your pardon? What did you say?"

Holly fanned the water as she turned to look at him. "I said you haven't been wrong about—"

"That's what I thought you said." He grinned at her. "Careful, Dr. McGinnis, you're on the verge of admitting that I'm a competent archaeologist."

Holly's jaw stiffened in irritation. "You're a competent treasure salvor," she corrected.

"What's the difference?" he asked. "Other than a diploma on a wall and little letters after your name?"

Holly shook her head sadly. "You used to know the answer to that, Logan."

"You make what I do sound like something obscene," he observed.

She sighed heavily. "We don't have time for an argument, Logan. There's a storm coming. Remember? We'd better get this basket topside. It's too heavy for the air bag, so we'll have to use the winch."

"All right. But I want you to go up with it this time and take a break."

Holly frowned and checked her dive computer. "I still have another forty minutes of air."

"I don't care. You're exhausted. This is your third dive today."

Holly glared at him mutinously. "Don't tell me what to do or how I feel, Logan. I've got forty minutes of air, so I'm staying down."

"Suit yourself." Logan scowled at her and flipped the switch on his communicator. "Duffey, you there?"

"Affirmative, boss. What's up?"

"Another load of gold bullion. Have Carl lower the hook."

"Done."

While they waited, Holly peered down the sloping walls of the crater at the men working twelve feet below. They were uncovering new pieces so quickly that there was no time to appreciate the extraordinary beauty of their finds. In a way, it was a shame. "It's not supposed to be this easy, Logan," she murmured.

"Would you rather have to chisel it out of a coral reef piece by piece?"

"Of course not. But there's something obscene about so much gold and silver. Usually you find an artifact in one spot, then sift for an hour or a day until you find another fragment."

"I know. We've found more treasure today than most archaeologists and salvors find in their entire careers."

Holly felt herself falling into a deep, dark well of sadness as she looked at the man she had once loved. "There's your answer, Logan."

His brow furrowed. "Answer to what?"

"The difference between archaeologists and salvors. To me, what they're finding are pieces of history. Answers to a hundred questions about how people lived and worked, what they valued.... They're important pieces of a mystery that I want to spend my life unraveling. To you, they're just pieces of treasure. A commodity to be sold on the antiquities market."

"Is that what you really believe, Holly?" he asked incredulously.

"Isn't it the truth?"

"No. I love that mystery as much as you do. I just chose a different way to pursue the answers to all those questions," he said with an intensity that startled Holly. "That doesn't make me and every other treasure salvor in the world a monster."

"Does that include the Dutchman?" she asked archly.

Logan's sapphire eyes glittered dangerously. "Don't put me in the same category as Voorhees, Holly. I don't deserve it. If you don't learn anything else from working with me, I hope you figure that much out, at least."

Holly felt an unwanted flush of shame. The intense, believable sincerity that she had seen before was back. At moments like these, she wanted desperately to trust him, to believe that he wasn't the corrupt rogue she'd made him out to be for the last decade.

If she was really honest with herself, Holly would also have admitted that she had begun to wonder if Logan was capable of dynamiting a reef. In the last month she had worked with his men enough to realize that their efficient and careful salvage techniques were a matter of habit; and habits only developed when they were employed consistently. In the very least, Holly was forced to concede that Logan really was competent and cautious.

But he was still a fortune hunter who might very well have a dangerous agenda. Holly wasn't about to lose sight of that important fact.

"Heads up, Logan. The winch is on its way," Duffey informed them.

Relieved to escape from their intense exchange, Holly looked up as the hook and ball descended. "I'll get the hook, you take care of the chains," she instructed, pushing up toward the surface. Because of her weight belt, she had to kick hard, straining against the weights and the water. The ball was only a few inches from her fingertips when the muscle cramp hit her. Her right thigh went into a massive spasm that made her gasp in pain. She fought down a surge of panic and tried to maintain her equilibrium in the water, but her leg was useless and her mind was numbed with pain.

Logan heard her strangled cry and looked up to see her sinking toward him. "Holly!" He pumped furiously and had a hold on her in seconds. "What is it?"

"Cramp," she managed to tell him, gritting her teeth against the pain.

"Hang on, beautiful. I'll take care of it." Logan flipped the quick-release on her weight belt and his own, then jerked the cord to inflate the bladder on his buoyancy vest, making it easier to get her to the surface.

"Logan, what's wrong?" Mike asked urgently. "Is Holly all right?"

Logan saw Mike swimming toward them, but he flipped his communication link to the cartographer's channel. "She'll be okay, Mike. It's just a cramp. You stay with the team while I get her topside."

Mike hesitated, watching them as they continued their ascent, then he reluctantly returned to the crater.

Duffey had been monitoring the exchange and had two men on the diving platform of the pontoon ready to pull Holly onto the deck.

"This is...stupid," Holly said through gritted teeth. While Logan removed her helmet, she tried to massage her leg, but the neoprene wet suit made it impossible for her to find any relief. Logan unhooked her buoyancy vest, and before Holly fully realized what was happening, he had her in his arms and was carrying her into the deckhouse.

"We've got to get you out of that suit," he said as he placed her gently onto a plastic-cushioned bunk. He removed her swim fins while Holly fumbled with the zipper, but it took both of them to get her out of the two-piece wet suit. By the time that was accomplished, tears of pain were streaming down Holly's cheeks.

Logan dug into a first aid kit under the bunk and found a tube of cream used to relieve muscle soreness. He slathered it onto his hands and began working it into her thigh.

"I can...do that," Holly grunted, but Logan didn't stop.

"Just shut up and lean back," he ordered as he massaged the corded muscles. He seemed to know just the right pressure points, because Holly felt the pain begin to ease almost instantly. She stopped fighting and leaned back against the bulkhead.

His strong hands worked magic on her, and as the pain gradually faded, Holly became increasingly aware of the intimacy of their positions. Logan was kneeling in front of her, his hands encircling her thigh, moving slowly up and down as his thumbs worked the offending muscle.

During the long years of her recovery from the accident, Holly had had countless physical therapists performing similar magic on her, but this was the first time she had ever found anything remotely sensual about a massage. Her thighs were parted, and she found it nearly impossible to take her eyes off his hands.

He had such strong hands. She could feel the slight abrasion from the calluses on them. She could see the fine dusting of light hair against the dark tan of his skin. She could remember quite vividly the other magical things he could do with his hands, how they felt stroking the small of her back or cupping her breasts. Logan had always known how to make her body come to vibrant, sensual life, as though he had more control of it than she did, and he was doing it again, now, without even trying.

As the pain in her leg receded, another pain just as sharp but far more pleasurable began growing very close to the place where his hands were working so diligently. When his hands moved higher, brushing almost against the junction of her thighs, Holly's breath hitched sharply.

"I think that's enough," she said, edging away from him.

Logan looked up at her. "It's better now?"

"It's fine. Thank you." She reached for a towel on the other end of the bench and began drying off.

Logan unzipped his suit and sank back onto his heels. Holly fixed her eyes on the equipment lockers on the other side of the room because she didn't want to look at the damp, curly mat of hair displayed so prominently in the V of his suit. "You scared me down there, Holly," he told her. "When I heard you cry out—"

"I didn't cry out. I gasped," she corrected him.

"Excuse me. When I heard you *gasp,* I thought—" He paused. "I don't know what I thought. I'm just glad it was nothing serious."

"No, nothing serious. Just humiliating," she said, trying to get control of her errant senses. She was still much too aware of Logan and how close he was.

"Holly, there's no shame in getting a muscle cramp. It happens to everyone, particularly when you're not diving every day. You have to learn to pace yourself."

"That's something I don't do very well," she admitted reluctantly.

"I know. You were always a fighter. You had to work a little harder, push yourself a little further, challenge yourself a little more than anyone else you worked with." His voice dropped to a soft murmur. "That's one of the reasons I fell in love with you."

Holly swallowed hard and somehow managed to look at him. "And you were the only one I could never get ahead of. That's why I fell in love with you."

"A perfectly matched set."

Holly felt tears stinging her eyes and she fought them back. She had believed that once, with all her heart. "Logan, don't..."

He came to his knees and took her face in his hands, his fingers lightly cradling her neck and his thumbs moving gently against her jaw. "Don't what, Holly?"

"Don't...touch me.... Don't remind me."

"Why? Because you're not young, it's not hot and you're not in love?" he asked lightly.

Holly could hear her heartbeat thundering in her head. "That's right."

"Then you won't feel anything if I do this...." He brought his face to hers and brushed her lips with his own, just a small grazing touch.

"Logan..." It was more of a moan than a fully formed word.

"Shut up, Holly," he whispered. His mouth closed over hers with his lips parted and his tongue demanding that she open to him, and Holly gave him what he asked for. Heat swelled up in her and she wove her fingers through Logan's hair as he deepened the kiss.

It went on forever, building in intensity, stoking fires that had been dormant for years. When Logan gathered her into his arms and pulled her to him, Holly went eagerly. Her body remembered what it was like to be controlled by him and it responded with impatience, reaching for that distant memory of the passion and fulfillment Holly had known with Logan a lifetime ago.

But this wasn't a lifetime ago, and the fiery couple who had taken such passionate delight in each other no longer existed.

With a strangled, frustrated cry, Holly pushed against Logan's shoulders and he released her.

Her face flaming, Holly stood and moved away from him, fighting to catch her breath and reclaim her senses. From the looks of him, Logan was doing the same. "Why did you do that?" she demanded.

Logan's eyes were smoky with hunger when he looked up at her. "Why did you let me?"

Holly didn't have an answer, but she knew she had just made the biggest mistake of her life. "It won't happen again, Logan. Do you understand that? I won't let it happen again."

He gave her an infuriatingly self-satisfied grin. "Are you sure about that? It seems to me that the temperature in hell just took a nosedive and it's getting colder by the minute."

"Damn you," she swore at him for reminding her of the promises she'd made the day she'd arrived. "Why don't you take a thermometer and go down to check that temp yourself?"

She whirled around and left, but it was several minutes before Logan regained enough control over his body to follow her.

Chapter Seven

Holly stood on the deck of the pontoon watching the approaching storm. It was only midafternoon, but night-black clouds were already closing in from the east, darkening the sky. The wind was creating whitecaps on the surface of the ocean, swells were buffeting both boats and she could hear the high-pitched whine of the pontoon straining against its anchor.

In many ways, the storm mirrored what had been happening inside Holly since Logan had kissed her. A maelstrom of emotions were buffeting her like driftwood in a hurricane, forcing her to examine feelings she had thought were long dead. The hunger Logan had created wouldn't go away, but that physical ache wasn't nearly as devastating as the emotional memories that were battering her—memories of what it had been like to be so close to someone, so close that it had seemed as if two people had really become one. She had felt that way about Logan once, and his kiss had made her realize how desperately she wanted to feel that way again.

But not with Logan. She was not going to fall in love with him again and risk the kind of pain he had brought her so many years ago. How could she love a man she didn't respect—or trust? She still blamed him for the threatening notes. She had good reason to believe that Logan might want to harm her.

So why was she finding it so hard to maintain her distrust?

A streak of lightning and the pitching boats brought Holly back to reality. She had a much more immediate problem than controlling her errant emotions.

"Duffey! It's time!" she called out, picking her way across the deck of the pitching pontoon. "We have to separate the boats now or they're going to break up! Get the divers out of the water!"

The dive master leaned over the bridge rail as Holly climbed the ladder to the *Fortune Hunter*. "I've already called down to Logan," he told her, shouting over the wail of the wind. "They're on their way up. We'll separate as soon as they're on board."

A violent swell pitched the boat, nearly dislodging Holly from the ladder. Her foot slipped, sending a scorching pain through her back, but she hung on and made it safely to the deck of the salvage boat.

Duffey came off the bridge in an instant, scrambling to help her. "Are you all right?" he asked.

Holly nodded, resisting the urge to rub the small of her back where the pain still throbbed. "I'm fine, but I don't think we should wait to separate the boats. They're already straining against the mooring lines."

"But we need the added stability of both boats to get the divers up," he told her.

"The divers can swim to shore on Sand Cay and take the helicopter back to base if they have to," she argued. "Stability won't mean a damned thing if the pontoon staves in the side of the *Fortune Hunter*." As if in agreement with her, the pontoon pitched against the boat hard enough to collapse one of the plastic bumpers that acted as a cushion between the vessels. Duffey heard the loud pop and stopped arguing.

"Skip! Release to mooring lines!" he ordered. "We're separating now!"

Skip Harding jumped to obey, and within seconds the two boats were drifting apart. Duffey hurried back to the radio on the bridge just as the divers began surfacing. Holly watched while Scanlon and his film crew struggled to their boat, the *Jupiter*, and succeeded in clambering aboard, but the men trying to mount the pontoon's dive platform weren't nearly so lucky. Without the stabilizing influence of the *Fortune Hunter,* the pontoon rode high on every wave, and since the men were heavily weighted down with the artifacts in their goody bags it was impossible for them to hang onto the boat, let alone lever themselves on board.

Holly was relieved when she finally heard Duffey on the radio instructing the divers to make for shore and the pontoon to make for port. But when Edgar Franklin, who had been tagging artifacts on the pontoon, saw the divers swimming away, he nearly had a conniption.

"But the treasure!" he began shouting as the pontoon's anchor was raised. "I have to tag the artifacts!"

"We'll do that at the lab," Holly yelled to him. Franklin turned his wrath on her, flapping his arms and shouting something at her, but a booming clap of thunder drowned out his tirade. Holly just smiled and waved at him as the pontoon's engine sprang to life and carried the boat farther away.

"What the hell is going on here?"

Holly heard Logan's muffled voice and whirled around in surprise. He had somehow managed to climb aboard the *Fortune Hunter*'s dive platform and was struggling to make it into the boat. Holly hurried to assist him.

"What do you think is happening? The storm blew up faster than we expected. We had to separate the boats," she said, taking his arm to steady him as he swung his long legs over the bulkhead. He was breathing heavily by the time he made it aboard and sank onto the gunwale.

"You couldn't have waited five minutes?" he asked.

Holly helped him remove the dive helmet. "No. You didn't see what was happening up here. One minute the sea was calm and the next, it was about to rip us off anchor."

Logan looked to Sand Cay. His men were just beginning to scramble ashore and Judd Cunningham was waiting to shepherd them to the helicopter.

"Welcome aboard, Logan," Duffey called down to him. "Glad you could join us."

Logan grinned up at the dive master. "No thanks to you and Holly. What about the other divers?"

"I just got off the radio to Mike. He says they all made it ashore, and that they're going to enjoy their ten-minute helicopter ride a lot more than we're going enjoy the next hour on the water."

Logan looked up as a flash of lightning streaked across the sky. "He's right about that. We're in for a rough ride. I'll be up to help you at the helm as soon as I get out of this gear," he said, unlatching his buoyancy vest as he started for the cabin.

Holly stayed with him, helping to ease the vest and dive tank off his back. "How much did you have to leave down there in the crater?" she asked him.

"Not much," he replied, flipping on the cabin lights as the *Fortune Hunter* got under way. "We managed to get most of the small artifacts that would have been dislocated by the storm. I don't think we're going to lose anything."

"Good."

"Here. Why don't you take charge of this?" Logan suggested as he removed the goody bag from his dive belt and handed it to her.

Holly couldn't believe she'd forgotten all about the artifacts he'd brought up. "Thanks."

"You're welcome."

He looked at her, and suddenly the cabin felt smaller than it ever had before. When Logan started unzipping his wet suit, the walls closed in even more, and Holly turned away quickly to escape the reminder of what had happened the last time he'd done that in front of her.

Fighting the pitching of the boat, she moved to the table in the galley area across from the lockers and tried to keep her tone casual. "We found an amazing number of artifacts today. It's going to take Mike weeks to turn Scanlon's videos into charts."

"Well, he doesn't need to be in any hurry. Those tapes aren't going anywhere and if we keep uncovering finds like this one, he's going to have his hands full keeping current."

"True." Holly heard Logan's wet suit plop onto the deck and wished that she was anywhere in the world but in the cabin with him.

"Holly?"

"What?" she asked, not daring to turn around.

"How long are you going to pretend it didn't happen?"

Damn him. Why couldn't he have just left it alone? But he hadn't, and since his question had the ring of a challenge, Holly had to acknowledge it. She turned toward him and willed herself not to respond to the sight of his perfectly tanned, gloriously masculine physique clad in nothing but the narrow band of his wet swim trunks. "I'm not pretending it didn't happen. I'm trying to forget about it. There's a difference."

"Are you having any luck?"

Holly could have cheerfully strangled him at that moment because he knew very well that she wasn't. "It was just a kiss, Logan," she said irritably. "It didn't mean anything."

"It did to me," he said in a soft, sexy tone that made Holly melt inside.

It was everything she could do to fight the emotions he evoked. "Then that's your problem," she snapped. "The love I felt for you died a long time ago."

"Are you sure about that?"

Holly gave a short, humorless laugh. "Of course I'm sure. I thought I'd made my feelings about you perfectly clear."

"So did I—" He took a step toward her. "—until you kissed me. Now I have to wonder if it's just easier for you to hate me than to acknowledge what you really feel."

"Don't flatter yourself, Logan. And don't read anything into that kiss. It didn't mean a thing."

Logan was fighting a few uncomfortable feelings of his own—and one of them was anger at Holly for being so damned stubborn. "Fine," he said irritably as he turned to his open locker. "If you want to pretend that you don't remember what it was like between us, go right ahead." He grabbed a towel off the shelf, unfolding it with a flick of his wrist, and stopped dead still as a flash of gold caught his eye. The object tumbled onto the deck and Logan frowned. "What the—"

Holly saw it fall, too, and bent to pick up the emerald encrusted necklace that was shining up at her. A botonée cross pendant four inches long dangled from a shiny gold chain. Stunned, she moved closer to the light, looking for the maker's mark.

What she found made her sick inside. For all her doubts, suspicions and accusations, Holly hadn't really wanted to believe that Logan was a crook. But here was the proof. She'd been right all along. Logan was smuggling artifacts from the site.

It was everything she could do to look him in the eye when she turned on him and demanded, "Where did this come from?"

"You saw where it came from," he snapped. "It was in my towel. The big question is, how the hell did it get there?"

"I think that's pretty obvious."

Logan glared at her. "Damn it, Holly, you can't seriously believe I stole that."

"What else should I think? The maker's mark is the same as the one we've found on at least a dozen other pieces of jewelry." She held the necklace up between them. "This is an artifact from the *Ambergris Isle,* and it fell out of your locker!"

Furious, Logan snatched the pendant out of her hand. "Right. I tucked this little two-hundred-and-fifty-thousand-dollar trinket into my wet suit, brought it in here, hid it in that towel, then forgot all about it! Jeez—" He swiped his hand through his damp hair. "Holly, I am not a thief, and if I were, I'd be a helluva lot better at it than this!" he said hotly.

He had a good point. Only an idiot would have hidden the necklace and forgotten about it. Logan might be a lot of things, but he wasn't stupid. "Then how did it get into your locker?" she demanded.

"Obviously someone planted it there to make me look like a thief."

"Why?"

Logan looked at her disparagingly. "Oh, come on. Is it really that hard to figure out? If I get arrested for theft, Avery Bedrosian has one less partner to share the treasure with."

"Don't be ridiculous," Holly argued. "Avery wouldn't do something like this."

"But I would," he flung back at her.

"Yes!"

Logan glared at her. "Are you sure enough about that to send me to prison for it?"

Holly shoved away an image of Logan behind bars. If he went to jail, it was his own fault. "Logan, I told you when I arrived that I planned to get proof of your criminal activities."

"That's right. You've made it clear that you've just been waiting to pounce on me, so why would I steal that and drop the proof right in your hands?"

"I don't know," she admitted. "None of this makes sense."

"It does if you will accept the fact that Avery Bedrosian isn't the altruistic saint he wants you to believe he is. Avery wants me out of the picture, Holly, and he'll do whatever it takes to keep from sharing the treasure with me."

"Logan, Avery wasn't even here today! He couldn't have planted that necklace."

"No, but there were at least a dozen people diving today who were hired by him."

Holly couldn't believe what he was suggesting. "Do you realize how illogical that is, Logan? If Avery wanted to get rid of you, why did he take you on as a partner in the first place? Why didn't he simply hire a salvor, pay the salaries and keep all the profits for himself?"

"Because buying the Ashcroft journals drained him of most of his resources, and there was no way to be certain that they would lead to the treasure—or if there even *was* any treasure. That's why he needed a partnership with an experienced, well-equipped treasure salvor. Teaming up with me cut his start-up expenses in half, plus he got the benefit of my intimate knowledge of these waters. I've spent a big chunk of the last twelve years looking for the *Ambergris Isle.* I didn't know where it was, but I sure as hell knew where it *wasn't.* All Avery had to do was wait until I found the treasure, then find a way to rid himself of an unwanted partner."

Logan tossed the necklace to Holly as he concluded, "And this seems like a pretty good way to do it, wouldn't you say? Plant a stolen artifact in my locker and hope that the woman who already believes I'm a crook will be around when it's discovered."

Holly had to admit that made a certain amount of sense, but only if she was willing to believe the worst of Avery Bedrosian—the man who'd taken a big risk by employing an archaeologist no one else would hire. Bedrosian had place an incredible amount of trust in Holly, and she wasn't about to betray him.

"I'm not buying it, Logan," she said with a shake of her head. "I'm not going to let you make me doubt Avery. He hasn't done anything to prove that he's untrustworthy."

"Whereas I have," he said coldly, gesturing toward the necklace.

"I don't know," she confessed reluctantly. "I can't believe that you put this in your locker and forgot about it. And you certainly wouldn't have wanted me to see it."

"Which means?"

Holly struggled to find another logical explanation. "It's possible one of your crewmen took it for you and didn't have the chance to tell you where he'd stashed it."

Logan just stared at her. "Do you also have a conspiracy theory about who shot JFK?"

"Don't be flippant, Logan. This isn't funny."

"No. It's deadly serious," he agreed, taking a shirt out of his locker and slipping into it. "I've been under investigation by the Bahamian police ever since they accused me of dynamiting that reef. They couldn't make that charge stick, so they're looking for any reason they can come up with to put me out of business. Avery knows that, and he's put my fate in the hands of a woman who's been waiting more than a decade to prove that I'm a crook." He stepped toward her and Holly fought the urge to back away from him. "So what are you going to do, Holly? Send me to jail?"

She met his gaze evenly, but it wasn't easy. She had no idea what she *should* do. There was no proof that Logan had stolen the necklace. Logic said just the opposite, in fact. The necklace in his locker gave every appearance of being a clumsy frame-up. But if the Bahamian police really were investigating Logan, this might be all they'd need to send him to prison.

Holly weighed her responsibility to Avery and to the project against a gut instinct that told her Logan hadn't stolen the necklace.

Though it didn't make a bit of sense to her, Logan won.

Praying she wasn't making a mistake, Holly turned and picked up Logan's goody bag from the table. With him watching her every move, she placed the emerald cross in the bag with the other artifacts he'd turned over to her earlier.

"Thank you, Holly," he said softly.

She looked at him coldly. "This doesn't change anything, Logan. I still don't trust you."

"Yes, you do," he replied, his voice gentle. "You don't *want* to, but you do." He took another step toward her, and for a second Holly was certain he was going to kiss her. Then he stepped away. "I'd better get up to the bridge and give Duffey a hand. You should probably get those artifacts into salt water."

He left the cabin and Holly sank onto the bench by the table. She had just made a tremendous leap of faith, and she had no idea if it had been the right thing to do—or a deadly mistake.

AS THE STORM RAGED through the night, Holly wrestled with her conscience. One indisputable fact haunted her. She had protected Logan today. By not coming forward with the necklace, she had lied for the man who had bullied her, threatened her . . . who may have even tried to kill her.

Why? she asked herself again and again as she tossed and turned in bed. Why was she covering for a man she didn't trust? Why had she even listened to his half-baked theory that Avery Bedrosian was trying to frame him? Logan had just as much of a reason to want to be rid of a partner as Avery did. That little scene in the cabin could have been a carefully staged act designed to make Holly distrust the man who had hired her—a tactic to divide and conquer. If anyone on the island was working on a nefarious scheme, it was undoubtedly Logan.

So why had she covered for him?

Because she didn't want to be the one to send him to prison; at least, not until there was more evidence than what she'd seen today.

That was the only answer that made sense to Holly. She recognized that it was a flimsy excuse at best, but accepting it as the truth was better than examining the other emotions that she was working so hard to suppress.

Somehow she managed to fall asleep, and awoke the next morning to find the sky clear and the island sparkling like a glittering jewel. She heard the boats leaving at six, but she made no effort to join them. Instead, she took her morning swim for exercise and headed off to the lab.

Halfway there, she found Avery strolling about the grounds with a handful of broken branches. Considering the bruised state of her conscience, he was the last person she wanted to see this morning.

"Good morning, Holly!"

"Good morning, Avery. Are you cleaning up the storm damage?"

He waggled some palm fronds at her. "Yes, indeed. I can't bear to see anything marring the beauty of this lawn. I've grown almost obsessively protective of this property."

"I can understand why."

"You're not diving today?" he asked.

"No. I think my time would be better spent cataloging yesterday's finds."

Avery nodded as he fell in beside her, strolling toward the lab. "It was a spectacular day. I was up half the night planning a special museum display for the jewelry we've found. There are some extraordinary pieces."

"Yes, there are," Holly said, feeling a flush of guilt when she thought about the emerald botonée cross. "I suppose it would be wishful thinking to hope that we could keep the entire collection intact."

"Um...wishful thinking indeed," Avery said regretfully. "I'm afraid that by the time Logan and the Bahamian government take their shares, the collection will be severely depleted. But there's nothing I can do about that, unfortunately."

"No, I suppose not."

Holly became vividly aware that Avery was looking at her curiously. "Are you all right, my dear?" he asked. "You were very preoccupied during dinner last night and you don't seem quite yourself this morning."

"I'm fine," Holly assured him. "That storm was a bit unnerving, that's all. I didn't sleep too well."

"Then you're not having any problems with Logan?"

The question startled her. "Why would you think that?"

"I know that working with him hasn't been easy for you."

"We've managed to keep our differences private," she replied, trying to keep her voice even.

"I'm glad. But I do hope you're keeping your guard up with him, Holly," he said gravely.

Good heavens, was Bedrosian psychic? she wondered. "I don't know what you mean, Avery," she said cautiously.

Bedrosian stopped, and Holly looked at him curiously as he glanced around. Even though no one was about, he still lowered his voice confidentially. "Edgar Franklin has been speaking with one of his contacts on the Nassau police force," Avery told her. "It seems that they are very concerned about Logan's involvement with this project. I hope you're being especially diligent in monitoring his activities."

Perhaps it was only because she had a guilty conscience, but his directive put Holly on the defensive. "Avery, I haven't found any proof of wrongdoing on Logan's part. And believe me, I've looked."

Bedrosian gave her a paternalistic pat on the shoulder. "I'm sure you have, my dear. I just want to be certain you maintain your vigilance."

"I plan to," she replied evenly.

"Excellent, my dear. Excellent," Bedrosian said, all smiles. "Well, I shouldn't keep you from your work any longer. I'll see you at lunchtime."

"All right."

Avery turned toward the house and Holly watched as he sauntered up the lawn gathering the palm fronds that littered his path.

Now, what was that all about? she wondered.

"IT WAS SUCH A STRANGE conversation," Holly told Mike that evening. "I felt as though Avery were fishing for something." They were taking an after-dinner stroll on the beach, but Holly's preoccupation with Avery left little room for either of them to notice the romantic atmosphere created by the secluded, moon-washed beach or the subtle pulsing of the surf.

"Fishing for what?" Mike asked.

Holly felt another flush of guilt—something that had been happening with disconcerting frequency since she'd made her decision to cover for Logan. But she hadn't told Mike about the necklace, and she didn't intend to. If Logan had somehow succeeded in making her an accomplice to a crime, Holly didn't want Mike implicated.

But unless she told Mike about the necklace, she couldn't very well explain why Avery's conversation had disturbed her so deeply. If Logan was telling the truth and Avery was responsible for planting the necklace, the antiquities dealer had to be wondering why his plan had failed—hence, his fishing expedition.

"I don't know, Mike," she hedged. "Avery just seemed very concerned with making sure I maintained an adversarial relationship with Logan."

"I suppose that's understandable."

Holly frowned at him. "Why?"

"It's obvious that Avery and Logan don't trust each other. This whole compound is one large armed camp, with loyalties almost equally divided between the two partners. It stands to reason that if Logan was to try something illegal, Avery would want him caught in the act. Or at the very least, he'd like you to keep so much pressure on Logan that he doesn't dare try anything."

"I'm sure you're right," she admitted reluctantly. "But I've made my distrust of Logan very clear. I don't know why Avery felt it was necessary to issue a reminder."

"Perhaps it's because you and Logan haven't exactly been adversarial lately."

Holly's thoughts flew to the kiss she and Logan had shared in the deckhouse of the pontoon yesterday, but Mike couldn't know anything about that. Still, she was glad it was dark because she was sure her face was flaming. "Mike, I've been trying very hard to keep things civil between Logan and me because I don't want our conflicts to affect our work or those people we work with. That doesn't mean I've started trusting him."

"Are you sure about that?"

Holly thought about the necklace, the notes and all the other things that had happened, and she laughed shortly. "Believe me, Mike. I've never been more sure of anything."

He stopped, forcing Holly to stop as well. "Then you're not falling in love with him again?"

The question stunned her. "Of course not! Why would you even think such a thing?"

Holly didn't need to see Mike's face clearly to hear the pain in his voice when he told her, "Because I've seen the two of you together and there are times that I could swear the clock has been turned back fourteen years."

Holly reached out and put her hand on his arm. "That's not true, Mike."

"Are you sure?"

"Yes!" she said irritably. "Why do you keep asking me that?"

"You know why, Holly. I love you. For years I've kept hoping that one of these days you'd turn to me—"

Holly didn't want to hear this. "Mike, please. Don't." She started down the beach again, but he grabbed her arm.

"Holly, please hear me out. You have to know how difficult this is for me. I love you, but Logan is my friend. I want the two of you to repair the bitterness between you, but I don't want to lose you to him."

Holly felt his conflict and it broke her heart. She didn't know how to tell him, though, that he couldn't lose something he didn't have. "Mike, I'm so sorry. I know you're in a difficult position, but..."

"But it's not your fault," he said sadly, completing her thought for her. "You've never led me to believe that we'll ever be more than good friends."

"But I've never closed the door, either, have I?" she realized.

"No."

Holly had never felt more like crying. "Maybe I should, Mike. If I'm hurting you—"

"No, Holly," he said sternly. "No. I won't let you close that door. I should never have brought this up. Let's just drop it."

"But, Mike—"

"I said drop it!" he repeated, then, softening his tone, he gently took her hands. "When we're finished with this job, we'll go away together, Holly. As friends. You will have buried Logan's ghost, and maybe we can finally figure out what you and I can become to each other. Until then, we won't mention it again."

Holly didn't know how to respond. Mike wasn't *asking* her to go away with him. He was telling her. Part of her resented his dictatorial attitude, but she couldn't bring herself to argue with him. She did love Mike, very deeply. It just wasn't the *kind* of love he wanted it to be.

"I've never been so far down the beach before," Mike commented mildly, making a very large and obviously deliberate change of subject and mood as they continued down the beach.

Holly knew she had to allow it. "Neither have I." She glanced over her shoulder and discovered that she couldn't see the lights from the dock. The manicured lawn had ended quite a ways back and a veritable jungle of tropical foliage and undergrowth had sprung up to their right. It was closing in on them as the beach narrowed sharply, and Holly was suddenly very uncomfortable. The beach was too isolated here; she was glad she wasn't alone.

"We must be getting close to the perimeter of the compound," she commented.

"Maybe we should go back now," Mike suggested. "Do you want to return the way we came or try to find one of the paths through the jungle?"

Holly smiled, trying to lighten the mood, which was still a bit tense and somber. "I don't know. How adventurous do you feel?"

Mike stopped and Holly turned to him as he gave her a tender smile. "I would follow you anywhere, Holly. You decide."

"Maybe we'd better stick to the beach. The guards patrol the paths every hour or so and I wouldn't want us to be mistaken for intruders."

"A wise—" Mike stopped abruptly as he looked over Holly's shoulder.

"What is it?" she asked, turning to look.

"A boat. I think."

Holly was barely able to pick out the shape on the beach just ahead of them where the narrow strip of sand and the jungle melded into one. "You're right. I wonder whose it is. It's hard to tell because of the shadows, but it looks too small to be one of our runabouts."

Intent on investigating, Holly started toward it, but Mike suddenly grabbed her hand and quickly pulled her into the deep shadows at the edge of the jungle.

"What—?"

"Shh...look."

"But—" Two men moved out of the jungle only a few steps from the boat, and Holly stopped questioning Mike's motives. This was one of the most remote parts of the estate, and the men might not appreciate the realization that their clandestine meeting had drawn spectators.

Their forms were still shadowed, but Holly could tell that they were deeply engrossed in conversation. The man closest to her was of medium height but very burly, and he wore some type of cap. The other was almost completely concealed by the shadows.

They stood talking for several moments. The burly one seemed agitated, waving his arms in a manner that suggested he and his companion were arguing, but Holly couldn't hear his voice well enough to catch any words. Then, abruptly, he stopped arguing and turned toward his boat. The moonlight caught him as he snatched his cap off his head....

His *completely bald* head, Holly realized.

She knew him! He was the rough-looking crewman on the Dutchman's boat who'd glared at her with such strange menace. The Dutchman had sent this man to the island! But why? Who was he meeting with? Was it possible that she had been right? Had Dutch Voorhees planted someone in the project?

Holly's head was reeling with questions, and she knew that she had to learn the identity of the second man on the beach, no matter what it took.

The bald man turned as he smoothed his cap back onto his head, and said something else to his companion. The other man came forward to help him push the boat into the surf, and the bald one hopped aboard, using the oars to take him beyond the breakers.

His companion turned back toward the jungle and disappeared, but not before the moonlight captured his face for just an instant.

That was all the time it took for Holly to recognize Logan.

Chapter Eight

"I'm sorry, Mr. Franklin, but those artifacts can't possibly be ready for shipment by tomorrow," Holly said testily for the third time. She didn't need yet another argument with the obnoxious bureaucrat. Not today, of all days. She'd had precious little sleep last night because she and Mike had waited in vain for Logan to return to the house and explain his mysterious behavior. She and Mike had agreed that they would mention the incident to no one until they spoke with Logan, but Holly felt guilty that she hadn't told Mike she'd recognized the bald man as being one of the Dutchman's men. Maybe she wasn't ready to implicate Logan so incontrovertibly—yet.

When Logan hadn't shown up by 3:00 a.m., Holly had given up and gone to bed, but she'd been at the dock early this morning to demand an answer from him. He hadn't put in an appearance there, either, and Holly had no idea where he was. Since she had responsibilities in the lab today, she hadn't been able to take time off to track him down.

And if she didn't have time for something that important, she certainly didn't have time for another petty argument with Edgar Franklin.

Franklin just didn't know when to quit, though. "That's not good enough, Dr. McGinnis. The excavation of Crater Four has left us with literally millions of dollars worth of artifacts—most of them gold and gemstone, which require very little restoration. They must be taken to Nassau immediately.''

Holly moved down the aisle between a long row of lab tables with Franklin hot on her heels. "Not until they've been processed through the lab," she argued. "I have very thorough recording measures—"

"Just how thorough?" Franklin asked.

Holly couldn't believe what she was hearing—or what he was implying. She stopped abruptly and Franklin nearly stumbled over her. "Very," she replied shortly. "And you ought to know that. You've been looking over my shoulder every day since I arrived."

"That's why I think there should be changes made," he told her. "I want the artifacts released immediately so that they can be taken to Nassau for accounting."

"Mr. Franklin, I don't appreciate your insinuating that there is something wrong with my accounting measures. Nor am I going to put up with having you second-guess my decisions," she told him. "I've been here less than a month, and it seems that I've spent most of that time arguing with you about artifact shipments. Now, I recognize that your job is to protect the government's interest in this project and I respect your devotion to duty," she went on, calming herself a little. "I just wish that you would respect my obligation to this project, which is to record every artifact and see that it receives the treatment it needs to prevent further damage and deterioration."

"I do respect the enormity of your responsibilities, Doctor," Franklin told her. "However—"

Holly shook her head. "There is no 'however,' Mr. Franklin. My word is law in this lab. No artifact is going to leave here until I say so. Period. End of story. No further argument allowed. Now, I can have a portion of the artifacts ready for shipment by the day after tomorrow, but that's absolutely the best I can do. Is that clear?"

Franklin eyed her imperiously, which wasn't easy because he was so much shorter than Holly. "It's clear that you are being very insubordinate, Dr. McGinnis."

"Mr. Franklin, one can only be insubordinate to one's superior—and you're not my boss," she reminded him.

"Well, we'll just see about that," he said huffily, turning on his heel.

Holly couldn't believe it. "Mr. Franklin, going to Avery won't help you," she called after him. "He gave me full control of this lab—without exception. He is not going to revoke my authority on your say-so! And neither would Logan, for that matter!"

Franklin stopped and turned to her. "Haven't you heard, Dr. McGinnis? Logan Tate is gone."

Holly froze. "What?"

"I said, he's gone. Vanished. Disappeared. Left the island, perhaps never to return. I would suggest you begin a thorough accounting of all the artifacts that were brought up yesterday to make certain none of them are missing." He gave her a thin, malicious smile. "And while you're at it, get anything Tate hasn't stolen ready for shipment by tomorrow at the latest. If he has made off with some of the treasure, you wouldn't want anyone assuming you were an accomplice, now would you?"

THE BODY WASHED ASHORE sometime during the night. One of the guards on patrol found him on the beach just before dawn, and the resulting commotion eventually got everyone out of bed early to see what was going on.

What woke Holly was the sound of a helicopter buzzing over the compound. Sleepily, she recalled that another shipment was being made to the bank today, but as the fog left her mind, she realized it was much too early for that. Then she heard the subdued voices in the courtyard and sounds of movement throughout the house, and she knew that something was wrong.

Fighting down a sense of panic, she threw on her robe and hurried into the courtyard where she found a knot of servants chattering away.

"Marianna! What's going on?" she called out.

Guilty for being caught gossiping, the other maids scurried away, but the lovely dark-skinned woman stayed behind long enough to tell Holly, "A dead man, Doctor. His body was found on the beach. The police have come."

"Oh, God," Holly whispered. She flew around the gallery to the front of the house, nearly knocking down a bleary-eyed Neal Scanlon as he stumbled sleepily from his room.

"Holly, what's—"

"I don't know!" she snapped and kept running.

A police helicopter sat in the middle of the lawn. Bedrosian, Edgar Franklin, security guards and several others were clustered around it or moving toward it. Mike was there, too, but when he saw Holly coming down the stairs, he hurried toward her.

"Holly—"

"Marianna said there was a body," Holly said frantically as she tried to rush past him, but Mike put out his arms to stop her.

"Yes," he replied stoically.

"Mike..." Holly couldn't remember ever having been so frightened. "Was it Logan?"

"No, Holly. No."

Relief flooded through her. It had been two days since Franklin had told Holly that Logan was missing, and the only clue they had to his whereabouts was the cryptic message Avery had received saying that Logan had been called away to Matthew Town, where the headquarters of his salvage operation was located.

Holly had alternated between concern and anger. Mostly, she had been just plain confused. Why had Logan been meeting secretly with a member of the Dutchman's crew? And why had he disappeared immediately afterward?

Holly wanted answers, but until Logan returned, she knew none would be forthcoming.

"Whose body washed ashore? Does anyone know?" she asked Mike, calmer now that she knew it wasn't Logan.

Mike shook his head. "From what little I heard, no one recognizes him. It's not one of our people."

"Thank God," she murmured. "What happened to him? Was it a boating accident? Was—"

"I don't know, Holly. The guards took the body to the lab while they waited for the police." Mike placed one arm around Holly's shoulders as he turned toward the helicopter. "That man there is in charge of the investigation. His name is Giradeaux. I heard him say he wants to speak with everyone in the compound."

Holly picked out the man Mike indicated. The tall, dark-skinned investigator would have been hard to miss under any circumstances because his commanding presence seemed to draw everyone's attention to him like a magnet. He chose that moment to lift his gaze and when he looked directly at Holly, she was startled by the intensity of his stare.

She felt an automatic flush of guilt, even though she had done nothing wrong, and she suddenly became conscious of her inappropriate state of dress. She tightened the belt of her robe and was greatly relieved when Giradeaux's attention shifted away from her. "I suppose I should change," she told Mike.

"Me, too," he said, indicating the dressing gown he had thrown on over his trousers. "I doubt that we're going to get much work done today."

Holly shuddered at the thought of a corpse reposing in her work area. "Certainly not in the lab," she murmured as she returned to the house.

"Good morning, Dr. McGinnis. I am Detective Inspector Xavier Giradeaux."

The elegant, courtly detective greeted her as she entered the parlor, and Holly was immediately struck by the feeling that she had stepped out of reality and into an Agatha Christie novel. Everyone was tense and watchful, as though they were just waiting for Hercule Poirot to step in and unveil the identity of the murderer.

But of course, there was no murderer in this scenario. Just some poor unfortunate victim of a boating accident, most likely. Holly had convinced herself of that while she was taking her shower, and so far nothing had been said to disabuse her of the notion.

"Good morning, Detective Inspector," she said respectfully. "One of the maids told me you wished to speak with me."

Giradeaux gestured her toward the only vacant chair in the room. "I am conducting interviews in the hope of learning more about the gentleman who was discovered on your beach this morning."

Holly resisted the urge to point out that it wasn't "her" beach; Giradeaux didn't seem like the sort who would appreciate being corrected. Instead, she responded, "I don't know what I can tell you, sir. I was as shocked by this as everyone else."

Giradeaux's dark eyes pinned her like a bug to a board. "Were you really?" he asked pointedly.

All of Holly's instincts went on the defensive, but she reminded herself that she had absolutely nothing to feel guilty about. "Of course. But naturally, I'll be happy to assist your investigation in any way I can."

The detective relaxed his piercing gaze. "That's very gracious of you, Doctor. Particularly since it will call for a degree of unpleasantness. As no one has yet been able to identify the body, I am going to have to request that you look at the corpse, as well."

Holly couldn't hide her dismay but she understood now why everyone around her seemed so shell-shocked. Obviously, Giradeaux had already been through this routine with them. "Is that really necessary? Since I arrived on the island last month I've had no contact with anyone outside this compound. I haven't even had time for a visit to the village."

"Nonetheless, you may know more than you think. When Dr. Villanova arrives, we will—ah, here he is now." Giradeaux moved across the room to greet Mike as he had done with Holly. The detective got the amenities out of the way, asked everyone else in the room to remain close by for further questioning, then politely but firmly ushered Mike and Holly out of the house.

"I am curious about something, Dr. McGinnis," Giradeaux said casually as they moved down the lawn. "You seemed quite panicked when you appeared on the gallery this morning. I noticed how quickly Dr. Villanova hurried to intercept you."

Now Holly realized why the detective had sounded so suspicious of her. She tried to look at Mike for a little moral support, but Giradeaux had very deliberately placed himself between the two of them.

"Dr. McGinnis?" he prodded.

"I was quite concerned," she admitted. "One of the maids told me a body had been found and my natural assumption was that it might be a member of my staff."

"Why was that a natural assumption?"

"As I said before, Inspector, my life has been quite cloistered since I arrived on Turtle Cay. I've been so focused on our work that I haven't really considered the existence of anything outside this compound."

"What a pity," Giradeaux said sadly. "My work doesn't often call me here, but it is a lovely island. You should consider becoming acquainted with it—and its inhabitants."

"I will," she promised out of politeness.

"But back to my original question."

"I thought I answered it."

"So you did. And your concern this morning had nothing to do with the mysterious disappearance of Logan Tate?"

Holly couldn't miss the sharpness of Giradeaux's tone or the emphasis he gave Logan's name, as though he disliked having the taste of it on his tongue. She should have realized someone would already have told him of Logan's absence. "The thought had entered my head," she admitted.

"May I ask the nature of your relationship with Tate?"

"They're colleagues. Nothing more," Mike said quickly.

Giradeaux glanced at him sharply, and Holly realized that together she and Mike had revealed a great deal to the detective. Frustrated, she stopped abruptly, forcing the men to do likewise. "Look, Inspector, I don't understand why any of this is necessary. You have an unidentified drowning victim—"

"What makes you say he was drowned?"

Holly stiffened. "Are you saying he wasn't?"

Giradeaux shook his head. "I am saying nothing," he replied, then calmly waited for her to answer his original question.

"I assumed he was drowned because—" Holly shrugged. "—I don't know. I just assumed. This is an island. There's a big body of water out there. People drown."

Giradeaux nodded slowly. "I suppose that would be a natural assumption. Accidents do happen with dismaying frequency. But in this case, our—how do your American cops say it?—our *John Doe* did not drown."

"Then how did he die?"

"I would not presume to make a definitive statement until a coroner examines the body, but my guess would be that his death had something to do with a rather untidy bullet hole in his head."

A wave of nausea rolled over Holly, leaving her too ill to even attempt a response. Giradeaux had to have seen how pale she turned, but that didn't stop him from asking, "Tell me, Dr. McGinnis, do you own a gun?"

The question took Holly's breath away, but Mike was far from speechless. "How dare you, Inspector?" he demanded angrily. "How can you even suggest that Holly might somehow be involved in a murder?"

Giradeaux turned a dispassionate eye on him. "That is my job. What about you, Dr. Villanova? Do you own a weapon?"

"Of course not."

"Neither do I," Holly told him.

"Does either of you know if Logan Tate owns a gun?"

Holly bristled at his insinuation. "Logan hasn't been on this island for two days. He's two hundred miles away in Matthew Town."

Giradeaux's broad shoulders went up and down slowly. "I will certainly make every effort to verify that. Did he speak to either of you before he left? Give any explanation for his absence?"

"No," Holly replied, resisting the urge to look at Mike. She couldn't erase the memory of Logan's meeting on the beach or the nagging fear that it was somehow connected to this murder, but she didn't want to believe that one was tied to the other.

Mike answered in the negative, as well, then asked, "Inspector, why is it that your investigation seems to be revolving around Logan?"

The detective took a moment, as though he wanted to measure his words before he spoke them. "Mr. Tate is not unknown to my department."

Holly wondered if this man could be Edgar Franklin's police contact that Avery had mentioned. "What does that mean, precisely?" she asked him.

"Dr. McGinnis, I'm sure you'll forgive me if I prefer to ask questions rather than answer them. It is the nature of my job." He gestured toward the lab. "Now, if you would care to move on."

Reluctantly, Holly complied, but she had never dreaded anything so much in her life. She had never seen a dead body before, and she didn't care to start now. In her work, she had been called upon to excavate human skeletons, but there was a big difference between hundred-year-old bones and a barely cold corpse.

Still, Giradeaux wasn't about to take pity on her. When one of his men snapped to attention at the door of the lab and opened it for them, the detective stepped aside to let Holly precede him. She hung back for a moment, but when Mike solicitously put a hand at her waist, Holly realized that she was behaving like a silly fainting female.

That was enough to shake her out of her lethargy. Stiffening her spine, she marched into the lab, fully expecting to see the corpse laid out in front of the door. What she saw first, instead, were several security guards. Their presence puzzled her until she realized why they were here; Edgar Franklin wasn't about to trust anyone with the *Ambergris Isle* artifacts—not even the Bahamian police.

"Back here, Doctor." Giradeaux moved past her and Holly followed him to a worktable that was draped in one of the canvas tarps used to cover artifacts. It didn't look too different from a half dozen other canvas-draped tables in the room, but every muscle in Holly's body tensed as the detective unceremoniously threw back the tarp. He stepped aside, and Holly gasped. This couldn't be happening.

She was barely aware of Mike's fingers biting into her shoulder, and she whirled to him, seeking the comfort of his arms. She buried her face in his chest and tried to erase the image of the man on the table, but the memory was already seared into her mind. For as long as she lived, she would remember his bloated face and the puckered entry wound where the bullet had pierced his head—his perfectly *bald* head.

There wasn't a doubt in Holly's mind that this was the man she had seen Logan with on the beach.

Oh, God, Logan. What have you done? she thought as a wave of anguish washed over her.

Chapter Nine

"Do you recognize this man, Dr. McGinnis?" Giradeaux asked as he recovered the corpse.

Holly hadn't liked Giradeaux much before, but she hated him now for the complete dispassion in his deep voice. She looked up at Mike, silently begging him to tell her what they should do, but it was clear he was as dismayed as she was.

"We have to tell him, Holly," Mike said softly.

"Tell me what, Dr. Villanova? Do you know him?" the detective asked.

With obvious reluctance, Mike shifted his gaze to Giradeaux. "No. I do not know him, but I have seen him once before. Briefly."

"Oh?" Giradeaux prompted.

"Three nights ago, Holly and I were walking on the beach when we saw this man and... another man come out of the jungle and move to a boat. They talked for a moment... rather argumentatively, it seemed," Mike said reluctantly. "Then this man got in the boat and rowed away."

One of Giradeaux's dark eyebrows went up. "They argued?"

Mike nodded slowly. "That was the impression I got. Yes."

Holly frowned up at him, wondering why he'd felt it necessary to mention that one detail. But he was clearly in agony over having to betray his friend.

"So the meeting seemed suspicious," Giradeaux deduced.

"It didn't make sense to us," Mike confessed. "But the location of their meeting made it clear they didn't want anyone from the compound to see them."

"And did you recognize the second man?"

Holly dug her fingernails into her palm, waiting for Mike to do what he had to... what she couldn't bring herself to do. But she was suddenly very glad that she hadn't told Mike that she recognized the bald man as being a member of the Dutchman's crew.

"It was Logan Tate," Mike said with obvious reluctance.

If that revelation pleased Giradeaux, he gave no sign of it. "I see. It appears we have a great deal to talk about," he said mildly. "But I don't feel the need to detain you any longer, Dr. Villanova. If you will return to the house and wait for me there, I will be along shortly to resume our discussion."

Mike frowned. "What about Dr. McGinnis?"

"I'll speak with her here."

Holly faced the detective. "What you mean is that you want to separate us so that you can be certain our stories match."

Giradeaux gave her a thin smile. "Apparently you watch a great deal of American television, Doctor. We receive a few of your detective shows down here, too. In syndication, of course." He looked at Mike. "You may go for the time being, Dr. Villanova."

Mike hesitated, taking Holly's hand, but she told him, "It's all right, Mike."

He left reluctantly, and Holly looked at the detective. The movement forced her to face the covered corpse again, and she turned away quickly. "Inspector, my office is up front. Could we continue this in there, or must we talk here so that you can keep me rattled by the presence of the body?"

"By all means, Doctor, let us adjourn to your office."

"Thank you." She led the way and took a chair that placed her back to the window that overlooked the lab. "I don't know what more I can tell you, Inspector. Frankly, you've sent Dr. Villanova away for nothing. He's already told you exactly what we saw."

Giradeaux slipped into the chair behind Holly's desk. "I sent Dr. Villanova away because he seems very protective of you, Dr. McGinnis. I thought some of my questions might be easier for you to answer if he wasn't present."

Holly's mouth went dry. "What questions?"

"Ones about the nature of your relationship with Logan Tate, to begin with."

"What bearing does that have on this murder?"

The detective gave a little shrug. "Perhaps nothing. Perhaps a great deal. I won't know until you've answered my questions."

Holly clasped her hands together with her fingers interlaced. "If you must know, Logan and I were engaged to be married at one time. I broke off the relationship twelve years ago, and hadn't seen Logan again until I joined the excavation."

"I see. Was your parting amicable?"

"No."

"And your reunion? How would you define your relationship now?"

Good grief. What was she supposed to tell him? Holly didn't know the answer to that herself. "We have tried very hard to maintain a professional relationship."

Obviously, Giradeaux recognized a nonanswer when he heard one. "Have you been successful?"

"Not always," she admitted. "Over the years I've made no secret of my professional distaste of Logan's work as a treasure salvor. We have exchanged unpleasant words on the subject more than once."

"I see. And where does Dr. Villanova fit in?"

She explained that the three of them had attended graduate school together, and that Mike had tried to maintain a friendship with both of them. "And before you ask your next question, Inspector, let me answer it for you," she added. "My relationship with Mike is purely platonic."

"Then what were you doing together on the beach that night?"

"Talking."

Giradeaux nodded slowly, as though he accepted her answer, then reached into the pocket of his suit jacket and extracted a Ziploc bag. "Do you recognize this?" he asked, holding it out in front of her.

Holly looked at the contents of the bag. "It's a key," she replied.

"More specifically, a locker key," he told her. "To locker twenty-seven at the Windjammer Club in the village. Have you ever been there?"

"No," Holly replied, though she knew that quite a few of the divers and members of the lab staff went there on their off-hours.

"Very well." He returned the bag to his pocket and finally moved on to more relevant questions about exactly what Holly had seen three nights ago. There wasn't much she could add to what Mike had already told him. At least, there wasn't anything she was willing to add. If the Dutchman had sent the bald man to the island as part of a plot to steal artifacts, it was possible that Logan was the engineer behind the plot. And even if that wasn't the case, if Logan had simply discovered the Dutchman's plan, how far would he have been willing to go to stop the smuggler in his tracks?

Would he resort to murder?

Just the thought of it sickened Holly, but she knew she had to face the possibility. More important, she had to face

Logan with what she knew and see how he reacted. She needed to look into his eyes when she asked him if he was a murderer. That was the only way she'd ever know the truth.

It didn't occur to her that by withholding this one piece of information she was impeding an official police investigation.

Giradeaux continued to quiz her until Holly thought she might scream with frustration, because he was asking questions about Logan that she wanted answered, too.

"Very well, Doctor. That is all for the moment," he said finally. "It is unfortunate that Mr. Tate disappeared before you could ask him for an explanation of his bizarre behavior. If he returns—"

"*When* he returns," Holly corrected him.

Giradeaux gave her a deferential nod, but he clearly had his doubts. "*When* he returns, he will have a great deal to explain. In the meantime, my office will issue a bulletin that he is wanted for questioning. If he is still in the islands, he will be found eventually."

She rose. "And he'll have a perfectly good explanation for why he was on that beach," Holly said, praying that she was right.

"No doubt."

"If there's nothing else, may I go?"

Giradeaux nodded and Holly turned toward the door, but she'd taken only one step when the detective said, "Oh, there is one more thing."

Holly swiveled to face him, wondering if those syndicated detective shows he'd mentioned included old reruns of "Columbo." "Yes?"

"Rumor has it that the excavation of the *Ambergris Isle* has been remarkably successful. Is it true that Tate has already found treasure worth more than one hundred million dollars?"

"Inspector, if you're insinuating that Logan might have taken some of the artifacts with him when he left, I can assure you that you are mistaken. I keep meticulous records of our finds, and nothing is missing." The defense of Logan came out of her mouth before Holly even realized what she was saying.

"Nothing that you are aware of, at least."

"I checked very carefully the day Logan disappeared, Inspector," she informed him.

"So the thought did at least cross your mind, Doctor," he said with a touch of satisfaction.

Holly flushed. "Mr. Bedrosian and Mr. Franklin insisted," she told him, wondering why it was so hard for her to admit that she, too, had been tormented by doubts. She still was. "Nothing was missing from the lab or the vault. And if you'll speak with Dr. Villanova, who has been diving on the wreck daily, he can verify my assertion that Logan's behavior there has been above reproach."

"I will certainly do that, Dr. McGinnis. And may I say I admire your impartiality. For someone who disapproves of Mr. Tate's profession, you have been exceedingly... supportive."

He was right, and for the life of her, Holly couldn't figure out why she was defending Logan at every turn. She had good reasons to distrust him, yet she was withholding information and misrepresenting her own suspicions—all to protect Logan. It didn't make sense.

"Are you finished, Inspector?"

"Yes," he replied. "Thank you for your cooperation."

Holly started to leave, glad to finally escape Giradeaux's intense scrutiny, but a sudden thought stopped her. As much as she disliked the Inspector, there might never be a better time for her to get the answer to something that had been bothering her for weeks. No, years. "Inspector, may I ask you a question?"

"Of course."

"You said earlier that Logan was known to your department. Were you involved in the investigation of his salvage of the *Nuestra Señora Suerte?*"

Giradeaux seemed surprised, but the question in his eyes didn't stay there long. "Yes. I was."

"And what did you determine?"

He paused a little longer than was necessary, Holly thought. "I am sorry to say that the case has not been solved. Until it is, it would be inappropriate for me to comment."

"But you *are* still investigating Logan's involvement in the dynamiting of the reef," she pressed.

"It was his salvage," Giradeaux pointed out. "Naturally, he would be our principal suspect."

"Do you also suspect a man called the Dutchman?"

"We suspect the Dutchman of many things, Dr. McGinnis. The rich history of shipwrecks in these islands has drawn a number unscrupulous men to our shores."

Holly knew how to recognize a nonanswer, too, and she realized Giradeaux wasn't going to tell her what she needed to know. Unless a miracle happened and the mystery surrounding the *Nuestra Señora Suerte* was solved, Holly was just going to have to make up her own mind about whether or not Logan had been telling her the truth.

"Thank you, Inspector. I'll be at the house if you have any more questions that I probably can't answer."

Giradeaux smiled. An actual, honest-to-God smile. "Thank you, Dr. McGinnis. If I think of one, I will let you know."

Holly turned and stepped out of the office, but she didn't get very far because she came face-to-face with Logan and the officer who was escorting him.

"Logan!" A dozen different emotions flooded through her, overwhelming any relief she might have experienced. "Where the hell have you been?" she demanded.

He looked confused, and not just by her harsh question. "In Matthew Town. Holly, what's going on? Why is the compound swarming with—" He stopped abruptly, his face darkening into a scowl, and Holly realized the inspector was right behind her. "Giradeaux."

"Mr. Tate. Welcome back. You're just in time to answer a few questions."

"Questions about what?" Logan asked insolently. "What's going on?"

It was clear they knew each other, and that their relationship wasn't exactly friendly, because Holly found herself caught in the middle of a high-voltage web of tension. That didn't keep her from beating Giradeaux to the punch. "A dead body washed ashore this morning, Logan. The man—"

"Dr. McGinnis!" The detective's sharp, commanding voice cut her off. "Why don't you return to the house?"

Holly whirled toward him. "Why? So you can try to catch him in a lie? But he's not going to lie, are you, Logan?" she rushed on, instinctively turning back to warn him. "You have a perfectly good explanation for your meeting with that man on the beach Tuesday night, don't you?"

All the animation left Logan's face, as though a curtain had slipped over it, freezing it in a cold, hard tableau. Only his eyes moved, and they flicked out sharply to Giradeaux. "Holly. Do what Giradeaux says. Go to the house. Now," he ordered, his eyes still locked on the detective's.

Holly couldn't believe it. She'd risked Giradeaux's wrath to warn him and he was ordering her around like a lowly peon! "I'm not going anywhere until I know why you left Tuesday night, where you've been and why you met that man on the beach!"

"Dr. McGinnis, I must insist. If you don't leave at once, I will have you arrested for interfering with a murder investigation."

"Murder?" Logan said sharply.

Giradeaux sighed impatiently and cast a disgusted glance at Holly. "That's right, Mr. Tate. During your timely absence someone murdered the man you secretly met on the beach Tuesday." Giradeaux gestured toward the corpse.

Logan turned and saw the draped body. He hesitated only a moment before moving resolutely across the room. The detective followed. He didn't seem to notice or care that Holly came along, as well.

Logan threw back the tarp, took one quick look at the man's face and replaced the drape. "How long has he been dead?" he asked without turning.

"That will be for the coroner to determine, but I would say somewhere between twenty-four and thirty-six hours. Would you care to tell me who he is?"

Logan faced the detective, his expression hard and unreadable. "I don't know his name. I was out for a walk when I ran into him on the path in the wooded area behind the laboratory. He said he was a reporter who wanted to do a story on the *Ambergris Isle.*"

Giradeaux cocked his head to one side. "Odd behavior for a reporter, wouldn't you say? Skulking about in the brush instead of knocking on the door?"

"That was what I thought, as well," Logan replied evenly. "I escorted him back to his boat and sent him on his way."

"Then you disappeared yourself. Strange coincidence."

"I don't see how the two could be connected, Giradeaux. After my walk, I went back to the *Fortune Hunter* at the wreck site."

Holly bit her lip to keep from asking why. For some reason, Giradeaux had given up on trying to get rid of her and it seemed wise to remain as inconspicuous as possible. Besides, the detective asked the question for her.

"Why did you return to your boat? Was that your habit?"

"Only when I planned to get an especially early start. Unfortunately, when I arrived I received a radio message that there had been a break-in at my warehouse in Matthew Town. I left immediately for the air shuttle on Port Long so that I could investigate."

"Duffey didn't tell anyone that," Holly couldn't keep from saying. "He said you got a message, took the runabout and left."

Giradeaux scowled at her, but Logan answered, "I asked him to keep it quiet. I didn't want anyone to worry until I knew the facts."

"I assume this break-in was reported to the authorities in Matthew Town," the detective said.

"Of course."

"Then it will be easy to verify."

"Yes."

"Good." Giradeaux looked at Holly. "It would seem that Mr. Tate has answered all of your questions, Doctor. Would you kindly leave now so that I can ask him a few more of my own?"

She looked hesitantly at Logan, but he only supported the detective. "Do as he says, Holly."

She didn't seem to have many options. "Very well," she said irritably. Logan had given answers, all right, but she didn't believe him. And judging from the look on Giradeaux's face, neither did the detective. He motioned toward the office, and Logan preceded him, ignoring Holly completely.

"Now, Mr. Tate. Perhaps you'd be good enough to tell me what really happened with the so-called reporter Tuesday night," Giradeaux said as he closed the office door.

"MR. BEDROSIAN, I must insist that you speak with Detective Inspector Giradeaux so that the shipment to Nassau can proceed this afternoon as planned," Edgar Franklin said.

The agitated little bureaucrat was adding to the tension felt by everyone else in the parlor.

Holly was no exception. It had been an hour since Giradeaux had begun his interrogation of Logan, and Holly's nerves were frayed to the breaking point. She didn't want to listen to Franklin rant and rave. "For heaven's sake, Mr. Franklin. That shipment is the least our worries," she said irritably. "There's been a murder here."

"Not precisely *here,* Holly," Avery corrected her. "The body only washed ashore on our beach. I'm sure that once Inspector Giradeaux completes his investigation he'll realize that no one on my staff had any involvement in the poor man's death."

Holly could have disputed Bedrosian's assessment, but she didn't because it would have meant telling him about the incident on the beach. For the time being, Holly felt, the less said about that, the better. At least until Logan was exonerated.

If he was exonerated.

It was easier to concentrate on the original problem posed by Franklin than deal with her doubts about Logan. "Be that as it may, Avery, I don't see why it's necessary to complete another shipment today. Why can't it wait until tomorrow?"

Franklin stepped toward her chair. "Because there are too many outsiders on the premises. The press will undoubtedly get wind of it and we will have that element to deal with as well. There is simply too much treasure in the vault to allow it to remain here when our own security controls are virtually suspended."

Holly looked up at him, her eyebrows raised. "You don't think the presence of a dozen policemen increases our security?"

"Dr. McGinnis, their job is to ferret out a murderer, not guard a fortune in gold," he said, giving her a condescending glare. "If you hadn't taken so long to catalog the contents of Crater Four, we could have done this yesterday—or the day before, as I wanted."

Holly was still seething over that encounter and the insinuations Franklin had made. Then, he'd accused her of conspiring with Logan to steal artifacts—or at least covering up for him. Now that she really *was* covering up for Logan, her guilt only heightened her anger.

"Mr. Franklin, those logs are the only written records of our discoveries. If we had done as you wanted, there would be no record and no way of proving what does *or does not* go into your precious bank vault in Nassau!"

"Please, please," Avery said, stepping between them. "This has been a difficult morning. Let's not allow tension to get the better of us." He looked pointedly at Franklin, who slunk away like a chastised puppy. "As for the shipment, I'm sure Inspector Giradeaux can be reasoned with so that it can go forward as scheduled this afternoon."

"What shipment would that be, Mr. Bedrosian?" Giradeaux asked as he entered the room through the French doors. Holly anxiously took a step to one side so that she could look around him, but Logan wasn't with him.

"Ah, Inspector. You're back," Avery said unnecessarily. "We were discussing the shipment of artifacts that was supposed to be flown to Nassau this afternoon. It is imperative that we keep to our schedule."

"I see. And who normally accompanies these shipments?"

"Mr. Franklin, myself and Logan Tate. And a security guard, of course."

Giradeaux frowned. "I have no objection to you or Mr. Franklin leaving the island, but I'm afraid I can't release Mr. Tate just yet."

"Release him?" Holly said, her heart in her throat. "Has Logan been arrested?"

"Not yet," Giradeaux replied. "It will be several hours before we can verify Mr. Tate's alibi. In the meantime, I intend to visit the excavation site to interview his men, and Mr. Tate is to accompany me. However, if you can complete the shipment without him, by all means, do so."

"Excellent," Avery said beaming.

"Wait a minute," Holly argued, stepping to him. "I thought your agreement with Logan specified that both of you had to accompany the shipments."

Bedrosian looked baffled by her attack. "Holly, that agreement was designed to allow each of us to protect our own interests in the treasure. Surely you're not suggesting that I would do anything to cheat Logan."

Holly flushed. "Of course not. But at the moment, Logan isn't here to protect his own interests, and someone should."

Bedrosian's brows arched in surprise. "Curious that it should be you, Holly."

"She's right, Avery," Mike said, stepping forward. "Logan's interests must be protected."

"What interests, Mike?" Logan asked as he came in from the hallway. The two policemen who had been flanking him waited at the door.

"Logan!" Holly took two steps toward him, then caught herself and scrambled for a measure of composure to cover her relief. "Are you all right?" she asked lamely.

Logan barely even glanced in her direction. "I'm none the worse for wear. The detective inspector didn't see fit to bring out his thumbscrews or rubber hose."

"I'm pleased to see that you find humor in this situation, Mr. Tate," Giradeaux said without showing any sign of being pleased.

Logan ignored him and looked to Avery. "What's going on here?" he asked.

Bedrosian explained the situation, and Logan clearly wasn't happy. "Odd that you would plan a shipment in my absence, Avery. What would you have done if I hadn't returned today?"

"I'm sorry, Logan. I really didn't think that would be an issue, because I assumed you would be back by this afternoon. Your message did say you'd be gone only a day or two at most."

"Of course." He looked at Giradeaux, who merely shook his head. Logan turned to Avery again. "Well, since the inspector says I can't go, and Mr. Franklin says the shipment *must* be made, I guess I'll just have to send someone else to protect my interests. Giradeaux, would you have any objection to Dr. Villanova leaving the compound for a few hours?"

"None whatsoever. I still have a few questions for him, but it shouldn't take long."

Logan turned to his friend. "Mike. Do you mind?"

"Of course not. It would me my pleasure."

"Then it's settled."

"Inspector?"

Everyone turned as a uniformed officer stepped into the room and waited just inside the door for her superior. "Yes, Jackson. What is it?" Giradeaux asked.

"We've completed the search of Mr. Tate's room, sir."

Giradeaux nodded and crossed to his subordinate. Together, they stepped into the hall and conferred for a moment in quiet tones, then the officer handed the inspector a clear plastic bag.

Holly couldn't hear them, but she could see the bag—and its contents. A single key that appeared to be identical to the one Giradeaux had shown her earlier.

Were they from the same locker? she wondered with a sickening sense of dread. Had Logan and the bald man been using the Windjammer Club as a drop-off point for smuggled artifacts?

She turned toward Logan, silently commanding him to answer the questions she hadn't even voiced, but he still wouldn't look at her. His gaze was fixed on Giradeaux and the key, and Holly was terribly afraid that the reason Logan couldn't look at her was because he knew she'd see the guilt in his eyes.

Chapter Ten

Logan leaned back against the headboard of his bed, staring at the wall opposite him, seeing nothing, and at the same time, seeing *way* too much. Like Seth Barnes's body. The image wouldn't go away.

Logan had expected a lot of things when he'd joined forces with Barnes. He'd known there would be danger. He'd known he would have to tell lies. He'd anticipated the possibility of betrayal, though he hadn't imagined that it would come from such a devastating source. He'd even expected that he would probably end up with blood on his hands before it was all over.

But the rewards had seemed worth it at the time. For a while, he'd even enjoyed the finer points of the deadly game he was playing. But in all the planning and plotting, figuring every angle he could possibly envision, Logan had never once imagined that he would feel so much guilt.

Knowing it wouldn't help, he got up anyway, poured a drink from the bottle of Scotch on the dresser, then moved outside to the balcony. The estate was quiet tonight. Too quiet, in fact. Avery, Mike and Franklin hadn't returned from Nassau yet, and the others had turned in early. The servants were all going silently about their business.

Giradeaux was gone, but he'd left two of his men on the island—to search for more clues, he'd said, but Logan knew the men were there to watch him. And he knew that Giradeaux would be back eventually. It was inevitable. Seth Barnes was dead and there was only one viable suspect. Logan knew that if it hadn't been for his alibi, Giradeaux would have cheerfully carted him off to jail. But unless the inspector could figure out how a man could be in two places at once, Logan was in the clear for the murder.

That didn't lessen his guilt, though.

He took another drink.

"Logan?"

He sighed deeply and looked down the balcony to find Holly standing there watching him. He'd expected this sooner or later, but he'd been hoping for later.

She looked so beautiful it made his heart ache. Just enough light spilled out of his room to cast a golden glow on her hair, reminding him of the night he'd watched her from the shadows in the garden, gloating because he'd succeeded in frightening her. Considering what she'd tried to do for him today gave him one more thing to feel guilty about.

"Drink?" he offered, raising his glass to her.

She shook her head and came closer. "We have to talk."

Logan gestured toward his room, and Holly preceded him. He shut the door and moved to the bottle on the bureau.

"That's not going to solve anything," she told him.

"I know." Logan put the glass down without pouring another drink. "But this hasn't been one of my better days."

Holly glanced around the room, which was a shambles. Giradeaux's men had done a thorough job of searching it, and Logan had apparently made only a halfhearted attempt at restoring order. Clothes were spilling out of drawers, books were piled in skewed stacks that looked ready to topple at any moment. The bed was mussed, and the shirt Logan had worn today was hanging drunkenly off the edge of the bed where he'd carelessly tossed it.

He was still wearing the loose-fitting trousers he'd arrived in this morning, and Holly wished he'd put the shirt back on, too, because she didn't like what the sight of his bare chest did to her.

She was determined not to let that distract her, though. "Why have you been avoiding me all day?"

"I haven't had a lot of free time, Holly. Good old Xavier has kept me pretty busy. If you're here to give me the third degree, too, you can save your breath. I'm in no mood to handle any more questions."

"That's too bad, because you're going to answer mine," she shot back. "Now, I don't care what you told Giradeaux, but I want to know the truth. What were you doing with that man on the beach?"

Logan's face stiffened into angles that were as cold and hard as granite. "I've already told you that."

"And I didn't believe your lame excuse any more than Giradeaux did. That man was no reporter."

"You're right about that," he admitted.

Holly felt a piercing stab of disappointment. She had wanted desperately for her suspicions to be wrong. "Then you did know him."

Logan shook his head emphatically. "This morning I didn't know anything more than what I told Giradeaux. But he faxed the man's fingerprints to Nassau, and got a response from his headquarters late this afternoon. The man's name was Seth Barnes."

"And he was a member of the Dutchman's crew," Holly added.

Logan was stunned. "That's right. How did you know?"

"I saw him on the Dutchman's boat the day of the shark attack. I find it hard to believe that you didn't notice him, too."

"Holly, I had never seen him before in my life until I found him on the grounds that night."

She didn't believe a word of it. "Then why didn't you take him to security?" she demanded.

Logan rubbed two fingers over his forehead in frustration. The lies were getting thicker and thicker, and he was getting in deeper and deeper. "I didn't want to create a scene or cause any undue alarm," he told her. "But that's why I took off for the *Fortune Hunter* after I got rid of him. I didn't buy his story about being a reporter and I wanted to make sure everything was secure at the site."

Holly shook her head slowly. "You're lying, Logan. There's something going on that you're not telling me about."

"Damn it, Holly!" He stopped and lowered his voice. "Do you think I killed that man?"

She hesitated a moment, agonizing over what she felt and what she believed, weighing it against what she *wanted* to believe. "I don't know, Logan. I honestly don't know. When I recognized the bald man on the beach, I assumed he was in league with someone on this project as part of the Dutchman's plan to steal artifacts. Then I saw *you* and didn't know what to think. And now..."

"Now, what?" he demanded.

Holly raised her head defiantly. "Now I have to wonder if you killed Barnes to put a crimp in Dutch's plot. Or worse—if you and the Dutchman have been working *together* to smuggle artifacts. Maybe Barnes was your go-between and you killed him because you found out he'd been cheating you."

Logan's eyes narrowed dangerously. "You can't really believe that."

"Oh, yes, I can. It fits the facts," she retorted. "Secret meetings, a trumped-up feud with the Dutchman, *keys to a locker at the Windjammer Club*," she said pointedly. "Why did you and Barnes both have locker keys, Logan? Were they for the same locker? Have you been using the club as a drop for stolen artifacts?"

It was everything Logan could do to keep from betraying his shock. How the hell had she found out about the keys? Undoubtedly, she'd seen the officer pass the key found in his room to Giradeaux, but why had the inspector let her know about the key that was found on Barnes, as well?

He tried to maintain his righteous anger. Tried to look like an innocent man being wrongly accused. "I have no idea where that key came from, Holly," he told her fiercely. "I'll tell you the same thing I told Giradeaux. It must have been planted in my room as a way to tie me to the murder."

Holly just looked at him. "You mean you're being framed."

"Yes."

"Just like someone tried to frame you by hiding an emerald necklace in your locker?"

Logan met her intense gaze evenly. "Exactly like that."

Holly shook her head. "Don't take me for a fool, Logan. I'm not buying it. And I can't believe that Giradeaux did, either. What amazes me is that you're not in jail tonight."

"For what? Murder?"

"Yes."

"You're forgetting one important thing, Holly. I have an alibi. I was two hundred miles away in Matthew Town."

Holly had heard him tell Giradeaux that, and it was the only glimmer of hope that she'd been able to hold on to all day. "You can prove that?" she asked him.

Logan gritted his teeth in frustration. "Well, let's just say that no one has been able to *disprove* it yet. But there are witnesses," he assured her.

"All right," she said, accepting his alibi for the moment. "But that doesn't prove you haven't stolen any artifacts from the site. Maybe you, Barnes and even the Dutchman are all tied into a smuggling scheme."

"Then why didn't you tell Giradeaux about the necklace?" he challenged her.

"Because I wanted to hear the truth from you before they cart you away to jail, not get secondhand theories from Giradeaux."

Logan laughed. "Holly, do you know how ridiculous that sounds? You didn't tell Giradeaux because you know that I'm not guilty of anything. You didn't want to watch me go to jail for something I didn't do."

"You're wrong."

"No, I'm not."

She denied it, but Logan knew he was right. For all her posturing and accusations, she didn't want to believe he was guilty. He didn't know *why* she felt that way, but he was damned glad she did. Right at this moment, he needed her trust. More than that, he needed *her*. "Holly-love, you are a wonder. A very *stubborn* wonder." He reached out to caress her face, but she jerked away from him and retreated toward the door.

"Don't, Logan. That's not why I came here, and you know it."

"Are you sure?"

She faced him defiantly. "Of course."

He nodded slowly, as though he accepted her answer. "Then why did you defend me to Giradeaux?"

The question put her right back on the defensive. "What makes you think I did?"

"Oh, come on," he said sarcastically. "Don't you take *me* for a fool, either. You didn't mention the necklace, and you didn't tell Giradeaux that you recognized Barnes as a member of Dutch's crew. And you went to great pains to warn me that you had seen me on the beach so that Giradeaux couldn't trap me in a lie. Didn't you?"

"Yes," she said reluctantly.

"Well, I can't say I'm thrilled that you believe I'm a smuggler and a murderer, but..." He moved toward her, lowering his voice to a seductive whisper. "But I'm very glad you wanted to protect me."

He was too close to her now, and Holly's heart was hammering. "Logan, please..."

"Please, what?"

"Leave me alone."

"The door's right beside you," he pointed out softly.

She stared at him mutinously. "I'm not going until I have the answers I came for."

He grinned. "That's as good an excuse as any for staying."

"It's not an excuse, damn it."

"No?"

He was too close. This was getting too personal. "Oh, this is ridiculous. Why did I even bother?" Holly turned and reached for the doorknob, but she froze when Logan lightly took hold of her other arm. He ran his hand seductively up, then down again, and Holly felt the effect of the contact clear to her toes.

"You were worried about me while I was gone, weren't you?"

His husky tone made her heart skip a beat, and she refused to look at him. "I was angry and confused. I wanted an explanation for what I'd seen on the beach," she said without much conviction.

"Nothing more?"

She turned her head sharply to look up at him. It was a big mistake. "No," she managed to tell him.

"You weren't afraid something had happened to me? And don't lie to me, Holly. I'll know it if you do. Your mouth turns down just a little bit, right here—" he lightly fingered the corner of her mouth "—whenever you lie."

Holly almost groaned at his feathery touch. "This is pointless," she murmured.

"Doesn't feel that way to me," Logan said, coming another step closer. "I want you, Holly. Despite all the years, all the bitterness, the accusations, I still want you very much."

Holly was trembling inside, but she managed to keep her voice steady. "I am *not* going to make love with you, Logan."

"Why? Because you think I'm a murderer?"

"No! I mean...yes." Holly didn't know what she meant. What she believed. She only knew what she wanted, and it had nothing to do with smuggling plots and murder mysteries. She tried to strengthen her resolve. Somehow she managed to look at him and repeated more forcefully, "I am not going to make love with you, Logan, because I don't trust you. Even if you could take away the fact that the police are investigating you for murder and ease my suspicions that you're a smuggler, we'd still have a world of differences standing between us."

"What differences?" he asked.

"The same ones that separated us twelve years ago."

His voice was soft and husky when he told her, "Holly, the only thing that separated us twelve years ago was your mule-headed stubbornness. You let the preconceived notions of a bunch of book-bound old men destroy everything that we had been trying to build together."

There was no heat in his words, just an all too visible hunger in his eyes that Holly wasn't sure she could fight. But she had to try. "You're the one who destroyed everything, Logan. It's too late to go back."

"I don't want to go back, Holly. I'd rather go forward. Haven't you learned anything in the last twelve years?"

Holly was too mesmerized to stop herself from asking, "Like what?"

"That you can't escape me. What we felt for each other was too strong. It didn't go away, Holly. You didn't stop loving me. You just channeled it into bitterness and suspicion. It's time to let that go and admit that we were always meant to be together."

"I don't believe that, Logan," she said breathlessly.

"Yes, you do," he whispered as his head bent slowly toward hers.

"I don't *trust* you, Logan," she murmured, but it didn't keep him from kissing her.

Holly's breath caught sharply as his mouth closed over hers. His hands went to her waist, pulling her closer until their bodies were fitted together like perfectly matched pieces of a puzzle. His lips and tongue demanded more than passive acceptance. They challenged her to meet him halfway, to give as good as she got, and Holly had never been able to refuse a challenge.

The deep, stirring kiss robbed her of thought and brought her to life in Logan's arms. A sweet, burning pain swirled between her thighs and her hands ached to touch him, to test the strength of the muscles in his corded arms and back, to feel the prickly silk of the pale hair on his chest. Her hands wanted to remember everything about him, so she let them. She gathered in the sensations...the taste of him, the smell, the feel...it was all so familiar that Holly felt as though she had come home.

She moved her hands over him, recalling rock hard thighs and the way his nipples tightened with just the slightest pressure of her thumbs. She remembered what it was like to feel him harden against her, and she arched into him, overwhelmed by her need, because this wasn't memory. It was real. Just as real as the things Logan was doing to her with his lips and his hands. And just as real as the heat of desperate urgency that scorched them both.

"Oh, God, Holly..." Logan reached for the buttons of her shirt, peeling it away, then flicked the front closure of her bra to free her breasts to his hands. He took a step forward, lifting and pinning her to the wall as his lips blazed a trail down her throat until his mouth closed over her breast.

With a hoarse cry, Holly wrapped her arms around his shoulders and wove her fingers through his hair. This was madness. It was insane. She couldn't respond to him—a man who might very well be a murderer. Might very well have tried to kill *her*. Her head was telling her not to trust him, but her heart wasn't listening. She knew she should stop him, but she couldn't. It had been too long. She wanted him too much. She needed more than just the memory of what it felt like to have Logan moving inside her, carrying her to a place that no other man had ever been able to reach.

Too fevered to think, she wrapped her legs around him, letting his hands and the wall support her weight, and she heard Logan's sharp intake of breath and a low, ferocious moan as she pressed against him intimately.

The knock at Logan's door brought Holly to her senses. He froze for an instant, and it was more than long enough for a burst of sanity to dampen the fire coursing through her.

Logan cursed viciously. This wasn't happening. He finally had Holly back in his arms again. He was so close to proving to her that they were two halves of the same soul, and he wasn't going to let anyone or anything take that away from him now. He kissed her again, hard, and then released her, but he didn't move away or take his eyes off her face.

"Who is it?" he demanded.

"Judd Cunningham."

"Damn," Logan growled. "Don't move," he ordered Holly. He whirled toward the door, but realized instantly that he couldn't possibly open it. His loose trousers did absolutely nothing to conceal his erection. "What do you want, Judd?" he demanded.

"Avery just returned from Nassau and he'd like to speak with you."

Logan ground his teeth in frustration. "Tell him I've already turned in for the night. I'll speak with him tomorrow morning."

"But—"

"Good night, Judd," Logan snapped. He heard Cunningham mutter something as he moved off down the hall, but Logan couldn't have cared less about Avery's request for a command appearance. He turned back to Holly.

The windows were open, the curtain was fluttering in the breeze and Holly was gone.

Chapter Eleven

Holly picked at her supper, only half listening to the conversation taking place around her at the dinner table. It had been nearly a week since the murder had rocked everyone in the compound, and on the surface things appeared to be returning to normal. At least Giradeaux had stopped coming around to ask questions, anyway. Logan hadn't been taken to jail, but in the days after the body had been found, Holly had heard enough to know that he was still in danger of being arrested. Giradeaux was trying to find a hole in his alibi, and it was a sure bet that the inspector hadn't believed Logan's lame excuse to account for the presence of the locker key in his room.

Holly still didn't know why she hadn't told Giradeaux about the necklace that had fallen out of Logan's locker. If the detective was trying to prove that Logan and Barnes had been collaborating on a smuggling operation, that one piece of information might have been all he needed to arrest Logan.

So why hadn't she told him? And why had she let herself get so out of control when Logan had kissed her? She couldn't escape the feeling that the answers to those questions were somehow intertwined. Despite all the evidence to the contrary, she wanted to believe in Logan's innocence.

All in all, it had been a miserable, confusing, emotion-charged week. The only good thing about it had been that she managed to avoid Logan for most of that time. This was the first time in days that he had joined the group for dinner, and apparently that wasn't by choice. Holly had the impression that it was a command performance, because Avery had spent most of the meal giving Logan the third degree.

"So you're convinced that Crater Four has been played out?" the host asked his partner.

"I think so. We expanded it three times today, and came up with nothing."

"I shouldn't find that surprising or disappointing," Avery replied. "The finds we made there were beyond my wildest expectations."

"And mine as well," Edgar Franklin said mildly. "We should make another transfer of the treasure to the bank as soon as possible. We have accumulated some incredibly valuable artifacts since the last shipment went out."

Holly forced her attention to the conversation. "I should be finished cataloging most of the finds later in the week."

"Can you be more specific?" Franklin asked.

Holly gritted her teeth. The little bureaucrat was still paying daily visits to her lab and generally driving her crazy. "Would Friday afternoon suit you?"

Franklin gave her a terse nod. "Very well."

"Excellent. I'm glad that's settled," Avery said. "In the meantime, Logan, I expect you'll be opening up a new crater."

"I don't know yet, Avery. That's something Holly and I will have to discuss."

Holly was surprised. She looked at Logan, who was directly across the table from her, but she had a difficult time meeting his eyes. The memories of what had happened between them were too powerful. "I thought we had already agreed on the location of the next dig," she said. "You wanted to move in a little closer to the shore of Sand Cay."

"Eventually. But there's still some work to be done in Crater Two, and I'd like to wrap that up before we open a new site."

Mike was sitting next to Holly, and she felt the tension in him almost as strongly as she felt her own. She caught the sharp look that he gave Logan and wondered what it meant. "Then you're ready to excavate the three cannons," she said, trying to keep her voice neutral.

Logan nodded. "I'd like to do it tomorrow if you have no objections."

Holly tried to ignore the queasy sensation that settled in the pit of her stomach. "No objections at all," she said evenly. "I'll have Paul take over the cataloging so that I can supervise the excavation."

"Surely that's not necessary, Holly," Mike said hastily.

Holly frowned at him. "Of course it's necessary. It's my job."

"But Logan has plenty of experience in bringing up cannon—"

"So have I," she replied tersely, irritated by his insinuation.

"But you almost died the last time," Mike said, his voice soft but underlined with anxiety. "Holly, you shouldn't have to face that reminder of what you suffered."

Holly knew she should have appreciated his concern, but she didn't. He had become increasingly protective of her ever since she had confided in him about the notes and her suspicions of Logan. But Holly didn't need a knight in shining armor to watch over her. "Mike, I was hired to oversee this excavation, and that's what I intend to do."

"But—"

"She's right, Mike. Leave it alone," Logan told him, earning a dark scowl from his friend. "Holly can do her job."

Holly looked at Logan in surprise. She certainly hadn't expected his support. "Thank you."

He shook his head. "No thanks are necessary. If you really plan to resume your career, you're going to have to face this sooner or later."

"Holly doesn't need to prove herself to anyone," Mike argued.

"Of course she does," Logan snapped. "She has to prove it to herself."

Holly found the animosity between Mike and Logan more disturbing than the thought of excavating the cannons, and she blamed herself. She should never have confided in Mike. That, combined with the murder investigation, had planted seeds of doubt that had put a strain on the men's friendship.

She reached out and gently touched Mike's arm. "Logan is right, Mike. I have to do this. Please understand. I'm going to help Logan bring those cannons up tomorrow."

She glanced at Logan and found him scowling at her hand on Mike's arm. The intensity of his frown made a chill run down her spine. Was he jealous? she wondered, or was there something else behind his icy glare?

THE DIVER MOVED SILENTLY through the dark ocean, surfacing only when necessary to get his bearings. He couldn't risk using his light yet, but he had to be certain he was on course, so he came up, took a quick look at the lights aboard the pontoon, then resumed his underwater trek.

The tools he would need were fastened to his belt, and he knew the location of the underwater alarm sensors. They wouldn't be a problem, because they were designed to protect treasure on the ocean floor, and that wasn't the diver's target. He had a few minutes' work to do beneath the pontoon, and then he would quietly return to the boat that was waiting for him in the darkness.

If he didn't get caught, that is. And he didn't plan to let that happen. The payment he had been promised more than compensated for the risk he was taking, and he didn't have enough of a conscience to feel the slightest bit guilty about what he was going to do.

After all, this wasn't the first time he'd orchestrated a murder. And it probably wouldn't be the last.

"WE'LL BRING THE falconets up first on the *Fortune Hunter,* but the culverin will have to come aboard the pontoon," Holly told the dive team that was gathered around a table on the deck where Mike's chart of the cannons' positions was stretched out. Holly looked at Logan. "You're certain the pontoon winch is rated for two tons?"

"Absolutely," he assured her. "The pontoon was built to take the weight of big boy heavy cannons like the culverin."

"All right." She went on to lay out the assignments so that every man knew exactly what he was supposed to do once they took to the water. Through the briefing, Mike stood just outside the circle, watching with unconcealed displeasure. Holly ignored him, and when she was satisfied that she had covered everything, she sent the divers off to the pontoon to suit up.

Holly stayed at the table, staring down at the map. Her mouth was dry and her palms were sweating. "Did I miss anything, Logan?" she asked without looking up at him.

"Not that I can think of. These are my best men, Holly. They've all done this before."

"I know. That's why I made you lead man rather than taking that job myself. They know how you work, and I don't want any risk of miscommunication."

Mike stepped forward. "But you shouldn't be diving at all," he told her.

Holly hadn't slept much the night before and her stomach was already churning. The last thing she needed was someone else's doubts bombarding her own. "We've been through this already, Mike," she said without much patience. "I'm not going to argue with you anymore. If you want to go back to Turtle Cay, by all means, take the runabout and go. I'll come back to the compound on the *Fortune Hunter* once we've finished."

Mike looked highly offended. "I am not leaving you. In fact, I'm going to dive, too."

Holly shook her head. "No. You're a cartographer, not a recovery specialist, Mike. I don't want anyone but the team in the water this time, and that's final. Come on, Logan, let's suit up."

Without waiting for a response from either of them, she went into the main cabin and stripped down to her swimsuit. Logan was right behind her.

"Don't be angry with Mike, Holly," he advised her. "He's only trying to protect you."

"No, he's trying to coddle me," she said as she jerked open her locker.

"With good reason."

She whirled toward him. "Not you, too? I thought you understood—"

"I do, Holly," Logan assured her quickly. "I know that you have to dive on this recovery or you'll never be able to look at yourself in a mirror again. But Mike was there when you were hurt. He knows what it's like to feel completely helpless while someone you love is suffering."

Holly understood what Logan was trying to tell her, but that didn't make Mike's opposition any easier to deal with. "Then he's trying to protect himself, not me. If I can handle this, so can he. But I do—" She hesitated a moment.

"What?"

"I . . . I appreciate your support."

He smiled at her. "That really hurt, didn't it?"

She straightened her shoulders. "I don't know what you mean."

"Sure you do," he said good-naturedly. "It galls you to say thank you to a man you think is a liar, a murderer and a smuggler... not to mention a wreck rapist."

She looked him squarely in the eye. "That's absolutely right."

Logan took a step toward her. "Then tell me something, Holly," he said softly. "If you *really* believe I'm all those things, why did you kiss me the way you did in my room that night?"

She didn't have an answer to give him because she didn't understand it herself. "The divers are waiting," she said shortly, but when she turned toward her locker, Logan took hold of her arm and forced her to look at him again.

"Damn it, Holly, admit it," he ordered with a fervor that struck at her heart. "You still love me. You still believe in me."

She jerked her arm away. "That's not true."

"No, you just don't *want* it to be true."

Holly felt like crying, and she couldn't afford the emotional toll this argument was taking on her. "Logan, stop it. Leave me alone and let me do my job."

He backed off a step. "All right, I'll leave you alone. For now. But sooner or later you're going to have to come to terms with what you're feeling, Holly."

She couldn't argue with that, but she wasn't going to admit it to him. Instead, she tried to put his accusation out of her mind so that she could focus on the job she had to do today.

Holly was intensely aware of Logan as they finished changing, but when they finally made it onto the deck, she checked all of the equipment one final time. By the time they took to the water, she was petrified, but she worked through the fear as the first falconet was brought up to the *Fortune Hunter*.

The three brass cannons in Crater Two were amazing finds. When the *Ambergris Isle* sank, a one-and-a-half ton

culverin and two smaller, eight-hundred-pound falconets
had fallen on top of each other, like a child's game of pickup
sticks. Sand had covered them quickly, prohibiting the
growth of coral encrustation, so that they were in nearly
mint condition. That would make them easier to bring up,
but it was still a herculean task.

The excavation of both falconets went smoothly, but
Holly knew they were only dress rehearsals for the big boy,
as Logan had called it. The ten-foot-long culverin lay in the
sandy seabed like a sleeping leviathan, taunting her, reminding her too vividly of the twelve-foot, two-ton demi-
culverin that had nearly crippled her in Mexico.

She suppressed those memories while Logan, Skip and
Carl secured ropes around the culverin in sling fashion and
attached them to the hook of the crane winch. Holly added
a guideline to each end of the cannon and took them up to
the pontoon, where a section of deck plates had been removed to allow the culverin to be brought up through the
center of the boat rather than over the side. Once the culverin was out of the water, the lines would be used to guide
it onto the deck and reduce the sway. Two more lines were
secured to each end to perform the same function while the
cannon was making its ascent.

Once the sling was secured, Holly double-checked the
rigging, then swam back out of the way, letting Logan take
charge. Carl and Skip handled the two guidelines and Logan, as lead man, stayed with the cannon.

As it had with the falconets, Holly's heart rose in her
throat when Logan ordered Duffey to start the winch. The
mechanical grind echoed eerily, and the whole ocean seemed
to groan as the pontoon took on the weight of the three-
thousand-pound cannon.

The culverin took a halting jolt off the seabed, creating a
small cloud of sand as it rose, but unlike the falconets, the
big boy didn't continue on a smooth, upward ascent. The
groan and grind of the winch was overpowered by a sudden

crack, and the cannon jolted downward, pulling Carl and Skip off balance.

"Back off, Logan!" Holly screamed, but it was too late. The culverin swayed drunkenly into Logan, knocking him to the bottom as a second crack like the splitting of timbers sent the cannon plummeting back into the sand, pinning Logan's foot.

"Logan!" Holly kicked hard, cutting through the water as quickly as she could. "Duffey! Take it up. Raise the cannon! Logan's trapped!"

"I can't!" the dive master responded from the pontoon. "The crane came loose from the deck mounting. If I start the winch again, the whole crane assembly will come down on top of you! How's Logan?"

"I'm okay," Logan replied as Holly settled on her knees beside him. He sounded controlled, but Holly could see the pain etched on his face as he struggled to pull his leg free.

"Don't do that," she ordered, barely able to breathe.

"I don't think it's broken, but my fin is wedged tight," he told her. "It's got my foot twisted like a corkscrew."

"Damn it." Holly tried to think, but she had to fight her own panic and a sickening flashback to her own accident. Carl and Skip were trying to lift one end just enough to free their boss, but it was pointless. Holly knew she had to do something. "Duffey, is there any way you can rerig the crane?"

"Not on the pontoon," he replied. "But we can use the *Fortune Hunter* winch."

"No," Logan said, grunting with pain. "It won't take the weight. We'll be right back where we started."

"Or worse," Holly muttered. "All right. I've got an idea. Duffey, get the pipe dredge down here fast!"

"What are you going to do?" Skip asked.

"We'll suck the sand away and dig a crater around Logan's foot," she told him. "If we can't raise the cannon, we'll lower the damn ocean!"

"THANKS, JUDD. I can make it from here," Logan said, shifting his weight off the helicopter pilot's shoulder and onto the post of his bed.

"No problem, Logan. If you need anything else, just yell."

"We will," Holly said as she accompanied Judd Cunningham to the door. "Thanks again for the lift."

"That's what I get paid for."

Cunningham gave her one of his irritating trademark salutes, but Holly was in no to mood deal with his flirtation. All her thoughts were focused on Logan. "How does it feel?" she asked him as she closed the door behind Judd.

"All things considered, not too bad," Logan replied as he eased onto the bed, propping his back against the headboard. The pain in his foot had been reduced to a dull throbbing and his head felt like he'd drunk one too many margaritas, thanks to the large dose of painkiller the doctor had given him. "I'm glad you called for the chopper to pick us up on Sand Cay. I don't think I could have handled a bumpy ride in the runabout."

"It was the quickest way to get you to the hospital on Port Long. And like Judd said, that's what he gets paid for."

He gave her a drunken smile. "You handled the whole thing very well today, Holly. You're a good person to have around in an emergency."

He patted her thigh, and Holly fought the urge to slap his hand away. He was a little high on the pain medicine, and she didn't have the heart to be too stern with him; not after the close call he'd had just a few hours ago. "Here." She picked up a pillow and gently slipped it under his foot. "The doctor said to keep it elevated until the swelling goes down."

"But at least it's not broken," he said with a lopsided grin. "Didn't I tell you it wasn't broken?"

Holly sighed impatiently. "About twenty times, all the way to the hospital."

"And I was right."

She frowned at him as she put the small bottle of pain pills the doctor had prescribed on his nightstand. "I swear, you're the only person I know who could be smug about a bone bruise. That smile ought to wear off about the same time as the painkiller."

"I could use a little TLC about then," he said suggestively. "And now, too, as a matter of fact. Wanna play doctor?"

"Don't push it, Logan, or I'll call one of the maids."

"Oh, come on, Holly, be a sport. At least fluff my pillows. All good nurses fluff pillows."

"So do good maids," she snapped, but she leaned over him to fulfill his request anyway. The movement brought her perilously close to him, and Holly could feel his breath on her cheek as he studied her.

"Mmm...you always did have incredible earlobes," he murmured. "Very delectable, as I recall."

"Don't even think about it," she warned him, measuring each word very carefully as she straightened up. "My sympathy has limits, and you can only get so much mileage out of this drunken sailor routine."

Logan snapped his fingers. "Shucks. Caught in the act. You're too smart for me, Holly-love."

"Don't call me that!"

She turned away, but Logan grabbed her hand. "All right. No inappropriate terms of endearment. Just don't go yet." He dropped her hand and patted the bed. "If I promise to behave myself, will you sit beside me for a few minutes?"

Holly hesitated. "I really should go downstairs and change clothes." She was wearing nothing but a blouse over her swimsuit, and for the life of her she couldn't remember who had thrown it to her in the chaos following Logan's rescue.

"Clothes can wait. We have to talk first," he told her, and Holly realized he no longer sounded tipsy. A sober Logan was more dangerous than a drunken one, but she accepted his invitation and sat on the side of the bed, facing him.

"What do you want to talk about?"

"You. The accident today."

Holly stiffened. "What's there to talk about? It's over. You'll be limping around for a few days, but you'll survive, so that's the end of the story."

"Not quite. I want to make sure you know it wasn't your fault."

Since the moment she took charge of Logan's rescue, Holly had been suppressing the terrible sense of guilt she felt. She didn't appreciate having it brought to the surface now, but she had to face it. "It was my excavation. The safety of the crew was my responsibility."

"But you couldn't have foreseen this. We both checked all the equipment. We did everything in our power to prevent an accident."

"I didn't check the deck plates under the crane," she argued.

"Oh, for crying out loud. What were you supposed to do? Swim under the pontoon and inspect the bolts? What good would that have done?"

"I don't know. I might have seen stress fractures, or something. I shouldn't have taken your word for it that the pontoon winch was rated for two tons."

"Holly, that rigging has supported cannons twice the size of that culverin."

"Then what went wrong?"

Logan had his own suspicions, but he wasn't about to express them to Holly. "I don't know, but whatever it was, you're not to blame," he told her.

"Well, that's good to know," she said with a touch of sarcasm. "You can tell that to the next research institute that refuses to hire me because I can't do something as basic as raise a cannon safely."

Logan sighed with exasperation. "Are you still worried about what your book-bound colleagues think, Holly?"

She came up off the bed in a huff. "It may not matter to you, Logan, but I have a career to consider. Granted, it's not much of a career at the moment, but it's the most important thing in the world to me."

"Then maybe you should reevaluate your priorities," he suggested lightly.

"And do what? Become a treasure salvor like you?"

He shrugged. "There are worse things in the world."

"Not to me," she said flatly, ending the discussion. "I'm going to shower and change now. Would you like me to bring you something to eat when I'm finished?"

"Thank you. I am a little hungry. And I could use a shower, too, you know." He grinned at her. "But I don't imagine you'd volunteer to help me with that."

"That's the first thing you've been right about today," she said testily. "Do you need me to get anything for you before I go?"

Logan nodded and pointed across the room. "In that closet, right front corner."

Holly stepped across the room. "What am I looking for?" she asked as she opened the door, but she didn't need to wait for an answer. The mahogany and brass cane Logan had given her was leaning against the wall. It brought back a flood of memories about her own accident that were already too close to the surface. It also brought up some unwanted emotions about Logan that she was in no shape to deal with, either.

She carried the cane to the bed. "Aren't you glad now that I returned this to you?"

"Not really," he said, seriously. "It was a gift that I hoped would have a special meaning to you. I never wanted it back." He reached for the cane, covering Holly's hand with his own. Her breath caught sharply when he touched her, but she didn't jerk away. "And no matter what you think to the contrary, I meant it as a gesture of support. It never occurred to me that you would think I was trying to be cruel.''

She believed him. How could she not, when his eyes held such tenderness? When it was so clear he *needed* her to believe him? The certainty that he was telling the truth caused something warm and wonderful to curl inside Holly. ''But why did you even bother to send it? With all the bitterness between us, why did you care what happened to me?''

''I don't know,'' he replied honestly. ''I was mad as hell about the article you wrote, but even as wrong as you were I still had a lot of respect for you. For your principles. For your strength and your courage. Even your stubbornness.'' He hesitated a moment before adding, ''I guess I was still in love with you, whether I wanted to admit it or not. And I still am, Holly,'' he added softly.

Holly wasn't ready to hear that. She certainly wasn't ready to believe it, not even when she could plainly see the love and tenderness in his eyes. Something inside her rebelled, and the warmth she had been feeling fled. All her doubts, suspicions and frustrations flooded back in an instant, and she jerked her hand away from his. ''Don't say that!''

''Why not?''

''Because it's a lie! You're just trying to manipulate me!'' Agitated, not knowing what to think or believe, she moved away from the bed. ''I know too much about your smuggling activities and you think you can keep me under control by seducing me with lies.'' She turned on him. ''But it won't work. I'm not going to melt like warm butter because you tell me you love me!''

Anger flashed in Logan's eyes, and when he sat up quickly, throwing his legs over the side of the bed, Holly backed away, suddenly afraid. ''Melt? Holly McGinnis, melt?'' he sneered, coming to his feet with the help of the cane. "Nothing could melt your heart—or any other part of you—because you're made of stone!"

Tears stung Holly's eyes, but she willed them not to fall. "That's right, Logan. Where you're concerned, I am made of stone. So you can stop playing games," she said with mounting fury. "You've done nothing but try to get rid of me ever since I arrived. When you saw that you couldn't scare me away you decided to seduce me into trusting you! But it's not working, Logan. I don't trust you," she told him coldly. "And I sure as hell don't love you!"

She whirled away from him, but Logan grabbed her arm. "Yes, you do, damn it."

"Let me go!" she shouted, struggling against his grip.

"No! Not until you admit that you love me."

Holly stopped struggling and glared at him defiantly. "What are you going to do if I won't? Beat a confession out of me?"

Logan released her abruptly and turned away, disgusted with himself. She had every right to mistrust him, and he had absolutely no right to want her love, let alone expect her to give it to him after everything he'd done.

"Get out of here, Holly," he said softly, in a hard voice.

"Gladly."

A second later, the door slammed, and Logan sank onto the bed.

Chapter Twelve

Holly kept her tears in check until she reached her room, but once her door was closed and locked, she let them run their course, hating Logan for what he was trying to do to her. Part of the blame was hers, though. Logan could never have succeeded in manipulating her so skillfully if she hadn't had feelings for him to prey on. Despite all her protests to the contrary, she wanted to believe in his innocence because she still loved him. It was as simple as that.

Facing that truth didn't bring her any peace. Not by a long shot. It only added to the conflicts roiling inside her. She didn't dare trust Logan, yet she wanted to with all her heart. She didn't dare believe that he still loved her, but that was all her heart wanted to hear.

It took awhile, but she finally succeeded in bottling up her emotions and corking them tightly inside, where they strained like a genie trying to get out of a bottle. She showered and changed clothes, then left her room, not sure where she was going. She just needed to move. To think. To forget the look in Logan's eyes when he had told her he still loved her.

The balcony was quiet. The sun had just set and everyone was gathering downstairs for dinner. The only light came from Logan's room, bleeding faintly through the curtains and a slender crack in the doors. Holly moved quietly on past, but when she heard Duffey's voice she froze in her tracks.

"I don't know who stripped those bolts, Logan, but I think that somewhere tonight, someone is very disappointed that you're still breathing."

"I agree with you, Duffey, but how the hell can I prove it?"

"You can't, I guess. Not without exposing the whole operation. But you're going to have to start being more careful."

"I know. I should have suspected he'd try something like this. The timing was just too perfect."

"Will it stop you from—"

"Absolutely not," Logan said firmly, cutting Duffey off. "As far as I'm concerned, the shipment can go ahead as originally planned."

There was a short pause. "Logan, if something goes wrong—"

Holly heard unsteady footsteps cross the room. "If something goes wrong, Duffey, you've got only one priority," Logan said, his voice hard. "I want you to take care of Holly. She's the only thing standing between my partner and a half billion dollars in treasure."

"I understand, Logan," Duffey said. "You just take care of yourself, all right?"

"I will," he promised. "Now, why don't you head on back to the site? I've got some thinking to do."

Holly heard their footsteps coming toward the door and didn't dare stay around any longer. She needed to get away, to sort through what she'd heard and make sense of it. Moving as swiftly and silently as she could, she fled down the balcony and around the corner to her room.

She shut the door, locked it and collapsed into a chair, trying to absorb it all. Logan's accident hadn't been an accident at all. Someone had sabotaged the winch—someone who had wanted Logan dead, or at least out of the way.

But out of the way of what?

And what had Duffey meant by "exposing the operation"? Was that the smuggling operation Holly desperately
wanted to believe didn't exist? Was the shipment he'd mentioned a transfer of artifacts that he'd succeeded in smuggling from the site? Who was the "partner" he'd mentioned—Dutch Voorhees or Avery Bedrosian?

And what had he meant when he told Duffey to "take
care of Holly"? Had he been asking his friend to protect
her?

Or kill her?

HOLLY STARED BLANKLY at the computer screen in her office, but she had no idea what was on the monitor. She'd
spent all night and all morning trying to make sense of what
she'd heard, and she was still no closer to figuring it out than
she'd been when she hurried away from Logan's door. She
had sorted through the facts she had, looking at them from
every angle, and the pieces still didn't fit together.

The most likely scenario, of course, was that Logan and
the Dutchman were smuggling artifacts away from the site.
With Duffey's help, Logan could silence the alarm sensors
so that Dutch could send divers in at night to loot the site.

Somehow, though, their partnership had taken a wrong
turn. One partner had betrayed the other, and Barnes—their
go-between—had gotten wind of the double cross. One of
them had killed him to keep him quiet.

Now, Dutch was trying to kill Logan.

It was the most complete theory she had formulated, but
there were several gaping holes in it. For one thing, Mike
sketched and charted every artifact before it was brought up.
If something disappeared overnight, he'd know it. In fact,
the whole dive crew would probably know it, too. Even if
only a piece or two at a time was taken, something would
have been missed by now.

And that brought Holly to an even bigger gap in her theory. Logan hadn't been talking about a *portion* of the artifacts. He'd mentioned a half billion dollars in treasure. That was the whole thing, not just bits and pieces.

None of it made sense. Logan had indicated that somehow Holly had the power to put an end to whatever was happening, and that power put her life in danger.

At the moment, she didn't see how that was possible. She didn't feel powerful at all. Rather, she felt like a marionette being manipulated this way and that, entirely against her will. The question was, who was pulling the strings?

"Well, you can forget about the shipment."

Holly nearly jumped out of her skin at the sound of Paul's voice. But this time it wasn't just his unexpected appearance at her office door that startled her. Was it possible that he'd been reading her thoughts? Or was he involved in Logan's operation, too? "What shipment?" she asked suspiciously.

Paul gave a short laugh of disbelief. "What do you mean, what shipment? The one Edgar Franklin has been demanding we have ready for the bank today. The one I *thought* you were in here working on."

Holly rocked back in her chair. That shipment. Of course! How could she have been so stupid?

Logan hadn't been talking about artifacts looted by the Dutchman in the middle of the night. He'd meant the artifacts that Holly scrupulously recorded and shipped off to a bank in Nassau whenever Franklin snapped his fingers. That was the shipment scheduled for today!

But what did that have to do with the operation? Or was the shipment itself the operation?

"Holly? Are you all right?" Paul asked. "If you're not finalizing the shipment log, what have you been doing all morning?"

"Looking at the forest instead of the trees," she muttered, coming to her feet. "What did you mean when you said I could forget about the shipment?" she asked, urgency coloring her voice. She was on the verge of something important. She just wasn't sure what.

"It's been canceled. I went up to the house for lunch and Avery asked me to return here and give you the message. Franklin came down with a case of food poisoning or something after breakfast. He's postponing the shipment until Monday." Paul laughed derisively. "Can you believe it? He makes us push our people to the breaking point to get these shipments ready because it's so incredibly urgent that the artifacts be taken to Nassau. But he gets a little green around the gills and suddenly it's not so urgent anymore."

No, Holly didn't believe it. Not for a minute. "Is anyone else sick?" she asked.

"Nope. Apparently Franklin raided the refrigerator and ate some leftover kippers. He's the only one who's feeling under the weather."

Holly was suddenly sorry that she'd skipped breakfast this morning. "Tell me something, Paul," she said, coming around the desk. "Did Logan come down for breakfast today?"

"Oh, sure. Everyone was surprised that he was getting around so well."

"I'll bet they were," she muttered under her breath.

"What?"

"Nothing. Did Logan say anything about accompanying the shipment this afternoon?"

Paul was looking at her strangely, obviously puzzled by her questions, but he answered anyway. "As a matter of fact, he did. As soon as he sat down, he announced that he felt well enough to fly to Nassau."

"How did everyone react?"

Paul shrugged and searched his memory. "I don't know.... Avery seemed pleased, I guess. I don't remember that anyone else really commented on it. Except, Franklin did tell Logan he probably shouldn't push himself too hard and encouraged him to stay here." He frowned. "Holly, what's going on? Why all the questions?"

"No reason," she said, turning away from him. She had another piece of the puzzle now. She just didn't know how it fit. "Why don't you go on to lunch now, Paul?"

"Aren't you coming?" he asked.

She sat at the desk. "No. I've got some work to do."

"All right." He shrugged and moved out of the office, leaving Holly alone with her jumbled thoughts.

The artifact shipments to Nassau. They were the key. But how? How did they fit into the puzzle?

Giradeaux had refused to allow Logan to accompany the last shipment because of the murder. If Logan's accident yesterday had been more serious, he wouldn't have been able to go today, either.

That wasn't a coincidence. Holly was certain of it. After Logan had disappeared last week, Franklin had pressed her mercilessly to get a shipment ready while Logan was in Matthew Town. Could Franklin have engineered the break-in at Logan's warehouse as a ploy to get him out of the way? Did the obnoxious little bureaucrat have some way of diverting artifacts between the lab and the bank?

But that didn't make sense. Mike had accompanied the last shipment and nothing had happened. Franklin would have to know that even if Logan couldn't go along this time, he would send Mike in his place.

Or maybe not, she realized, with a jolt of inspiration. Mike had left for the wreck site as usual at six this morning; Bedrosian and the staff members who worked in the lab never gathered for breakfast until seven. It was possible that Franklin had counted on Mike not coming back to stand in as Logan's watchdog.

But if something was happening to the artifacts before they reached the bank—something that *couldn't* happen if Logan was along as a witness—then Avery had to be in-

volved . . . just as Logan had claimed weeks ago when the
necklace had fallen out of his locker.

This certainly made a lot more sense than her other theory. It didn't explain Barnes's death or the Dutchman's involvement, but it had one very important feature: it meant
that Logan was innocent, that he wasn't a smuggler or a
murderer. Someone *had* tried to frame him, and when Giradeaux hadn't come up with enough proof to arrest him,
that same someone had tried to kill him.

Who was that someone? Holly had to know the truth. All
of it, not just the fragments she had collected. Because if she
was on the right track, Logan was marked for death.

And for some reason she still didn't understand, her name
was the next one on the list.

LOGAN STARED UP at the ceiling, feeling very much like a
caged and tethered animal. His leg was better, but he needed
more than just a reduction of pain. He needed to be in the
best physical condition of his life. The net was closing in on
him. He hadn't seen the danger coming this time, and that
had been a stupid mistake. He couldn't afford another one.
The next time his partner made an attempt on his life, Logan had to be ready.

So he forced himself to lie still with his foot propped up,
feeling like an idiot, chafing against the self-imposed inac-
tivity.

It gave him too much time to think, and most of the images that ran through his head were of Holly. The way she'd
looked last night when she'd sworn she didn't love him, the
accusations she'd made . . .

The words played over and over in his head, taunting him.
Haunting him. And the worst part of it was, he couldn't
deny her accusations. Not to himself, anyway. He *had* tried
to frighten her. He *had* tried to intimidate her. He *had* tried
to seduce her.

And nothing in the world would ever make her believe that he'd done it all because he loved her. Even when he had been hurt and angry and bitter for the accusations she'd made against him years ago, he had still loved her. When he learned that she was coming to the island, he hadn't wanted her in the middle of the deadly game he had let himself be drawn into.

Unfortunately, his chances of convincing Holly of that were even slimmer than his chances of coming out of this mess alive. The stakes had already been raised and Logan wasn't sure he was clever enough to beat the odds that were stacking up against him. The most he could hope for now was that he could somehow keep Holly safe.

And the only way to do that was to continue the charade until he got caught. Or killed. Either way, it was only a matter of time.

When he heard the rapid drumbeat of footsteps on the balcony, Logan tensed and reached for Holly's cane. He sat up and faced the open French doors just as Holly stormed through and locked them behind her. When she turned to him, her beautiful face was set with determination, and her eyes held a glow that was lit by some inner fire that Logan didn't begin to understand. She looked like a gorgeous lion tamer who'd bearded her prey in its den. This was the Holly that Logan loved most—the stubborn, determined spitfire who believed she could take on the world single-handedly.

Seeing her like this only made the memory of her stinging rejection more painful. He tried to inure himself against everything she was making him feel. "What's wrong, Holly? Did you suddenly remember something else that you forgot to accuse me of last night?" he asked sarcastically before she could get a word out.

Holly didn't waste any time. "Who tried to kill you yesterday, Logan?"

Logan leaned back a bit, stunned. This wasn't at all what he'd expected. "I don't know what you're talking about," he said cautiously.

"Yes, you do." She moved toward the bed. "I want to know who stripped the bolts and created that accident. Was it the same person who killed Seth Barnes?"

Logan frowned. "Haven't you heard? I killed Barnes."

"Oh?" she questioned lightly. "I thought you had an alibi."

"I did. But up to now, you haven't seemed inclined to believe it."

"I'll tell you what I believe, Logan. You're up to your ears in something very messy and it's about to get you killed. The question is, by whom?"

Logan leaned back against the headboard and watched warily as she circled the bed like a predator on the prowl. "I don't know what you're babbling about, Holly."

"I heard you and Duffey last night, Logan! I know someone tried to kill you!"

Logan went very still inside and out. "How much did you hear?" he asked, his voice low.

"How much is there to know?" she countered.

He came to the edge of the bed. "Damn it, Holly. Don't play games with me. How much did you hear?"

"Someone sabotaged the crane, but you can't prove it without exposing your whole *operation*," she replied. "What operation, Logan? Is the Dutchman trying to kill you because you and Barnes double-crossed him? Or did someone just want to keep you off the helicopter with the artifact shipment today? It would have been the second one you'd missed, wouldn't it?" she asked shrewdly.

Damn, Logan swore inwardly. She was so close to the truth. How the hell had she put it all together? "You're treading on thin ice, Holly," he warned her.

She laughed shortly. "Look who's talking. Someone's trying to kill you, and I want to know why. I have a *right* to know, Logan!"

He shook his head. "Holly, stay out of it."

"I can't! I want to know who killed Barnes!" she demanded, moving toward him. "Who put the necklace in your locker? Who planted the key in your room? Who stripped the bolts on the winch?"

Logan came to his feet. "I don't know."

"Yes, you do!" she insisted, coming face to face with him.

Frustrated, Logan grabbed her shoulders. He wanted her trust but he couldn't tell her the truth. "Holly, stop it. You're asking questions I can't answer."

"Can't or won't?" she flung back.

"Can't."

"But you do know who tried to kill you. Was it Avery? When that necklace fell out of your locker, you told me he was trying to frame you. Did he also try to frame you for murder?"

Logan moved away from her, frustrated by her barrage of questions because there were too many things he couldn't tell her. A little knowledge was a dangerous thing, but giving her too much knowledge would get her killed.

He had to tell her *something* though. "Yes, it's Avery," he said, turning to her. "I can't prove it, but he's the only one with anything to gain if I'm arrested. Or killed. Frankly, I don't think he much cares which. If I go to jail, I forfeit my share of the lease and he gets it all."

Holly recognized a bare bone when she saw it, but at least he was talking. "But what does that have to do with the artifact shipments?" she asked him. "If you forfeit the lease, he gets whatever is already in the bank and anything else that's brought up in the future. What difference does it make whether you go on the shipment run or not?"

Logan shook his head. "I don't know, Holly. I don't understand it, either. The circumstances just seem too convenient. After I got back from Matthew Town and learned that Avery had been preparing to make a shipment without me, I started getting suspicious. And then the accident happened just in time to keep me off the next one. I don't know what Avery is up to, but I don't want you involved in it."

"But I am involved! I heard what you said to Duffey about taking care of me if something happened to you. I know you believe I'm in danger, but I don't know why."

"Because you have a habit of sticking your nose in where it doesn't belong," he said forcefully, moving to her again. "People are dying, and I don't want you to be one of them."

He meant it. Holly could see it in his eyes. He was frightened for her—maybe even more than he was frightened for himself. Whatever else he'd done, he hadn't lied to her last night when he told her he was in love with her.

The wall that Holly had built up to protect her heart from being broken collapsed, leaving her feeling more vulnerable than she had at any moment since she arrived.

"Oh, Logan, what have you gotten yourself into?" she murmured, as she sank onto the bed, trying to absorb what she was feeling.

Logan sat beside her. "A whole boatload of trouble. And I want you to stay out of it."

She looked at him. "How do you expect me to do that, Logan?"

"Very easily. Just keep quiet. Whatever you do, don't let Avery or anyone else on this island know what we've talked about tonight. If you tell someone who is involved in Avery's plot, it will put you in danger. If you tell someone who *isn't* involved, it will put him in danger."

"You mean Mike," she said, and Logan nodded.

His advice was good. Holly couldn't dispute that. Not until she had separated the good guys from the bad guys, anyway.

She had to know without any doubt which one Logan was. She looked into his eyes. "I have to know the truth, Logan. I have to hear it from you. Did you have anything at all to do with Barnes's murder?"

Logan's eyes never wavered from Holly's. "No."

"Are you involved in any kind of scheme to smuggle artifacts from the site?"

"No."

She nodded, accepting his answers. But there was one more thing. "When I arrived here, someone sent me two threatening notes. Was it you?"

Logan frowned at her. "Notes?"

"That's right. Telling me I was going to die if I didn't leave. I thought you sent them."

Logan shook his head, knowing he couldn't tell her the truth. She was on the verge of trusting him. He could see it in her eyes, hear it in her voice. She wanted answers that would convince her he wasn't guilty of any of the things she'd accused him of. If he told her about the notes, that fragile thread of trust would snap. He had to lie. "It wasn't me, Holly. I have no idea who might have sent them."

Holly believed him. "Then who did?" she asked. "Avery is the one who hired me. He wouldn't have gotten me here just to frighten me into leaving."

"Unless he wanted another reason to make you distrust me. He knew our history. He may have figured you'd blame me."

"And I did. I'm sorry, Logan," she said, not knowing how to juggle the incredible guilt she felt. "I've accused you of terrible things because I needed to believe the worst." She stood and moved away from the bed, because it was the only way she could confess, "I had to have something to protect myself, so I invented doubts and suspicions."

She heard Logan stand up, heard the soft tread of his footsteps, but all she could feel was warmth that turned quickly to heat the closer he came to her. "What were you protecting yourself from?" he asked softly.

Holly gave a short, miserable laugh. "Don't be coy, Logan. You know exactly what I was hiding from. You've been bellowing it at me for weeks."

Logan put his hands on Holly's shoulders and gently turned her toward him, but he waited until she looked up at him before he told her, "I need to hear you say it, Holly."

She couldn't. The words were there in her heart, but she couldn't make them come out. "I...I can't," she told him, hating herself for not being able to say the words he'd said to her.

His reaction wasn't at all what she expected. He didn't curse, he didn't demand. He laughed. It started as a slow, sexy grin, then a smile, a chuckle, then a full-fledged laugh. "God, I love you," he told her, his shoulders still shaking with mirth. "You are the most stubborn, prideful, infuriating woman in the world, and if you ever change, I think I may wring your neck."

Holly felt tears welling in her eyes. "I don't plan to change, so I guess my neck is safe."

Logan sobered and slipped his hands around her waist, slowly pulling her close. "No, it's not. But I won't let anything happen to you. I swear it. If you don't believe anything else, believe that," he said as he brought his lips to hers.

Without even thinking about it, Holly wrapped her arms around Logan and surrendered to the kiss. There was no question of pulling away this time, no debate about whether or not she was doing the right thing. She wanted Logan, and no matter what it might cost her, she was going to do what felt right.

Holly parted her lips eagerly, delighting in the hard, teasing pressure of Logan's tongue as he took possession of her mouth and her senses. She drank in the sensations, and when his hands caressed the soft curves of her back, moving downward, cupping her buttocks to pull her tight against him, a breathless moan rose in her throat. Her hands moved insistently over his chest, and Holly reveled in the impatient sounds he made as she touched him.

He reached for the buttons of her blouse, and Holly shared his impatience when the first one refused to yield to him. It finally popped free, and another followed it, then another, until he peeled the soft cotton away from her skin.

Touching, kissing, sighing, they moved to the bed, and Logan laid her gently onto the mattress. Holly moaned as his lips left a moist trail along her throat while he moved down, inching his body tantalizingly along hers until she began to tremble.

His mouth covered one pink nipple, suckling gently through the sheer fabric of her bra while his tongue rasped over the hardening peak, and Holly gasped. She wove her hands into Logan's hair, urging him to continue, arching into the pleasure he gave her. Heat suffused her, leaving her breathless and making her ache so badly that she thought she might die from it.

Mindlessly, she clutched at Logan, frantically caressing his shoulders, testing the strength of his back and the sleek curve of his spine. When her hands moved lower, Logan tore his lips away from Holly's breast with a low growl and reclaimed her mouth in a blinding kiss. They strained toward each other, Holly tugging at Logan's trousers while he unfastened her shorts. Somehow, he had the presence of mind to retrieve a small foil package from his wallet as he discarded his clothes, and finally there was nothing between them but scorching heat.

Logan's hands caressed her hips and thighs, then moved inward, searching for the moisture his caresses had created, and Holly arched against his questing hand. He slid over her, and she parted her thighs to accept his weight between her legs. She reached out and captured him in her hand, caressing the silken length of him.

Logan groaned, and their kiss took on a frantic desperation as Holly guided him to her. Her hips rose to accept his first deep thrust, and they moved together wildly, circling and arching, giving and taking as the pleasure built.

Smothering her face and throat with hot kisses, Logan pressed into her again and again until heaven and hell blended into one incredibly sensual, earth-shattering moment just before the first wave of pleasure overtook Holly. For just a second, she was suspended in time, completely lost to herself and the world. And then the world exploded as wave after wave of pure sensation coursed through her.

A hoarse cry burst from her lips as her senses shattered, but Logan continued to thrust deeply, taking her to another plane of pleasure until his own explosion had them crying out in one voice. Slowly, the white-hot pleasure receded, leaving nothing but their soft sighs and an achingly gentle kiss. Holly gradually reclaimed her senses, and she was no longer lost. She knew who she was, where she was...

And to whom she belonged.

Chapter Thirteen

Logan had never felt such total contentment. Holly was curled in his arms, her sun-streaked hair cascading across his chest like a silken sunrise, much softer and far more beautiful than the sunset outside his window. Her breath played softly against his skin, and her long eyelashes rested like entrancing feathers on her cheeks.

He had her back. Finally. After years of telling himself he didn't need her, didn't miss her, didn't still want her, she was finally his again.

Now, the big questions was, what was he supposed to do with her? Every rational instinct he possessed warned him to send her away from Turtle Cay. It was the only way he could possibly protect her from the dangerous game being played out on the island. But ordering Holly to leave would be about as pointless as asking the tide not to come in. Her ruthless stubbornness was one of the things he loved most about her, but it didn't make her the most malleable of women. If Logan told her to go, she'd tell him *where* to go. And she'd probably provide him with a road map.

So getting her out of harm's way wasn't an option.

Since that was the case, should he tell her the truth? She'd already pieced most of it together on her own—but could she accept the *whole* truth?

He didn't think so. In fact, he was sure of it. If he told her, what had happened between them this afternoon wouldn't mean a thing. Considering what she suspected now, Logan could keep her safe only if he could keep her trust.

Holly stirred in his arms, her hand running lightly across his chest as she stretched like a sleepy, contented kitten, and Logan smiled. He remembered the gesture well, but he didn't realize until that moment how deeply he had missed the small, sweet moments like this that he and Holly had once shared. They had wasted a lot of years because of her stubbornness. He didn't intend to waste any more.

Not quite awake, Holly started to roll over, but Logan tightened his arms around her waist to keep her where she was. Her eyes fluttered open, and for just an instant they widened as though she couldn't quite believe what she was seeing. After a moment, though, a little smile tugged at the corners of her lips.

Logan smiled, too. "If you tell me this was a mistake, I'll break your neck."

Her eyes widened again. "Ooh. The stakes are rising. We've gone from wringing to breaking. I stand warned. I wouldn't dream of telling you it's a mistake. But I wouldn't say it was the smartest thing I've ever done, either," she added ruefully.

"Do you regret it?"

She swirled her finger around a lock of hair on his chest. "Ask me that when we've got some clothes on," she said coquettishly, snuggling against him.

"You slept a long time this afternoon," he told her.

"That's because I didn't sleep at all last night. After I heard you and Duffey, I had more important things on my mind."

"I'll bet you haven't eaten, either."

"Nope."

Logan grinned. "I seem to recall that you used to enjoy eating in bed. That tray on my desk is the lunch Marianna brought me before you arrived. I don't know what's on it, but we could probably salvage something."

"Just so long as it's not kippers."

Logan's chuckle rumbled in her ear. "Should we flip to see who goes for the tray?"

Holly raised up on one elbow and looked down at him. "What are we going to flip with?"

"Never mind. I'll get the tray," he said without making any effort to rise. "My ankle doesn't hurt that bad, really. I'm sure going for the tray won't put any strain on it at—"

"Oh, all right. I'll get it." Holly twisted, taking the sheet with her, draped like a Roman toga, as she rose and moved across the room.

Logan couldn't conceal his disappointment. "That's funny. I don't remember you ever being shy."

Holly carefully tucked the sheet so that it wouldn't fall when she picked up the tray. "You don't remember Holly McGinnis as a thirty-four-year-old, either. I'm not the twenty-two-year-old nymph I used to be."

Logan shook his head. "You're beautiful, Holly. Even *more* beautiful than I remember."

She gave him a wistful smile. "As the saying goes, Logan, it's not the years, it's the miles." Her smile faded. "I've got a lot of scars."

"From the accident?"

She nodded.

"Scars don't matter, Holly. You're whole again, and that's all that counts."

A flash of sensation flooded Holly as she remembered how she'd felt making love with Logan, and she knew he was right. She *was* whole again. For the first time in twelve years.

But that feeling also made her remember why the two halves of one soul had been torn apart.

She set the tray down in the middle of the bed, and saw the cane that was leaning against the wall by the nightstand. Another reminder of their differences. Holly reached for the cane and sat on the end of the bed, facing Logan.

"Tell me the truth, Logan," she begged him. "Did you get this from the wreck of the *Nuestra Señora Suerte?*"

Logan wasn't offended by the question. Holly no longer believed he was a smuggler and a murderer, but he was still the same "wreck rapist" he'd been before she had arrived on the island. He knew that she still had issues to settle in her mind before she could ever commit herself to more than an afternoon between the sheets.

"No," he told her honestly, without any rancor. "I got it in London after I heard about your accident. And before you ask the next question, let me save you the trouble. I *was* telling the truth when I said Dutch dynamited the reef."

"Why couldn't you prove it?" she asked him.

"Because except for the word of my men, whose testimonies were considered biased, I didn't have an alibi. I was adrift at sea between Matthew Town and the wreck site at the time that reef was blasted."

Holly raised one eyebrow. "That was awfully convenient, wasn't it?"

Logan ignored her sarcasm. "Rough seas had forced us to go into port the night before, but we only got halfway to the site the next morning when the engines conked out."

"Why didn't you radio for help?"

"Because the radio was on the fritz, too."

"Oh, come on, Logan. No wonder the government is convinced you dynamited that reef."

Logan sat up straighter in bed. "It was no coincidence, Holly. The Dutchman planted a spy on my crew to keep him informed of what we found and what my plans were. He paid that man to sabotage the *Fortune Hunter* while it was in port. The guy didn't show up for work the next morning, so we left without him, but five miles out to sea, the entire electrical system on the boat failed. While we were drifting, Dutch moved in and dynamited the reef.''

His story sounded implausible, but Holly believed him.

"I want to show you something," he told her, twisting toward the nightstand by the bed to retrieve a paper from the drawer. "Read this. I took it from my files in Matthew Town when I was down there to check out the break-in. I thought it might come in handy if you ever softened up enough to listen to the truth."

Holly shot him a exasperated glance as she accepted the paper. She read through it quickly, and was stunned. The document was a petition asking the Bahamian government to declare the wreck site of the *Nuestra Señora Suerte* a protected area, off-limits to all treasure reclamation efforts. In exchange, Logan's company would relinquish all treasure already recovered and allow his two-year lease of the site to return to the government.

"That's the reason Dutch moved when he did. He knew that I was planning to get the reef declared off-limits to everyone. You see, core samples had shown that the main portion of the treasure was buried in a large pocket of silt beneath three hundred and fifty years of coral growth," he told her as she read the document. "The easiest way to get at it was to dynamite, but even without a blast, excavating the treasure would have completely decimated the reef."

"So you were willing to give it up?" she asked with a touch of incredulity. If this document was for real, she'd made a horrible, unforgivable mistake five years ago.

"Under certain conditions. I knew if I simply vacated the lease, the Dutchman or someone else would take over, so I was going to try to prevent that as soon as we had excavated as much as we could without creating environmental chaos. To prevent that from happening, Dutch dynamited the reef and set me up to take the blame for it. The government revoked my lease."

"And Dutch took it over?"

Logan shook his head. "No. That one dynamite blast made it possible for him to excavate a large part of the treasure in a twenty-four-hour period, but there was still a lot left. When Xavier Giradeaux came in to investigate, he couldn't prove who did it, but he figured it had to be either me or Dutch. Since Dutch was under suspicion, too, the Treasury Ministry moved in and took over the excavation themselves."

Holly frowned as she folded the paper. "Why didn't you show this to me before? Last week? Or five years ago?"

"Because it doesn't prove anything. For all you know, I could have written that document last week in Matthew Town."

She regarded him suspiciously. "Did you?"

Logan just looked at her. "Holly, if you're going to believe me, you'll just have to take my innocence on faith alone."

"You're right," she conceded.

"Do you believe me?"

She nodded very slowly. "Yes. I do."

Logan felt as though the world had just been handed to him on a silver platter. "If you were on this end of the bed, I'd kiss you," he told her, grinning like an idiot.

Holly pushed the tray toward him. "Eat first. Kiss later," she said, then frowned as a thought suddenly struck her. Another piece of the puzzle slipped into place. "Logan, do you believe in an eye for an eye?"

The question caught Logan totally off guard. "What do you mean?"

"Five years ago, the Dutchman planted one of his men on your crew as a spy and saboteur. Did you do the same to him? Was Seth Barnes working for you, feeding you information about the Dutchman's plans? Is that why you were meeting secretly on the beach?"

Damn. He hadn't even considered the possibility that she would make a connection like this one. He couldn't tell her the truth. Though it killed him to tell yet another lie, he nodded and let her believe what she wanted to believe. "Yes."

"What did he tell you that night?"

Logan shrugged as he tried to come up with the most plausible lie he could think of on short notice. "Not much. Dutch was trying to figure out a way to disarm the alarm sensors on the site, and Seth wanted me to know that Dutch was going to try to bribe one of Avery's guards."

"Did you tell that to Giradeaux?"

"No."

Holly frowned. "Why not? If Dutch murdered Barnes because he found out he worked for you, that would let you off the hook."

"Holly, do you remember me telling you that Dutch had government officials on his payroll?"

"Giradeaux?" she asked, aghast.

"I think so."

"Oh, God, Logan," she murmured, shoving the tray to the foot of the bed so that she could slip into Logan's arms. "What have you gotten yourself into?"

Logan shoved aside his guilt and pulled her close. "Something I wish you weren't in the middle of," he told her. It was the most truthful thing he'd said in the last five minutes.

"If wishes were horses..." She murmured wearily. "Logan, what's going to happen to you?"

"I'm going to prove that Avery is setting me up."

"How?"

"I don't know."

A terrifying thought struck her. "Logan, Franklin postponed the artifact shipment until Monday. What if Avery tries something between now and then?"

"I'll deal with it."

She slipped out of his arms and glared at him. "Oh, good answer. *How* will you deal with it?"

"I don't know. And I won't know until he makes his next move." He looked at her sternly. "Until that happens, I want you to stay out of the way."

"Oh. You mean you want me to just stand by and do nothing while he tries to kill you."

"I want you to be safe!"

"Well, don't I have the right to want the same thing for you?" she shot back. "Should I send flowers to your funeral or just make a donation in your name to the Old Treasure Salvors Home?"

"I'm not going to get killed, Holly."

"You're right. You're not, because I won't let it happen."

"What are you going to do, Holly? Glue yourself to my side? We won't get much work done that way." His look of irritation evolved into a devilish grin. "On the other hand, the idea does have a certain appeal."

"Logan, be serious," she commanded.

"I am."

"Put your libido in park, Big Fella," she advised him, ignoring what his sexy grin did to her stomach. "We have to formulate a plan."

"I've got a good one," he said promptly. "I go back to work at the wreck site tomorrow, and you keep a low profile in the lab. And no matter what happens, you don't breath a word about our suspicions of Avery to a living soul."

Holly shook her head. "I'll keep my mouth shut, Logan, but if you're diving tomorrow, so am I."

"No, Holly. I don't want you on the site tomorrow, and that's that," Logan said sternly.

Holly studied his face for a long moment before telling him, "You know, you're very handsome when you set your jaw like that. There's something about your steely-eyed resoluteness that I find very sexy."

Logan sighed. "Forget my steely-eyed jaw and stick to the subject. I don't want to have to worry about you tomorrow. I'm going to have enough trouble looking out for myself."

"Exactly. That's why you need me. Since we suspect that you're an accident waiting to happen, I'm going to be there to watch your back—and anything else that needs watching."

"Holly—"

"You can't argue with me, Logan. I outrank you, remember? This is my excavation. If I want to dive, there's not a blessed thing you can do to stop me."

"I could tie you up and throw you in a closet."

Holly grinned. "You wouldn't do that. You're not that kinky."

"Don't bet on it. A woman as stubborn as you can push a man to do a lot of things he wouldn't normally do."

"Well, you're going to have to come up with something better than that, because I do plan to be on the runabout with you at six o'clock tomorrow morning." She pointed a finger at him. "And don't even think about leaving without me. I'll just get Judd to fly me to the site."

"Damn it, Holly—"

"Face it, Logan. You've lost this argument," she said with absolute finality. "I don't know what's going to happen tomorrow, but I'm going to be there when it does."

"DOES IT LOOK LIKE sabotage?" Holly asked Duffey quietly. She was kneeling across from him on the deck of the *Fortune Hunter* with Logan standing over them as Duffey carefully inspected Logan's air tank.

Duffey shook his head. "I wouldn't be able to tell for sure without taking it apart, but I doubt it. My guess is that the internal O-ring has lost its seal. It happens to all tanks from time to time, and this one has seen an unusual amount of use lately."

"I agree with Duffey," Logan said as he sat on the gunwale. "No one who knew anything about diving equipment could possibly believe that this would be a danger to me. My dive computer warned me that I was losing pressure in plenty of time for me to make my ascent. The only way it could have caused me any trouble is if decompression time was a factor, and it's not." He stretched his legs out and crossed his ankles. "I think this is exactly what it looks like—a case of equipment in need of maintenance."

He looked at Duffey. "Why don't you put it with the artifacts to be loaded onto the chopper when it gets here? I'll take it in with me tonight and drop it off at the dive shop on Turtle Cay before I head for Nassau on Monday."

"*If* you head for Nassau," Holly muttered.

Logan smiled at her. After she'd won their argument last night, he'd decided it was probably for the best. Her determination to keep him safe was a two-way street—as long as she was on the *Fortune Hunter* he could keep an eye on her, too. "Stop worrying so much, Holly. The day's half-over and I'm still in one piece," he told her, though he wasn't quite as confident as he sounded. *Something* was going to happen today, or tomorrow at the latest.

He'd just have to do his best to survive whatever it was.

BY THE TIME she finished her last dive, Holly was exhausted and her back was aching more than it usually did after an active day, but despite all her fears for Logan's safety, nothing had happened. The day had been so routine that she had wondered several times whether she and Logan were crazy to be so paranoid.

When Logan offered her a ride back to Turtle Cay on the helicopter with the artifacts, she accepted gratefully, knowing the passenger seat of the chopper would be a lot more comfortable than the runabout.

It took another thirty minutes to load the helicopter, and by the time they completed the flight, Mike was just pulling in to dock the runabout. Neal Scanlon's cruiser wasn't far behind him.

"Now, that's what I call timing," Judd said, gesturing toward Mike as he shut down the engines. "We're going to need all the help we can get unloading this lot."

"Yes," Holly said, removing her headset.

Judd turned to her. "You okay, Doc?"

Holly glanced at Mike in the distance. He'd been very cool toward her all day, and she'd wondered several times if he had sensed the change in her relationship with Logan. If that was true, she knew he must be very hurt. She was going to have to talk to him soon. There had to be a way to make him understand that it was useless for him to hope that they would ever be more than friends. "I'm fine, Judd," she said sadly.

Judd shrugged. "If you say so."

He slipped out of his seat and joined Logan and Franklin in the cargo bay as guards and lab staff members began converging on the helicopter. Even Avery came sauntering down the lawn, but Holly didn't imagine he'd help unload. He certainly hadn't so far, though he'd begun to make a habit of meeting the daily shipments.

"A productive day, Holly?" he asked her as she came around the chopper.

Given her newfound suspicions about him, it was hard for Holly to be friendly, but she painted on a smile anyway. Logan was right. If Avery was guilty, Holly was much safer if he thought she was still on his side. "Very much so," she replied, joining him just out of the way of the workers. "We started bringing up the silver bullion and the olive jars today. I'm anxious to do some testing to see if we can determine what was in those jars originally. Oh, and we found several wine bottles with their contents intact," she told him, her eyes dancing with genuine excitement. "That's very rare."

"Indeed it is," he replied, seemingly as excited as she was, but as he went on to question her about what still remained in the crater Holly noticed that he focused almost exclusively on the items with the greatest monetary value. Franklin joined them, and he, too, waxed rapturous about the "treasures" that had yet to be brought up.

With so many people working, it didn't take long to off-load the chopper. "I guess that's all of it," Holly heard Logan say. He jumped to the ground as the last load was wheeled off to the lab, and started to follow it.

"Wait a minute, Logan," Judd called out from the bowels of the cargo bay. "Is this yours?"

Logan turned as Judd appeared at the hatch cradling the defective scuba tank in his arms. "Yep. Thanks, Judd. I didn't see it back there." He reached up for the tank, grasping it by the T-valve assembly at the top. Judd let go, and the tank swung down to Logan's side.

Logan knew almost instantly that the weight of the tank was wrong. It was too heavy to be devoid of compressed air. In fact, it was too heavy to be fully loaded. But that was as far as his thoughts traveled, because the bottom of the tank suddenly popped off, and a wad of white rags fell out. The rags unfurled, and a glittering array of gold chains, jewelry and sparkling emeralds scattered across the grass.

Logan was so shocked that he couldn't do more than stare down at the cache of treasure that had fallen at his feet.

Holly was stunned. "Logan?"

"Good heavens!" Avery exclaimed, hurrying to the chopper. "What is going on here, Logan?"

"I demand an explanation, Tate!" Franklin chimed in as he dropped onto the grass and began collecting the treasure. "Look at this broach! That wasn't brought up today. I've never seen any of these pieces!"

"Let me see it," Holly demanded, reaching for the broach. A huge square-cut emerald sparkled in the center, accentuated by diamonds in the gold filigree of the setting. She looked at Logan. "Where did this come from?"

Logan searched for his voice and found it. "It would seem that someone is trying to smuggle some unreported treasure away from the site."

"*Someone*?" Edgar squeaked, glaring up at Logan. "Isn't this your tank?"

If the situation hadn't been so serious, Logan would have laughed. Instead, he looked at his partner. "You've outdone yourself this time, Avery," he told him, with a mockingly appreciative nod of his head.

"I don't know what you mean, Logan," Bedrosian replied huffily. "Are you going to explain how these pieces came to be hidden in your scuba equipment?"

Holly picked up the false bottom of the tank. She was only vaguely aware that Neal Scanlon had arrived, camera in hand, and had started filming. "They were planted there, obviously," she said indignantly, coming to her feet.

"She's right," Logan said. "Someone is setting me up."

"Can you prove that?" Avery challenged.

"No more than you can prove that I'm the one who hid this treasure in a tank specially designed for smuggling. But then, you have circumstantial evidence on your side," he said derisively. "The tank is identical to mine, right down to the red stripe and my name stenciled on it. I'm the one who ordered it be put on the chopper—the real tank, that is. Somewhere along the line, my tank was switched for this one, which was rigged to fall open at just the right moment. And it worked."

"I'm sure Detective Inspector Giradeaux will be very interested in your theory," Avery told him coldly.

"You can't be serious!" Holly exclaimed. "Avery, you know damned good and well that—"

"What is going on?" Mike asked as he returned from the lab.

Holly whirled to him. "Logan is being set up." She hastily explained what had happened, then urged Mike, "Please. Tell these men that Logan is innocent."

Mike's face took on a cast of sadness that Holly didn't understand as he looked at the man he had once claimed was like a brother to him. "I can't, Holly. I've tried for weeks to believe in Logan's innocence, but this is the last straw."

Logan felt sick. He had expected Avery to pull something today; he just hadn't expected this much finesse.

"I agree with Mike," Avery said with disgust. "Guards! I want you to escort Mr. Tate to his room and see that he remains there until Giradeaux arrives. We'll let the inspector sort this out and decide what is to be done. Although I must say, Logan, that I can't imagine our partnership continuing as it has."

"Certainly not!" Franklin said indignantly. "I'm making a call to the Home Office immediately to see that your name is removed from the lease license!"

Logan glared at Bedrosian. "Very nicely done, Avery. Scratch one unwanted partner."

"Guards, take him," Avery ordered.

"Now, wait a minute," Holly said, but Mike intervened.

"Holly, please. Don't make this worse than it already is. Let Avery do what he must."

"But this isn't right! It can't be!" She turned to Logan, looking up at him beseechingly. "Logan—"

"Stay out of it, Holly," he warned her.

"But—"

"It will be all right," he said forcefully, but only to shut her up before she said too much. The noose was tightening around his neck, and he had no idea how he was going to slip out of it this time.

Two guards stepped forward with their guns trained on him, and Logan had no choice but to accompany them up to the house.

Chapter Fourteen

"It's just so hard to believe," Paul Kyte said.

"I know," one of the technicians agreed with him. "I've heard that Logan had a shady reputation, but I never imagined he'd try something like this."

"I guess a billion dollars is enough to turn anyone into a crook."

From the refuge of her office, Holly listened as her staff vilified Logan, and it sickened her, mostly because she couldn't march out there and defend him. They believed he was guilty. They had tried and convicted him on circumstantial evidence alone—and who could really blame them? Logan *did* look guilty.

But he wasn't. He couldn't be. Just the sabotage of the cannon alone proved that someone was out to get him.

But of course, no one knew about that except Logan, Duffey and Holly, since Logan had insisted on keeping it a secret so as not to alert Avery that he was on to him. And even Holly couldn't testify to the sabotage because she hadn't seen the damage herself. She had only Duffey's word that the bolts had been stripped.

A sickening thought struck her but she couldn't turn away from it. Was it possible that *she* was really the one who had been set up? Had Logan invented the sabotage story, turning a simple accident into an attempt on his life to gain her sympathy?

Stop it! Don't be an idiot, she berated herself. Logan couldn't have invented the sabotage story because he had no way of knowing that she would be on the balcony to over-hear his conversation.

But the door had been ajar....

Don't do this to yourself! she commanded. She had known that Avery was going to try something to get rid of Logan this weekend. And this was it. He had set Logan up. End of story. Holly couldn't allow any room for doubt about that. She'd let herself fall in love with Logan all over again, and she couldn't bear the thought that he had played her for a fool. She *had* to trust him, because as doubt-ridden as her mind was, her heart was equally sure that he was in-nocent.

It was just a matter of deciding which one she would lis-ten to, and it wasn't a hard choice to make.

"Well, that didn't take long. The inspector must have been in the neighborhood," she heard Paul comment. She raised her head, listening to the sound of a helicopter cir-cling the compound. Giradeaux had arrived.

Holly stood and hurried out of her office.

"I guess this means Logan will be spending the night in jail," Ron said.

"Probably a lot of nights," Paul commented.

"Not if I have anything to say about it," Holly snapped as she stormed past them.

As IT TURNED OUT, Holly didn't have anything to say about it at all. Giradeaux disappeared into Avery's study before Holly could even reach the house. He questioned Mike, Avery and Franklin, but when it came to Holly's turn he refused to listen to her protests of Logan's innocence. He was only interested in how Logan's air tank came to be on the helicopter in the first place, and once she had explained the leak he'd discovered, Giradeaux dismissed Holly and went off to interrogate Logan.

"This is madness!" Holly said as she stalked into the parlor where she had been ordered to wait along with the others who had just been questioned. She marched up to Avery. "I want you to put a stop to his, Avery. Now. You know Logan didn't steal those artifacts!"

"On the contrary, Holly," Bedrosian said placidly. "I believe everything is beginning to make a great deal of sense."

"What do you mean?"

"Think about it. This certainly explains what Logan was doing with that man Barnes last month. Obviously, he's been smuggling treasure away from the site from the very start of the excavation, and he was using Barnes to get it off the island."

"That's absurd!" Holly insisted, even though she had believed the same thing until just a few hours ago. She hurried across the room to Mike, entreating him privately, "Tell him he's wrong, Mike."

Her friend shook his head sadly. "I can't, Holly. Even Inspector Giradeaux believes that's what Logan has been up to all along. He told me that himself not fifteen minutes ago."

"I don't believe this! Mike, Logan is your friend. You trusted him even when I didn't. How can you turn on him now?"

"Because too much has happened, Holly. We can't make excuses for him forever. And you can't cover for him this time, either."

Holly frowned. "What do you mean?"

"The necklace in Logan's locker," he replied, his voice soft and sad. "I know you were there when it fell out of his towel, but you kept silent to protect him."

"How did you know about that?"

Mike seemed surprised by the question. "Logan told me, of course."

"He did?" Holly didn't understand that, but a horrible thought struck her before she could even begin to make sense of it. "Mike, you didn't tell Giradeaux, did you?"

"No, Holly, I didn't," he assured her. "But you should. If Giradeaux discovers it on his own, he could name you as an accomplice. Holly, please, don't let Logan drag you down with him. You have to face the facts. As I have."

Holly stiffened as a sudden realization hit her. "You've turned on him because of me, haven't you? You're letting your jealousy get in the way of what you know is the truth."

"No," he told her sternly. "You are the one who's letting emotion cloud her judgment. Holly, I've watched for weeks as Logan worked some form of insidious magic over you, wearing away your suspicion of him and trying to make you love him again so that he could laugh at how easily he conquered you. And now he's making you look foolish because you're defending him like a woman blinded by love. He is guilty. Accept that, Holly!"

Holly couldn't believe what she was hearing. Jealousy had turned Mike against Logan, and Avery had probably capitalized on it, encouraging him to distrust Logan as he had tried to do with her. Mike was too hurt by her relationship with Logan to see that he was placing his trust in the wrong man.

It was everything Holly could do to keep from hurling that accusation at him, but common sense warned her to keep quiet. Logan had flatly accused Avery of setting him up, but Bedrosian had no way of knowing whether Logan had taken Holly into his confidence. He might suspect that she knew he was responsible for the acts that had been perpetrated against Logan, but he couldn't be sure.

Holly knew she had to keep it that way. She would be of more use to Logan in helping prove his innocence if Avery didn't view her as an enemy.

But at the moment, she didn't have a clue about how to even start proving his innocence. Frustrated by Avery's duplicity, Mike's defection and her own impotence, she turned away from Mike and moved to the French doors. If they wanted to believe that she was overwrought and close to tears, let them. Because it wasn't far from the truth.

She wasn't surprised when Mike joined her a moment later.

"Holly—" he said softly, but she cut him off.

"I don't want to hear it, Mike," she said, not caring that her voice sounded broken. "Logan is innocent."

"I want to believe that, too," he replied sadly. "Even after we saw him on the beach and that man was murdered, I believed he was innocent."

Holly faced him. "And then you saw that I was growing closer to Logan, and you started having doubts."

Mike's face hardened into austere lines. "I saw him manipulating you. Why do you think he encouraged you to oversee the excavation of the cannon?"

"Because he knew I had to face that responsibility, no matter how hard it was for me."

"No, Holly. It was nothing more than a ploy to earn your trust and place you at odds with me. Don't you see how skillfully he has turned you against me?"

"Mike, that wasn't Logan's doing. It was yours. You've been wearing your jealousy like a coat of armor, and I got fed up with being caught in the tug-of-war between you two."

"That didn't keep you from turning to Logan, did it?" he asked harshly.

"No," she was forced to admit.

Mike's dark eyes were like a cold, bottomless well. "And now you're in love with him again."

She couldn't deny that, either. "Yes. I love him."

"Then I'm truly sorry for you, Holly," he said tenderly, though his eyes didn't mirror the gentleness of his voice. "When the full truth about Logan's guilt is brought out, you're going to be forced to admit that he used you. I can't take away the pain that you'll feel then, but I will always be here for you."

Holly knew exactly what Mike meant. He was hoping that she would eventually turn to him, but that wasn't going to happen. "I'm sorry, Mike. Truly, I am, but no matter what happens between Logan and me, it won't change my feelings for you. I do love you, but it's not the kind of love you want it to be, and we've got to stop pretending that it ever could be."

Clearly, that wasn't what he wanted to hear. "You're wrong, Holly. When all this madness has ended and Logan is out of your life for good, you'll see. I'll *make* you see how much you love me," he said with an intensity that frightened her. "I've waited too long for you, Holly. I won't let you go now."

He walked away, leaving Holly more frustrated than ever. But despite her desire not to see Mike hurt, he wasn't the most important problem she had to solve. Finding some way to prove Logan's innocence was her first priority.

"Mr. Bedrosian?"

"Yes, Inspector?"

Holly whirled around when Giradeaux came into the parlor.

"We will be leaving shortly to take Mr. Tate to Nassau," he told Avery. "Will it be possible for you to come to headquarters tomorrow to sign a complaint against your partner?"

"Certainly," Avery replied. "In fact, I had planned to be in Nassau tomorrow, anyway. Mr. Franklin has made arrangements with an officer of the bank to open the vault for us so that we can complete a treasure shipment that was postponed yesterday."

Holly couldn't believe what she was hearing. What better proof did she need that Logan was right about Avery. Somehow, he was diverting artifacts from the bank shipments. Unfortunately, there was no way she could prove that to Giradeaux. Yet.

"You're not arresting Logan," she said, going to him.

"Oh, but I am, Dr. McGinnis," he told her briskly. "I have more than enough evidence to convict him for artifact smuggling, and by the time I finish the investigation, I expect that the charges against him will include an indictment for the murder of Seth Barnes."

"What?" she asked, aghast.

Giradeaux nodded. "We have a witness who claims that he saw a man matching Tate's description chartering a private helicopter in Matthew Town around the time of Barnes's death. So far, we haven't been able to locate the pilot of that helicopter, but when we do, I believe Tate's alibi will collapse."

Oh, God. This couldn't be happening! Was Avery paying for witnesses now? "What does that prove?" she challenged him. "Even if he was in the area, it doesn't mean he killed Barnes!"

"I'm afraid the evidence to the contrary is compelling, Dr. McGinnis. The key we found in his room—"

"Was planted there!" she insisted. "Logan had never seen it before!"

Giradeaux regarded her coldly. "Then how did his thumb print get on the key ring, Doctor?"

Holly felt as though he'd just delivered a blow to her solar plexus, robbing her of air. How could a key Logan had never seen bear his prints?

Was it just trumped-up evidence created by a crooked police inspector? Was Giradeaux helping frame Logan on the Dutchman's orders, or had Avery paid him off, too?

Or was it possible that Logan had lied to her?

No. She wouldn't believe that.

But she knew that she had to stop arguing. Giradeaux wasn't going to listen to reason. Flinging accusations at him would only place her in danger. As Mike had said, Giradeaux had the power to arrest her as Logan's accomplice, and she couldn't allow that to happen.

Holly stopped protesting and turned to pleading. "Inspector, please. Let me see Logan."

He shook his head. "That's not possible."

"Why not?" she asked. "You have him under guard. What harm could it do?"

"I'm sorry, Doctor—"

"Please," she begged. "I have to talk to him. I have to know if what you've told me is true."

Giradeaux's stern demeanor melted a bit and a look of pity crept into his face. "He will not tell you the truth, Doctor." He hesitated a moment, then nodded. "But if you insist on seeing him, I will permit it."

"Thank you," Holly said breathlessly, then hurried off before the inspector could change his mind.

She ran upstairs, but she got no farther than the door of Logan's room. The guards there refused to admit her and wouldn't change their minds until Giradeaux appeared behind Holly and gave one of them a nod.

The sentry unlocked the door and stepped aside.

"Logan?" Holly stepped into the room and was appalled. Giradeaux's men had conducted another search and had torn the room to pieces in the process.

"Holly! What are you doing here?" Logan asked, trampling on clothes and books to reach her.

Holly slammed the door and stepped into Logan's arms. "I had to see you. Giradeaux is arresting you."

"I know," he said, pulling her tightly against him. "Don't worry, Holly. It'll be all right."

She looked up at him, fighting tears. "How can it be, Logan? They've trumped up more evidence to convict you of Barnes's murder. You've got to tell Giradeaux that he was working for you!"

"That wouldn't help right now, Holly."

"But you can prove it, can't you?"

Logan nodded hesitantly. "I think so."

"And the sabotage on the pontoon. We can prove that, too. The damage hasn't been repaired yet. We can prove there was an attempt on your life—"

"Maybe," Logan agreed. "But Giradeaux won't lift a finger to help me, Holly."

"Then you have to get to someone else. Someone Avery or the Dutchman hasn't paid off."

"I will," he told her. "But for now, there's nothing I can do but let Giradeaux take me in."

Holly knew he was right. Miserable and frightened, she laid her head against Logan's chest. "Oh, God, this is a nightmare."

"Yes it is," he agreed, holding her tightly. "But it will be over soon."

Holly shook her head, not seeing how it could be. "We have to find more proof," she said. "I'll—"

Logan grabbed her shoulders. "You'll do nothing, Holly. Do you understand me? Nothing! Giradeaux won't be able to make these charges stick. You have to keep quiet and stay out of it!"

"How can I?" Holly said, her fear boiling into anger. "There has to be some way I can help you!"

"There isn't!"

"Damn it, Logan—" She jerked away from him and nearly tripped over the rumpled bedclothes at her feet. Frustrated and furious, she picked them up and threw them onto the bed. She only succeeded in uncovering another layer of debris, though. Papers from the desk were strewn everywhere, but Holly would have ignored them if she hadn't caught a glimpse of red and green lying half-hidden among the other white sheets of paper.

Christmas stationery. A border of red-and-green holly. Just like the one on the threats she had received. The threats Logan had denied sending her.

"Oh, God, no," she whispered as a wave of nausea flooded through her. Lies. Everything he had told her...lies. The evidence Giradeaux had against him wasn't a frame. Avery hadn't paid off the inspector. Logan had created an intricate tapestry of plausible lies, and Holly had swallowed them because she wanted so desperately to believe in his innocence.

But she couldn't. Not now.

"Holly?"

Fighting back a flood of anguished tears, she bent to pick up the stationery. When she turned to Logan and held the paper out to him, the look on his face told her everything she needed to know.

His guilt was inescapable.

"Holly, let me explain," he said.

She stiffened her jaw against the tears and the swell of rage that was building inside her. "Explain what, Logan? How you seduced me into trusting you? Defending you? Lying for you? Why did you do it? Did you decide it would be more fun to seduce me into silence than killing me?"

"No!" he exclaimed. "Read the notes again if you still have them Holly. They weren't threats! They were warnings. I knew that you wouldn't believe me if I told you that you shouldn't trust Avery, but I had to warn you that something was going on here. Something that could be dangerous for you. The only way I could think of to put you on guard was to send you those stupid, half-veiled threats."

Holly wanted to believe him with all her heart, but she couldn't. She was hurt and humiliated, but more than that, she was in agony. She had allowed herself to love Logan again, and the pain of his betrayal was a thousand times worse than it had been twelve years ago.

"I don't believe you, Logan," she told him. "And I don't believe what I let you do to me." She turned toward the door.

"Holly, wait," Logan said, snatching at her arm, but she jerked away from him.

"Don't touch me! Don't ever touch me again!" she shouted, then turned and fled from the room.

Logan took two steps after her, but the guard at his door brought him to a halt.

"The inspector is waiting for you downstairs," the guard told him. "It's time to go."

Logan looked down the hall as Holly disappeared around the corner. The pain in her eyes was etched into his soul, but there was nothing he could do to take it away. He had lost her.

It was all for the best. Yesterday he'd thought he could keep her safe if she trusted him. Now, her hatred of him would achieve the same thing.

THE SUN WAS JUST SETTING as Holly watched from the gallery while four armed policemen escorted Logan across the lawn to the helicopter. As long as she lived, she would never be able to wipe the image of Logan in handcuffs from her mind—or the image of the pain etched in his face when he'd stood silently in the parlor, watching her as she told Gira-

deaux about the necklace that had fallen out of his locke.
weeks ago.

Admitting her stupidity in front of everyone had been
humiliating, but she was beyond caring. She had made a
fool of herself because of Logan. She deserved whatever she
got.

The inspector had postponed his departure long enough
to take a full statement from Holly, and though he had
hinted that there might be repercussions, at least he hadn't
arrested her as an accomplice. Not yet, anyway.

A crowd had gathered to witness the spectacle of Logan's arrest, and when Holly caught a glimpse of Neal
Scanlon and his video camera, she almost snapped. The
drama that had unfolded this afternoon had been too juicy
for him to miss, and he had captured every last bit of it on
film like a vulture circling its prey.

Holly watched as Logan reached the helicopter and
stopped. He turned, looking back at the house. Looking at
her.

Something inside her broke and shattered into a thousand pieces. He was guilty. He had lied to her. He had seduced her, and she hated him for it. So why did she still
imagine that she could feel the strength of his love for her,
even from this distance?

Tears coursed down her cheeks, and she turned her face
away, unable to bear looking at him and equally unable to
return to the house. When she glanced back at the helicopter, drawn by the magnetic power that Logan always had
over her, he'd disappeared inside.

Holly wiped away the tears.

Down the gallery, Giradeaux and Avery were just emerg-
ing from the house, and when Giradeaux caught sight of
Holly, he changed course and moved toward her. Holly was
too exhausted and too battered by her emotions to care.

"Thank you for your honesty, Dr. McGinnis," the inspector said without preamble. "I don't expect that we'll be pressing charges against you for obstruction of justice, but you will be asked to testify at the trial."

Holly just nodded numbly. "Whatever you need."

Avery placed a comforting hand on her shoulder, and Holly almost cringed. "I know how difficult admitting the truth must have been for you, my dear. But Logan is a very persuasive man. Please don't blame yourself for being taken in by him."

Holly managed to look up at him. "That's very generous of you, Avery, but I should have come forward when it happened. Maybe Seth Barnes would still be alive if I had."

Bedrosian shook his head. "Don't take that burden onto your shoulders, my dear. You couldn't have known the lengths Logan was prepared to go to."

Like telling me he loved me, and making me believe it with all my heart, she thought, tears welling in her eyes.

Giradeaux had the good grace to pretend he didn't notice the tears. "I will expect to see you tomorrow in Nassau, Mr. Bedrosian," he said, turning to Avery. "Can you be there by eleven in the morning?"

Avery nodded. "Of course."

"Good day to you both, then."

The inspector turned briskly and marched off toward the helicopter with Scanlon filming him every step of the way.

"Holly, my dear, please come inside," Avery encouraged her. "We'll be dining shortly, and I do hope you'll join us. We should all rally together at a time like this."

"Thank you, Avery, but I'd like to be alone for a while."

He sighed regretfully. "Very well. But don't cut yourself off from everyone, Holly. Your friends can be a great comfort to you at a time like this." He patted her shoulder again and slipped through the parlor doors behind her.

Friends? Holly thought derisively. She didn't have any friends here, and no one could possibly offer her any comfort. Mike would be only too happy to have her turn to him, but she couldn't do that to him. He would view it as more than it was, and his love for her had cost him too much already.

And his love for Logan? That was costing him, too. Obviously, even when he'd had his doubts, he'd kept silent about the necklace. Just like Holly, he'd wanted to believe in his friend until the evidence against Logan became too overwhelming to ignore.

The necklace... The image of it flashed in Holly's mind, but she was too numb to think.... The image wouldn't go away, though. There was something about the necklace... and Mike.

She saw Giradeaux climb into the helicopter and slam the door.

The necklace and Mike. Holly knew she was reaching for something important. She forced her pain away and focused on the inconsistency that she hadn't had time to consider before.

The rotors of the helicopter began to churn sluggishly.

Why had Logan told Mike about the necklace? Holly asked herself. He had seduced her to buy her silence about it. What possible reason could he have had for confessing the incident to Mike and in the same breath denying that he was guilty?

No reason, she realized. No reason at all. Logan would never have confided in Mike about the necklace, and there were only three people who knew that it had been in that locker—Logan, Holly and the person who had put it there.

Holly couldn't believe what she was thinking. It wasn't possible. Mike *couldn't* be involved. But he had accompanied Avery, representing Logan's interests on the last artifact shipment. When Barnes's body was found, he had told

Giradeaux that he had seen Logan arguing with him on the beach.

Holly didn't want to believe her suspicions about Mike any more than she wanted to believe in Logan's guilt. He was her dearest friend. He loved her. He had stood by her for years, and he had stood by Logan, too. He couldn't be guilty of betraying him now.

But the doubts were there, and Holly had to know the truth. There was only one way to know for sure. Desperate to get the answers she needed, Holly darted down the gallery and down the stairs, flying across the lawn as fast as she could run.

But she was too late. The helicopter roared and the wind whipped at Holly's hair as it lifted off and sailed away.

Logan was gone.

Holly would just have to find some other way of getting the answers she needed.

HOLLY RETREATED to her office where she could think without any interruptions. All the technicians had long since quit work for the day and the lab was as silent as a tomb. There was no one to disturb her as she collected her thoughts. She shoved aside the emotional impact of everything that had happened today and tried to think logically.

There had to be some way to prove or disprove Logan's innocence and the extent of Mike's involvement. But what was it? After all this time, how could she possibly prove who had smuggled the emerald cross from the wreck site and put it in Logan's locker? For that matter, how could she prove who had stolen the artifacts that had fallen out of Logan's scuba tanks today?

Frustrated, she swiveled her chair toward the barred window behind her desk and caught a glimpse of Neal Scanlon's two camera assistants as they made their way around the lab to the mess hall used by the guards and other non-supervisory personnel. Beyond them, at the dock, she could see the lights in the *Jupiter*'s main cabin, and the documentary director himself was headed up the lawn toward the main house.

Too bad Neal didn't get the thefts on camera, she thought sourly. If he'd been as diligent about filming the site as he'd been about capturing Logan's arrest on—

Holly sat upright in her chair. Of course! Why hadn't anyone thought of it before? There *was* a chance that Neal had captured the thief on film! Somewhere in the mounds of videotapes he'd made there might be at least one scrap of proof that showed who the real thief was.

Of course, the proof wouldn't be obvious. If Scanlon had caught the culprit in the act, he surely would have said something. Unless he, too, was part of Avery's scheme. And if that was the case, he wouldn't have been so foolish as to videotape one of his confederates committing the crime.

Those realizations caused Holly's bubble of excitement to deflate a little, but it didn't burst entirely. Her chances of finding the proof among Scanlon's tapes weren't good, but it was the only chance she had at the moment.

She came out of her chair in a flash. The *Jupiter* would be deserted for several hours. Scanlon and Paul always played chess after supper, and the staff poker game in the mess hall had become legendary. It was now or never.

Holly didn't stop long enough to give a second thought to what would happen to her if she was caught.

DESPITE HER DETERMINATION, getting aboard the *Jupiter* wasn't a piece of cake. If any of the guards saw her go aboard, there was a good chance they would challenge her— or worse, report her to Avery. He might not know what she was up to, but he would certainly find her behavior suspicious.

To avoid the guards, she headed toward the house, then doubled back onto one of the paths leading into the jungle. Eventually, she emerged on the beach and made her way back toward the dock. She encountered a guard, but he didn't seem to find anything strange in her excuse that she was just out for a stroll.

As she approached the boats, she had to pause for a few moments against the trunk of a palm tree while one of the roving patrols made its routine pass by the dock, and then she was home free. She hurried onto the planking and climbed aboard the *Jupiter*.

Holly had been aboard the boat enough to know her way around. She'd ridden back from the wreck site with Scanlon a few times, and he'd invited her and several others aboard on more than one occasion to view edited footage of the documentary. His editing area was at the back of the main cabin, and his tapes were stored in a climate-controlled chest beside the console.

Holly opened the chest, and her heart sank. There were at least a hundred of them. Two months worth of videos, neatly arranged according to the date they had been shot.

This wouldn't take hours, it would take days!

Or maybe not. Holly didn't have to go through months worth of footage. The botonée cross was the first artifact that had been used to frame Logan, and it was far more distinctive than a simple gold chain or uncut emerald. Very little jewelry had been found prior to the opening of Crater Four, so if she concentrated on the day they found the necklace in Logan's locker and then worked backward, she probably wouldn't have more than a few days to cover.

Holly remembered that day very well—it was the day Logan had kissed her in the deckhouse—but pinpointing the exact *date* was a little tougher. A pinup calendar over the editing console helped her with that, and she set to work, fast-forwarding through everything Scanlon had shot aboard the boats.

His underwater footage on that day was particularly meticulous. With the storm heading in, he had been recording the exact positions of the finds so that Mike could chart them later. As a result, there were very few shots of any of the dive team. Occasionally she would see Mike setting out reference markers, but everything else was artifact footage.

It went on forever, through one tape, then another as Scanlon had made slow scanning shots of the crater bed. But at least the slow pace allowed Holly to fast-forward through the tedious footage.

If the tape had been moving any faster, she would have missed it.

With a flush of excitement, Holly punched the rewind button, then froze the frame she wanted. There, in the middle of the screen, was the botonée cross lying in the midst of a knot of gold chains.

"Please, God, please, let me see who picks it up," she muttered fervently, advancing the tape again. "Let it be one of the divers who works for Avery. Let it be Neal or Duffey or Carl or *anyone* but Logan or Mike."

Holly leaned forward, watching with total concentration, but suddenly, the camera jerked away from the bed of artifacts. There was a blur of motion, and when the picture came into focus again, Holly saw herself in the distance as she floated down from the surface, her body contorted as she tried to cope with the muscle cramp that had struck her.

She watched as Logan swam to her and released her weights, then Mike swam into the picture briefly. Logan waved him back, and Mike disappeared, but Scanlon kept the camera on her ascent with Logan. Moments later, she was pulled onto the boat, and Scanlon returned to the crater.

His movement as he turned this time was much slower, and he scanned past the other divers working in another part of the crater, until he was focused once again on the spot he'd been filming moments before. He captured Mike pointing to the place where he'd left off filming, and then the close-up returned to the knot of gold chains and the botonée cross.

Except, the cross wasn't there anymore...and the only person who'd been even close to the spot where it had lain was Mike.

Chapter Fifteen

Holly stared at the frozen image in disbelief. It couldn't be! Mike couldn't be in league with Avery. He couldn't be a part of this whole sordid setup.

And yet, there was no escaping the truth. Neal and Mike had been the only divers in that section of the crater. One of them had to have taken it, and Neal's whereabouts were accounted for every minute that the camera had been off the cross.

"Oh, Mike . . . Why?" she whispered as a wave of misery washed over her. "Why?"

But Holly knew she didn't have time to figure it out or to grieve over the betrayal. Logan was innocent and Avery had set him up with Mike's help. And Holly had the proof. She was in big trouble.

When she glanced at her watch and realized she'd been on the *Jupiter* for nearly three hours, she knew she had to get out fast before anyone returned. She also had to get the tape to the authorities, but how was she supposed to do that?

Logic told her to make a copy so that there would be no possibility that Scanlon might notice the original's absence, since he often returned to the *Jupiter* to work on his editing before turning in for the night. But the editing equipment in front of Holly was a lot more complex than a simple VCR, and she didn't have a clue how to operate it.

She would just have to take the tape with her and find a way off the island tonight before Neal realized it was missing and raised an alarm.

Ejecting the tape from the machine, Holly did her best to return everything to the way she'd found it. She slipped out onto the deck and scanned the dock to make certain there were no guards about. Two runabouts were moored across from the cruiser, and Holly made her decision in an instant. She would commandeer one of the speedboats, paddle away from the dock and make her way to the village. With any luck, she would be able to hire a water taxi to get her to Port Long and be off Turtle Cay by the time anyone realized the runabout was missing.

She had to wait nearly five minutes for the roving patrol guard to pass by the dock. She watched him closely as he moved on down the beach, and once she was sure he wouldn't hear her, she stepped onto the dock.

Her focus on that one guard was her undoing. She had taken only two steps toward the runabout before she realized that a second guard was back at the entrance to the dock. Watching her.

"Dr. McGinnis?"

The guard stepped toward her and Holly got a better look at him. "Gordy? Is that you?"

"Yes, Ma'am. What are you doing out here? Mr. Bedrosian was worried sick about you when he found out you weren't in your room and no one had seen you since you left the lab. He asked me to look for you."

"As you can see, I'm perfectly fine," Holly said, doing mental gymnastics trying to come up with a reasonable excuse for being there. "I went for a walk, and then decided that I'd like to see some of the video footage Neal Scanlon shot today. When I saw the lights in the cabin, I assumed he was here, but—" She shrugged her shoulders. "—no luck."

"I see you found the tape you wanted, though," the guard said, gesturing toward the cassette in her hand.

"Oh. Yes. I didn't have a clue how to work his equipment, so I thought I'd take it up to the house. There are several VCRs in the house."

Holly realized she was talking too fast, because she could see the guard's suspicion. "I see. Well, before you do that, I think you should have a word with Mr. Bedrosian."

"I'm sorry, Gordy, but I'm really tired. Could you just tell Avery I'm fine and I'll see him in the morning?" She tried to bluff her way past him, but Gordy wasn't buying her act.

"I don't think so, Doctor," he said, taking hold of her arm.

"How dare you! Let me go!" she demanded as she tried to jerk away, but Gordy had a grip like iron.

"Doctor, please. Don't make this difficult. You're going to see Mr. Bedrosian the hard way or the easy way. Make up your mind."

Since he outweighed her by a good fifty pounds and also had a gun slung over his shoulder, Holly didn't see any choice but to accompany him. She was truly terrified, because Avery wasn't going to buy her lame story any more than Gordy had.

FROM A CHAIR beside the desk, Holly watched as Avery stood in front of the television set in his office viewing the videotape. It didn't take him long to spot the same thing Holly had seen.

Breathing a heavy sigh and shaking his head, he switched off the TV and turned to Holly. "Rather incriminating for Dr. Villanova, isn't it?" he asked her mildly.

"Yes."

"And it would prove without a doubt that Logan is as innocent as he claims."

Holly just nodded.

Avery extracted the videotape from the machine and held it up. "This was a fine piece of deduction, Holly. I thought when you betrayed Logan this afternoon that we'd finally convinced you of his guilt once and for all. It's most unfortunate that Mike was so clumsy. I had hoped to complete this affair without any harm coming to you. Once Logan was safely out of the picture, I'd have found an excuse to fire you, of course, but that was the extent of my plans regarding you."

The knot of fear in Holly's stomach doubled in size. Avery wasn't making any attempt to deny the fact that he had engineered the entire plot against Logan. In a way, she appreciated him for not insulting her intelligence by denying it, but overall, she would have preferred it if he'd lied. She could have pretended to believe him, and her life expectancy might have extended beyond the next few hours. As it was, she didn't see much hope.

"I guess that makes a certain amount of sense," she told him, scrambling to put all the pieces into their proper places. At least she'd have the satisfaction of knowing what was going on before she died. "Firing me, I mean. Somehow, you're diverting the artifacts between here and Nassau, and you're doctoring the manifest logs from the bank to show that everything is safely stored there when in fact, it's not. When it comes time to ship the artifacts to the museum, you can't afford to have anyone involved with that transfer who knows exactly what should be in the bank vault."

Bedrosian beamed at her like a proud parent at his child's spelling bee. "Precisely. I see that I was right, though. Logan did confide a great deal to you, didn't he?"

"Not willingly, I assure you. And I figured most of it out for myself. All except—" She gestured toward the TV and her facade cracked for a moment.

"Your dear friend, Mike?" Avery asked sympathetically. "That must have come as a terrible disillusionment."

Holly collected herself. "To say the least. How did you do it, Avery? What did you use to turn a kind, honorable man into a liar and a thief?"

"I did what I do best. I found his weakness. While I was researching Logan's background and trying to formulate his downfall, I learned of his friendship with Miguel Villanova. Upon investigation of Mike, I discovered that he had a number of unpleasant gambling debts, which I was only too happy to help him pay off."

"No." Holly shook her head emphatically. "I don't believe you. Money wouldn't be enough to make Mike turn against Logan!"

Bedrosian laughed. "My dear Holly, I'm afraid you have greatly misinterpreted Mike's feelings toward Logan Tate. He despises him with a passion almost equal to his love for you. And he *does* love you, you know. One might say almost fanatically, in fact. So in a way, I suppose you could say *you* are really to blame. It was his idea to bring you in as head of this project because he had the misguided notion that throwing you and Logan together would 'exorcise Logan's ghost from your heart,' as he so eloquently put it. Even now, when it's blatantly obvious that you love Tate, Mike continues to believe that he will be able to win you over."

Holly didn't know what to feel. Revulsion was there, certainly, but she also felt an incredible sense of loss coupled with guilt. Without realizing the damage she was doing, she had maintained a friendship with Mike that had caused something truly evil to fester inside him.

But she didn't want to think about that now. "All right, Avery, let's cut to the chase. What are you going to do with me?" she asked bluntly.

"I? Nothing. I'm afraid I lost my taste for unpleasant work like this long ago. Fortunately, my partner isn't so squeamish."

Holly looked at him in horror. "You think Mike will—"

"No, no. Of course not. I was referring to Dutch Voorhees."

"Dutch works for you?" Holly asked as the final piece of the puzzle dropped into place.

"Of course. I have to have some way of getting the treasure out of the islands and into the hands of my brokers. When the shipment is made to Nassau, Dutch meets us at a charming little island called Key Perilous, where he off-loads part of the treasure onto his boat." Avery smiled. "And he has other uses, as well."

Holly suppressed a shudder of fear, determined not to let Bedrosian see how much the thought of the Dutchman terrified her. "What are you going to do? Invite him up to the house and turn me over to him?"

"Nothing so obvious. No, a subtler touch is called for, and I must also be prepared to explain your absence tomorrow."

Holly wasn't sure she wanted to know, but she asked anyway. "How will you do that?"

Avery leaned back in his chair, tenting his hands thoughtfully. "It will be tricky, but Judd and Riva should be able to assist me. I'll have Judd drop you off on Key Perilous tonight, then he'll continue on to Nassau, where Riva, my secretary, will disembark and disappear into the airport, making her way back here on one of the ferries. No one will miss her. Her inconspicuousness is one of her chief assets."

"But how does that explain my disappearance?"

"Simple. Judd will claim that you were so distraught over the arrest of your lover that you couldn't bear to remain on the island a minute longer. You came to Judd in the middle of the night, begging him to take you to Nassau, and he complied out of pity. He had no idea what became of you after he left you at the airport. Witnesses will attest that they saw a woman getting off the helicopter, and from that point on, your disappearance isn't my problem."

Holly stared at him, appalled by the intricate workings of his mind. "Is there anyone on this island who *isn't* in on your plot?"

"Oh, of course. Most everyone is quite legitimate. Scanlon and Paul Kyte are completely in the dark, as are most of the guards."

"What exactly is going to become of me, Avery?"

He waved his hand dismissively. "I'll leave that up to Dutch, but if it will make you feel any better, I will request that he make your death as quick and painless as possible."

"As painless as Seth Barnes's death?" she said coldly.

Avery nodded. "If possible."

"Did you kill him, or did Dutch?" Holly asked.

"Oh, Dutch did, of course. After Mike saw Barnes with Logan on the beach, he realized that a spy had been planted on the Dutchman's crew. Barnes had to be eliminated."

So Mike had been responsible for Barnes's death just as surely as the Dutchman. At that moment, Holly was too terrified to feel anything at all about this new revelation, but she did have one more question. "What about the sabotage of the pontoon?" she asked him. "Another of Dutch's masterpieces?"

"Yes. One of his men took care of that." Avery rose and came around the desk. "You know, Holly, I must admit that I felt no remorse over the removal of Barnes. It served to put the police on Logan's trail, and that was an important element of my plan. I do regret what's going to happen to you, though. Quite deeply, in fact. You are a remarkable woman—not at all the gullible fool I took you for after our first interview. I shall miss your outspokenness. And your expertise with my artifacts, of course.''

Considering the fact that he was going to have her killed, it didn't seem necessary to acknowledge his compliment. Avery moved on to the door and asked Gordy, who was standing just outside, to surreptitiously fetch Judd Cunningham. Holly began a frantic mental scramble for some way out of her predicament, but unfortunately she couldn't find one. Bedrosian's office was so heavily soundproofed by books that no one would even hear her if she screamed, and by the time she was taken out of the office two hours later, that wasn't even a possibility....

Bound, gagged and terrified, Holly was on the helicopter headed for Key Perilous.

BY DAY, KEY PERILOUS was a tropical paradise—albeit a small one. According to the description a chipper Judd Cunningham gave Holly before he deserted her, the uninhabited island was a coral atoll about two miles in diameter. Dense vegetation made the interior difficult to traverse, but it was worth it to see the magnificent blue hole that had given the island its name. The seemingly bottomless crater came up through the coral and for years had enticed divers to their deaths as they searched for the outlet from the blue hole to the sea.

Eventually the island had been declared off-limits, making it a perfect rendezvous spot for anyone whose motives were less than legitimate.

"I really appreciated the travelogue," Holly told Judd just before he left her. "But I'd rather know when I can expect the Dutchman to come calling."

"Probably pretty early," Judd replied. "Mr. Bedrosian sent a message telling him to pick you up and have you hidden on board the *Treasure Trove* before the chopper arrives."

"And when will that be?"

"About nine."

Holly glared up at him from her uncomfortable position in the sand. He was standing between her and the chopper, and the harsh landing lights made it hard for her to see him clearly. "I don't suppose you'd be willing to untie my hands so that I can see my watch?"

Judd looked at her sympathetically, but shook his head. "Sorry. I wasn't even supposed to undo the gag."

"It's okay," Holly said casually. "I wouldn't want you to do anything that might get you in trouble."

The sarcasm was hard to miss. "I'm really sorry about this, Doc. But if you knew what Avery was holding over my head, you'd understand."

Holly's feigned good humor left her. "I understand that after tonight, he's going to have a helluva lot more to hold over you."

Judd just shrugged and turned back to the helicopter. A few minutes later, it lifted off, throwing up a swirl of sand that sparkled in the landing lights. The lights disappeared, the drone of the engine eventually vanished, and Holly was left completely alone on the dark, eerie island.

"Some tropical paradise," she muttered as she began methodically tugging at her bonds.

BY DAWN, Holly's wrists were bleeding, but she hadn't succeeded in slipping out of the ropes. She had freed her feet, though, and she had a plan—for all the good it would do her. As soon as it had grown light enough to see, she set out for the interior of the island. Judd had said the blue hole was located in the south, so that's where she was going. The irregular, sharp-as-glass coral walls of the hole could be used to cut her rope, and if she was very lucky, might also provide her with a hiding place.

She estimated that it took her about two hours to find the blue hole. The island wasn't very big—from one vantage point she'd been able to see the ocean on both sides of her—but having her hands tied behind her back threw off her balance, and made walking difficult. Stumbling back and forth through the small patch of jungle searching for a medium-size hole in the ground was like looking for a needle in a haystack.

When she did finally stumble into the clearing surrounding the hole, she almost shouted for joy. The hole, with its crystal blue depths, seemed too clear to be real. The jagged coral structures that formed its walls dropped down ten feet before disappearing into the ocean pool, and the twenty-foot-wide, irregular circle was more like an artist's painting than one of nature's most spectacular wonders. Holly knew she didn't have time to enjoy the incredible beauty, though.

Sitting down at the edge of the crater, she used the sharp coral to saw through the ropes, then checked her watch. It was only seven-thirty. She still had time, but she couldn't afford to waste any of it. Circling the perimeter, she inspected it carefully for any cavity above the waterline that might serve as a hiding place.

When she saw what looked like the opening of a small cave just above the waterline, she summoned all her courage and began the painful climb down to it. The coral cut into her hands and lacerated her limbs, but she ignored the pain because faintly, in the distance, she could hear the deep rumble of a boat engine.

Dutch was early. Holly's time had run out. But no matter what, she wasn't going to make it easy for him to kill her.

Chapter Sixteen

The sleek white cruiser approached the island and came to a stop just long enough to disgorge two inflatable boats and twenty heavily armed men. The boats zipped toward shore and the cruiser sped off as the men scrambled onto the beach. With stunning efficiency, they hid their boats, erased all traces of their landing and disappeared into the dense tropical foliage. Within a matter of minutes, there was no sign that they had ever been there.

"I must admit, Gerry, I'm impressed," Logan said as he settled into the underbrush, well hidden, but with an excellent view of the beach. "You've been bragging about the efficiency of your men for years, but this is the first time I've really seen them in action. They're good."

"Thank you, Logan," Xavier "Gerry" Giradeaux replied. Dressed in camouflage gear instead of his pristine white suit, the detective inspector looked very much like the tough-edged guerrilla fighter he had been trained to be. But the smile he gave Logan contained none of the animosity that he'd had to work to generate these last months. "The proximity of the Bahamas to Florida makes us a prime target of smugglers. These men are our best weapon for stopping the flow of drugs through our islands."

"I won't dispute that." Logan heard a rustle in the brush and turned just as Larry Hamilton poked his way through the foliage. Thin-faced and wiry, the U.S. Treasury agent was a bundle of controlled energy, and though Logan didn't know him as well as he'd known Hamilton's partner, Seth Barnes, he was pretty certain Hamilton would be a good man to have around in a tight spot.

"Everyone is in place," the agent announced as he settled in beside Logan. "We've got complete coverage in this section of the beach. Our reconnaissance after their last shipment run showed that this is the exact spot where Cunningham lands the chopper, so we should be able to close them in a very tight net when they get here."

"Then we're ready. All that's missing are the bad guys," Logan said as he checked the safety on his revolver. He knew he was going to need the gun. Seth Barnes had died because he'd learned that Avery and Dutch were making artifact transfers on Key Perilous. That was the information he'd passed to Logan that night on the beach; he'd considered it so important that he had bypassed the locker at the Windjammer Club that they had established for passing messages.

Seth's information was the only thing that had allowed them to piece together what Avery was up to, but being seen with Logan had cost him his life.

Logan wasn't about to forget that. Avery and Dutch would both pay for what they had done—not only to Barnes, but for what they had cost Logan, as well. He still couldn't escape the memory of the pain he'd seen on Holly's face when she realized he'd lied to her. He didn't think she'd ever forgive him, not even when she learned that he had been working from the very beginning with the Treasury agents who had been trying for years to prove that Avery Bedrosian was smuggling antiquities into the States illegally.

Logan's only consolation in this whole sordid mess was that Holly was safe. Telling Gerry about the necklace had put her back on Bedrosian's side of the fence, and the deadly game they were playing would be over today—long before Avery had to get rid of her to keep her from exposing his scheme.

"I just got word that Voorhees left Port Long about an hour ago," Hamilton told Logan and Giradeaux. "That would put him here sometime around nine if he doesn't make any stops."

"Good," Logan said. "I was afraid I'd have to miss this little surprise party. I'll have to remember to thank Avery for setting me up to be arrested instead of killing me outright."

"You've done good work, Tate," Hamilton told him. "And you, too, Giradeaux. It couldn't have been easy for you guys to pretend to be mortal enemies."

"Oh, it wasn't so bad," Logan said. "All those hours of interrogation gave us the perfect opportunity to pass information back and forth with absolutely no risk. And it certainly gave Avery a false sense of security. He never had a clue that we were manipulating him far more effectively than he was manipulating us."

Giradeaux chuckled softly. "I especially appreciated that, too. It's what you would call poetic justice."

"I'll settle for some real justice that puts an end to this," Logan replied. "I'm ready for it to be over so that I can get back to Turtle Cay."

Giradeaux nodded. "I know that will please the beautiful Dr. McGinnis."

Logan shook his head grimly. "I don't think so, Gerry. She's never going to forgive me," he said, then shoved those thoughts aside so he could concentrate on the confrontation that was coming. By the time an hour had passed, he was growing restless, but Gerry and Hamilton—old hands at this waiting game—were as cool as proverbial cucumbers.

Logan heard the *Treasure Trove*'s engine before he actually saw the boat. Giradeaux was connected to his assault team via a wireless communication network, and he adjusted his headset, alerting the men that it was time. A small chorus of clicks indicated that weapons were being readied, and they all waited tensely as the *Trove* dropped anchor just beyond the breakers. A longboat was lowered over the side, and moments later, Dutch Voorhees and three of his men clambered into the boat and rowed for shore.

Logan noted with dismay that all of the men were armed—three with rifles and Dutch with a holstered revolver. The situation just got a little stickier.

"Remember, we wait for the helicopter," Giradeaux said softly into his microphone. "We want them all here before we spring the net. Just hold your positions until I give the word," he told his men. He didn't have to add that he wouldn't give that word until he saw the artifacts being transferred from the helicopter to the longboat. He had to be sure his case held up in court.

The island was absolutely hushed as Voorhees's boat landed, so hearing their conversation would be no problem at all. Comprehending their behavior was another matter. All four men glanced up and down the beach as though they were looking for something, and Logan tensed. Did they know about the trap? If so, coming onto the island at all was downright stupid, and Dutch was anything but a fool.

"Well, where the hell is she?" one of the men demanded.

"How should I know?" another one replied.

Dutch shook his head in disgust. "The idiot probably dropped her off on the other side of the island. I'll be damned if I'm going to walk two miles around the beach looking for her."

Logan and Giradeaux exchanged puzzled, concerned glances. Who on earth were they expecting to find waiting for them?

"Maybe she got away," the first man suggested.

"And went where?" Dutch asked disparagingly. "You see any water taxis waiting around to pick up passengers?"

"She could be hiding in the jungle."

"Yeah, she could be, but I'm not going to waste time looking until I know where Cunningham left her. He lost her, he can damn well help find her."

"Bedrosian is going to be pissed," the first man told him.

"You think I care? If he wants a say in how the good doctor dies, he should have killed her himself."

Logan's heart stopped beating. Holly. They were looking for Holly so that they could kill her. The world tilted on its axis and Logan couldn't think straight. What the hell was Bedrosian up to? Why would he want to kill Holly? There was no reason for it . . . unless she had done something that made it impossible for him to allow her to live.

Logan couldn't imagine what that could possibly be, but it didn't matter at the moment. The important thing was that Holly was obviously somewhere on the island, in hiding and undoubtedly terrified.

Logan finally realized that Giradeaux was gripping his arm as though to hold him in place. But Logan wasn't going anywhere, and he told his friend with a look and a nod that he was all right. Wherever Holly was, she was safe for the moment. The best thing he could do for her would be to snag Voorhees and Bedrosian as quickly as possible. Once that was done, it wouldn't take more than a well-worded shout on Giradeaux's bullhorn to bring her out of hiding and into Logan's arms.

Hang tight, Holly-love. I'll have you safe in no time.

His silent message proved prophetic as the drone of the helicopter reached his ears. He waited, scarcely able to breathe, as it came in for a landing. Cunningham jockeyed into position with the cab facing the ocean, and Logan had a clear view of the cargo bay as the door slid open. Mike was crouched in the hatch with three boxes at his feet and Edgar Franklin standing over him.

Dutch waited until the rotors stopped before he swaggered toward the chopper. "Cunningham, you idiot! Where did you leave her?"

Avery was climbing down from the passenger seat, and he nearly stumbled when he heard the Dutchman's question. He cast a concerned glance back at the cargo bay, but his consternation passed in an instant and he walked out to greet his partner. "Don't you have her?" he asked imperiously.

"If I did, would I be asking where she was?"

"I left her right here," Judd said, hurrying around the chopper.

"Tied up?" Avery asked.

"Of course," Judd answered.

"She must have broken free. She could be anywhere," Avery said.

"Hey, it's a small island. She can't have gone far," Judd told him.

"Avery, what's going on?" Mike asked as he jumped out of the cargo bay. "What are you talking about?"

Avery sighed heavily as he faced Mike. "I'm afraid we had a little problem last night. Of your own making, I might add. It seems that Holly had sufficient intelligence and determination to search Scanlon's videotapes for proof that someone other than Logan had picked up that botonée cross. She found what she was looking for and was trying to get off the island when Gordy discovered her."

Mike's face turned ashen. "She knows? She saw me take the cross?"

"I'm afraid so."

Logan felt simultaneous surges of pride and anger. His brilliant, beautiful Holly had put her life in danger looking for some way to prove his innocence. He couldn't imagine a more telling demonstration of love, and as soon as he found her, he was going to kiss her senseless. Right after he strangled her.

"Oh, God," Mike murmured, then collected himself quickly. "What have you done with her? You told us this morning that she had begged Judd to take her to Nassau. If that's not the truth, where is she?"

"I had Cunningham bring her here so that Dutch could dispose of her," Avery said bloodlessly. "But apparently our plan has gone slightly awry."

"Dispose of her?" Mike repeated, outraged. "No! I won't allow it! We had an agreement! Holly wasn't to be harmed under any circumstances!"

"Oh, good Lord," Avery snapped. "It's over, Mike. Holly knows that you've been working with me from the beginning. Whatever affection she felt for you is gone, and I assure you she will do everything in her power to put us all behind bars unless we silence her!"

"No!" Mike roared as he whirled away and headed down the beach.

"Where do you think you're going?" Bedrosian demanded.

"To find her! To explain! I have to make her understand! Holly!" he shouted into the jungle. "Holly, where are you?"

Logan held his breath, fearing that Mike might plunge into the underbrush and trip over one of Giradeaux's men, but that didn't happen. He kept moving on down the beach, calling Holly's name as though he really expected that she would coming rushing out and fling herself into his arms.

Logan had known ever since Barnes's death that Mike was involved, but he hadn't realized until that instant that his onetime friend was quite probably mad.

Dutch looked at Avery and frowned. "You want me to stop him?" he asked, fingering the pistol strapped to his waist.

"No. Let him go. Someone has to find her and as Judd pointed out, it's a small island. Let's make the transfer and then your men can go look for them."

"Whatever you say."

Logan tensed, ready to spring, as Dutch signaled his men to move to the chopper. They slung their rifles onto their shoulders and accepted the boxes Edgar Franklin shoved at them.

Giradeaux let them get halfway to the longboat before he quietly spoke the word, "Now," into his headset.

The result was stunning and startling. As one, twenty armed men came charging out of their hiding places, guns at the ready.

"Drop the treasure and your weapons!" Giradeaux thundered. "Freeze where you are!"

All of them froze for just an instant, but their shock didn't last long. When Dutch drew his revolver and made a diving lunge for the belly of the chopper, his men took their cue from him.

"Don't do it, Dutch!" Logan shouted, but his men dropped the boxes and unslung their rifles with surprising efficiency. Giradeaux opened fire, and a spate of shots cut one man down before Dutch began returning fire from his sanctuary beneath the helicopter.

Logan and Giradeaux's men scrambled for cover, and that pause was enough to allow the two remaining men in the open to join their boss. Avery sought refuge behind the cab of the helicopter, but Logan knew there was no way for him to escape. He just prayed that Dutch would give up his futile fight before anyone else got killed.

The rain of gunfire that pounded in his ears didn't make that seem likely.

FROM HER HIDING PLACE in the small coral cave, Holly heard the shots, but it took her a moment to recognize them for what they were, because they echoed so eerily against the walls of the blue hole.

She couldn't imagine who was shooting, or why, but a tiny sliver of hope swept through her. She prayed that somehow Logan had learned of her predicament and had come to rescue her. She didn't see how that was possible, of course, but she prayed just the same—for herself and for Logan, if he was in the middle of the ferocious gun battle she heard raging in the distance.

It went on for what seemed like an eternity, but in reality it was only a few minutes before everything returned to the silence she had grown accustomed to.

Now, what? she wondered. She didn't dare go investigate, but a frightening possibility occurred to her. Her imagination painted a scenario in which the police had somehow learned of Avery's plan to meet the Dutchman on Key Perilous, but had no idea that she was here as well.

What if everyone who knew of her presence had been killed in the gun battle? What if the police left the island without her? Avery had invented a story that placed her in Nassau last night. If everyone believed him, Holly knew she would die of thirst before anyone would think to look for her here—if they ever did.

She was faced with an agonizing decision. Pray that Avery and Dutch Voorhees were no longer a threat and come out of hiding, or stay where she was and risk a slow, painful death.

Holly didn't see that she had much choice. If Dutch was still a threat, he probably wouldn't give up looking for her until he found her. There were only so many hiding places on the island, and he would eventually find this one. She'd known that from the beginning, but she hadn't been willing to accept her fate without some kind of a fight.

She had to take the chance.

Dreading the difficult climb back up the coral wall, she carefully inched her way out of the cave. Finding footholds and handholds was easy—as long as she could ignore the pain of the lacerations the coral made on her hands. She kept climbing, fighting tears, and willing the pain to go away.

"The trail leads this way, to the blue hole."

Holly heard the deep, silky, accented voice and couldn't believe her ears. It was Giradeaux! She opened her mouth to scream, but the second voice she heard brought tears flooding to her eyes and down her cheeks.

"God help her if she tried to hide in the hole, Gerry. That thing is a death trap."

"Logan!" she screamed. "Logan, I'm here! Down here!"

"Holly?"

Forgetting caution, Holly scrambled up the few remaining feet to the lip of the blue hole. Torn and bleeding, she struggled to stand, ready to throw herself into Logan's waiting arms—and came face-to-face with Avery Bedrosian.

He had a gun, and it was pointed at her.

Chapter Seventeen

"Holly!" Logan burst into the clearing with Gerry on his heels, but the sight that greeted him made his heart skid to a halt faster than his feet stopped him.

On the opposite side of the blue hole, Avery was holding Holly in front of him like a shield. He was also holding a gun.

"As they say in the movies, that's far enough," Avery said, pressing the gun to Holly's temple.

He was trying to sound calm and collected, but Logan could see the gaping chinks in his facade. Though her eyes were wide and she was standing stock-still, Holly looked in better shape than Bedrosian. Logan didn't dare make a move that might spook her captor. "Let her go, Avery," he ordered. "You can't possibly get off this island. Voorhees is dead and everyone else is in handcuffs. I still haven't figured out how you slipped past Gerry's men, but this is the end of the line."

Avery wiggled the gun a little against Holly's forehead. She winced but wisely kept silent as Bedrosian explained, "Cunningham keeps this tucked under his seat in the helicopter, and Inspector Giradeaux's men were a bit haphazard in seeking cover when Dutch opened fire. I managed to slip through."

"Obviously. But you won't slip out, Avery. I can promise you that."

"On the contrary, Logan. I believe I can escape, because we are going to return to the helicopter, where you will release Judd from his handcuffs so that he can fly us out of here."

"That is not going to happen, Mr. Bedrosian," Giradeaux told him gravely.

"If it doesn't, Dr. McGinnis will die," Avery replied. "And since I have absolutely nothing to lose, that's a promise I'll make and *keep*. Now, both of you toss your guns into the hole and do a smart about-face. You may precede me down to the chopper, but I would suggest you move slowly. We wouldn't want anything to happen to Holly."

Logan and Giradeaux looked at each other, but clearly there was nothing to do but comply. They threw their weapons into the blue hole. "Are you all right, Holly?" Logan asked her, needing to make some kind of contact with her.

"Do I look all right?" she asked with an exasperated defiance that made Logan love her all the more.

"Yeah. You do," he said tenderly.

"Move," Avery commanded him. Logan turned reluctantly. Giradeaux took the lead, and Avery shoved Holly in front of him as he circled the hole to follow Logan. "While we're taking such a pleasant stroll, perhaps one of you gentlemen would be good enough to explain to me how this debacle came about. I must confess, I was completely surprised."

"That's what we intended," Logan replied without turning. "After I agreed to a partnership with you, I asked Gerry to do some checking on you."

"Gerry?" Holly queried.

"Detective Inspector Giradeaux," Logan replied. "We've been good friends ever since I convinced him that it was Dutch who dynamited the *Nuestra* site."

Holly gasped. "Why, you—"

"Anyway," Logan went on, cutting her off in midcurse, "Gerry learned that the U.S. Treasury Department had been investigating Avery for illegal antiquities smuggling and he put me in touch with Seth Barnes, the agent in charge of the case."

Using the most matter-of-fact, calming voice he could muster, Logan explained how he had agreed to work with the Bahamian police and the Treasury Department in their cooperative effort to capture Avery in the act. He didn't leave anything out, not even the distress he'd felt when he'd learned that Mike was involved.

"Damn you," Holly said. "Why didn't you tell me?"

Logan almost turned around, but he checked himself. "For the same reason I sent you those notes. Considering all the doubts you had about me, you never would have believed that Mike was involved."

"You're right," she admitted. "I guess I wouldn't have. I had to see it for myself."

"Any more questions, Avery?" Logan asked him.

"No. You covered everything quite nicely. And just in time. I believe I see the beach up ahead and several of the inspector's men. Be very careful how you proceed from here, gentlemen."

Six of Giradeaux's men had remained near the helicopter to guard their prisoners while the others had gone in search of Holly and Avery. All six men snapped to attention as soon as they saw the inspector emerge onto the beach, but none of them brought their guns up until they saw Bedrosian and his hostage.

"Careful," Avery warned them.

"Put down your weapons," Giradeaux ordered.

"Have them uncuff Judd, if you please."

Gerry gave Logan a what-else-can-I-do look and ordered one of his men to comply with Bedrosian's command. Judd didn't think twice about scrambling to his feet and heading for the chopper.

"We will be going now," Avery announced as he began backing toward the helicopter, keeping Holly between himself and the armed policemen.

"Leave her here, Avery!" Logan demanded, taking an angry step toward him.

Bedrosian jammed the gun into Holly's temple, and Logan froze. "I don't think leaving her would be wise. The moment I release her, you would most certainly open fire. She's my only hope of escape."

He started backing toward the helicopter again, and the look on Holly's face nearly tore Logan's heart out. She was so frightened, but so obviously determined not to cry out or beg for help.

"I'll be all right, Logan," she promised him, unshed tears brimming in her eyes. "I love you."

Those were the words Logan needed to hear, but not now. Not like this. Not when he couldn't take her in his arms— when he might never be able to take her into his arms again. "Damn you, Avery, if you kill her, there's not going to be a hole on this planet small enough for you to hide in!" Logan swore viciously.

"Frankly, Logan, your threats don't concern me." Avery knew he was almost at the chopper, but he chanced a quick glance over his shoulder to make sure he was headed for the open cargo bay door. Smiling with satisfaction, he returned his full attention to Logan, which was unfortunate, because he didn't see the man crouching beneath the helicopter, ready to spring at him.

Avery was completely unprepared for Mike's attack. He grunted in surprise when his hand was grabbed from behind and drawn away from Holly's head.

The rest happened almost too fast to comprehend. With her captor off balance, Holly wrenched away from him and Logan darted forward, grabbing her and thrusting her toward Giradeaux in one swift movement. He didn't see her stumble and fall as he lunged on toward Avery.

But he was too late. Mike was grappling with Bedrosian, locked chest to chest with him as they fought for possession of the gun. When it fired, Holly twisted toward the sound, and everything seemed to freeze ... Giradeaux, his men, Logan, Avery and Mike. All were frozen in time for just an instant.

Then, the tableau ended, and Mike fell at Avery's feet, a dark red stain spreading out across his chest.

Holly screamed his name and the echo chilled the island.

Logan grabbed Avery, wresting the gun from him as Holly scrambled across the sand to Mike. She cradled his head in her lap, but it was too late. He was already dead.

Holly didn't know if a second or an hour had passed before the shadow fell across her. She was completely unaware of Avery being led away, or Logan standing over her, until he quietly spoke her name.

Holly looked up, tears streaming down her face. "Why, Logan? Why?"

Logan knelt beside her in the sand. "He loved you enough to kill for you, Holly. I guess he knew that you were worth dying for, too."

A sob wrenched her body, and Logan gently took her away from their friend, gathering her into his arms so that she wouldn't have to mourn Mike's death alone.

"HOW DO YOU FEEL?"

Holly held up her bandaged hands for Logan to see, then

used them to gesture toward her legs, which were stretched out in front of her on the sofa. Matching bandages covered them, making her look like a modified mummy. But at least she was feeling human again, after a much needed twenty-four-hour nap. "How do you think I feel?" she said waspishly. "Pretty damned lucky to be alive, actually."

Logan smiled and moved on into the parlor. "That's how you should feel. You're propped up here on a comfy sofa like the Queen of Sheba, receiving homage from your court of admirers. I'd feel lucky to be alive if someone pampered me like this, too."

"After all I went through, I deserve it," she told him. She slid deeper toward the back of the sofa, and Logan accepted the unspoken invitation to sit on the edge, facing her.

Her hair was hanging down around her face, and Logan tenderly brushed a lock of it over her shoulder. "All wise-cracking aside, how are you really feeling?"

"Sad," she told him, sobering. "Very, very sad. I don't think I'll ever forgive myself for what happened to Mike."

"Holly, his death wasn't your fault, and neither was the way his love for you twisted into something totally insane. Don't torture yourself with guilt over something you couldn't have controlled or prevented."

Holly nodded, but Logan knew it was going to be a long time before the sorrow in her eyes faded—if it ever did. Whatever Mike had done, his love for her couldn't be questioned. Logan wasn't surprised that she changed the subject.

"Is your good friend *Gerry* coming back today?" she asked him with a hint of exasperation.

"I don't think so. He rounded up all of Avery's confederates here and at the wreck site yesterday. He's probably got a mountain of paperwork to do."

"Logan, why didn't you tell me Giradeaux was only pretending to suspect you?"

"Because that would have meant telling you all of it—about Barnes, Hamilton, Mike and everything else. The Treasury agents had sworn me to secrecy, but I truly believed you'd be safer if you didn't know."

"Smart thinking, Sherlock," she said sarcastically.

"How was I to know you were going to go skulking around the compound looking for clues to prove my innocence? And thank you for that, by the way. I thought you were convinced I was guilty."

"I was. Until I realized that Mike had lied when he said you told him about the necklace. You never would have done that."

"No. I wouldn't have. But you shouldn't have taken such a risk for me, Holly."

"I thought I was saving your hide from a murder rap! How was I supposed to know that all the time Avery was setting a trap for you, *you* were baiting an even bigger trap for him?"

Logan couldn't keep himself from saying, "You could have trusted me."

"How, Logan?" she asked, pleading with him to understand her doubts. "When I saw the stationery and realized you'd lied, how was I supposed to believe anything else that you'd told me?"

"I know. I'm sorry for that, Holly. I'm sorry for everything." He pressed a gentle kiss to her lips. "Thank you for trying to come to my rescue, despite all the lies."

"What else could I do? I love you."

"Holly—"

She read the tender look on his face and knew what he was going to say. She quickly raised a bandaged hand to his lips. "Don't, Logan. Not yet. I'm not ready to talk about vine-covered cottages."

"Will you ever be?" he asked quietly.

"I don't know. Probably," she said reluctantly. "I love you too much to walk away this time. But..."

When her voice trailed off, Logan picked up for her. "But you still don't want to team up with a greedy, no-account wreck rapist."

"That's not what I meant, Logan."

He reached out and tenderly brushed a lock of hair off her forehead. "Yes, it is. But is working with me really such an unappealing notion? Doing the work you love to do without having to scramble for grants? Having no one to answer to but yourself?"

Holly reciprocated his gesture and ended up running her fingers through his hair. She found herself getting lost in his eyes, but she managed to match his tone of voice. "Being shunned by my colleagues.... Having unscrupulous partners who try to kill me.... Staying one step ahead of murderous pirates who dynamite my salvage sites...." She dropped her hand. "You're right, Logan. That has a lot of appeal," she said dryly.

He grinned at her. "Before you give me your final answer, there's someone I want you to meet, Holly. He should be here later this afternoon."

"Who?"

"Victor Simms."

That took a moment for Holly to digest. "*The* Victor Simms? The new Director of Special Projects at the Smithsonian Institute?"

"The very same. Dr. Simms and I had an interesting conversation yesterday afternoon while you were sleeping. I asked him if the Smithsonian would have any interest in taking over the excavation of the *Ambergris Isle*."

Holly frowned in disbelief. "Are you serious?"

"Absolutely. And we came to a mutually beneficial agreement. The Institute will take sixty percent of the finds and preside over the excavation. They'll sell off some of the pieces, of course, to finance the venture, but most of the *Ambergris Isle* will reach the museum floor."

"But why, Logan?" Holly asked him. "After the Bahamian government takes its twenty-five percent, that leaves you with next to nothing. Why give it away when you could have it all now that Bedrosian is in jail?"

"Because if I did that, I couldn't have you," he told her. "You see, this way, I can remain with the project and have plenty of time to convince the woman who's taking charge of the excavation for the Smithsonian that she can't live without me."

Holly realized what he was getting at, and her heart leapt into her throat. "You didn't."

He nodded. "I did. I told Simms that if the Smithsonian wanted the *Ambergris Isle,* you had to be left in charge of the excavation."

"And he agreed?" she asked, astonished.

"Gladly. He knows that you've worked for the Smithsonian before with excellent results. He thought you'd be perfect for this job."

Holly sank back into the pillows and let the enormity of what Logan had done seep through her. One question kept surfacing, though. "Why?" she asked, tilting her head to one side. "Am I really worth half a billion dollars to you?"

Logan nodded. "That much, and a whole lot more. I'm not going to let you go again, Holly," he told her with a fierce tenderness that brought tears to her eyes. "Your love and the joy of working beside you is all the wealth I'll ever need."

He took her face in his hands and brushed at the tear that slid down her cheek. "What do you think? Can we make it work?"

Holly managed a nod. "I don't see why not."

Logan's smile lit up the room and Holly's heart. "Oh, God, I love you, you stubborn, opinionated, obstinate, beautiful woman," he said, gathering her into his arms.

"I love you, too, Logan," she murmured, but when he brought his lips toward her, Holly put up her bandaged hand again. "But we do have a whole new problem now."

Logan saw the mischief in her eyes. "What?" he asked suspiciously.

"If we're using love as our currency of choice, I'm not sure we can afford our new tax bracket."

Laughing, Logan pulled her into his arms again and didn't give her a chance to stop him from kissing her this time.

Not that she would have, of course.

HARLEQUIN®

Deceit, betrayal, murder

Join Harlequin's intrepid heroines, India Leigh and Mary Hadfield, as they ferret out the truth behind the mysterious goings-on in their neighborhood. These two women are no milk-and-water misses. In fact, they thrive on

MISCHIEF & MAYHEM

Watch for their incredible adventures in this special two-book collection. Available in March, wherever Harlequin books are sold.

REG4

HARLEQUIN®

I N T R I G U E®

Into a world where danger lurks around
every corner, and there's a fine line between trust
and betrayal, comes a tall, dark and handsome man.

Intuition draws you to him...but instinct keeps you
away. Is he really one of those...

Don't miss even one of the twelve sexy but secretive
men, coming to you one per month in 1995.

In March, look for
#313 A KILLER SMILE
by Laura Kenner

Take a walk on the wild side...with our
"DANGEROUS MEN"!

Available wherever Harlequin books are sold.

HARLEQUIN®

INTRIGUE®

Brush up on your bedside manner with...

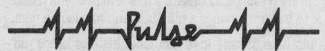

Three heart-racing romantic-suspense novels that are just
what the doctor ordered!

This spring, Harlequin Intrigue presents PULSE, a trilogy of
medical thrillers by Carly Bishop to get your blood flowing,
raise the hairs on the back of your neck and bring out all the
telltale of reading the best in romance and mystery.

Don't miss your appointments with:

#314 HOT BLOODED
March 1995

#319 BREATHLESS
April 1995

#323 HEART THROB
May 1995

HARLEQUIN®
INTRIGUE®

What if...

You'd agreed to marry a man you'd never met, in a town where you'd never been, while surrounded by wedding guests you'd never seen before?

And what if...

You weren't sure you could trust the man to whom you'd given your hand?

Look for "Mail Order Brides"—the upcoming two novels of romantic suspense by Cassie Miles, which are available in April and July—and only from Harlequin Intrigue!

Don't miss

> #320 MYSTERIOUS VOWS
> by Cassie Miles
> April 1995

Mail Order Brides—where mail-order marriages lead distrustful newlyweds into the mystery and romance of a lifetime!

On the most romantic day of the year, capture the thrill of falling in love all over again—with

Harlequin's

Bachelors

They're three sexy and *very single* men who run very special personal ads to find the women of their fantasies by Valentine's Day. These exciting, passion-filled stories are written by bestselling Harlequin authors.

Your Heart's Desire by Elise Title
Mr. Romance by Pamela Bauer
Sleepless in St. Louis by Tiffany White

Be sure not to miss Harlequin's Valentine Bachelors, available in February wherever Harlequin books are sold.

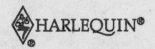

Harlequin invites you to the most
romantic wedding of the season.

Rope the cowboy of your dreams in
Marry Me, Cowboy!

A collection of 4 brand-new stories,
celebrating weddings, written by:

New York Times bestselling author

JANET DAILEY

and favorite authors

Margaret Way
Anne McAllister
Susan Fox

Be sure not to miss Marry Me, Cowboy!
coming this April

HARLEQUIN®

Don't miss these Harlequin favorites by some of our most distinguished authors!
And now, you can receive a discount by ordering two or more titles!

HT#25577	WILD LIKE THE WIND by Janice Kaiser	$2.99 ☐
HT#25589	THE RETURN OF CAINE O'HALLORAN by JoAnn Ross	$2.99 ☐
HP#11626	THE SEDUCTION STAKES by Lindsay Armstrong	$2.99 ☐
HP#11647	GIVE A MAN A BAD NAME by Roberta Leigh	$2.99 ☐
HR#03293	THE MAN WHO CAME FOR CHRISTMAS by Bethany Campbell	$2.89 ☐
HR#03308	RELATIVE VALUES by Jessica Steele	$2.89 ☐
SR#70589	CANDY KISSES by Muriel Jensen	$3.50 ☐
SR#70598	WEDDING INVITATION by Marisa Carroll	$3.50 U.S. ☐
		$3.99 CAN. ☐
HI#22230	CACHE POOR by Margaret St. George	$2.99 ☐
HAR#16515	NO ROOM AT THE INN by Linda Randall Wisdom	$3.50 ☐
HAR#16520	THE ADVENTURESS by M.J. Rodgers	$3.50 ☐
HS#28795	PIECES OF SKY by Marianne Willman	$3.99 ☐
HS#28824	A WARRIOR'S WAY by Margaret Moore	$3.99 U.S. ☐
		$4.50 CAN. ☐

(limited quantities available on certain titles)

	AMOUNT	$
DEDUCT:	**10% DISCOUNT FOR 2+ BOOKS**	$
ADD:	**POSTAGE & HANDLING**	$
	($1.00 for one book, 50¢ for each additional)	
	APPLICABLE TAXES*	$_____
	TOTAL PAYABLE	$_____
	(check or money order—please do not send cash)	

To order, complete this form and send it, along with a check or money order for the total above, payable to Harlequin Books, to: **In the U.S.:** 3010 Walden Avenue, P.O. Box 9047, Buffalo, NY 14269-9047; **In Canada:** P.O. Box 613, Fort Erie, Ontario, L2A 5X3.

Name:_____

Address: _____ City:_____

State/Prov.:_____ Zip/Postal Code:_____

*New York residents remit applicable sales taxes.
 Canadian residents remit applicable GST and provincial taxes.

HBACK-JM2